THE IF-NODES OF ANTAN:

"I have to bring you to our headquarters in Hell, Pan, so . . ."

"Headquarters, Althea? In Hell? What organization?"

"Sometimes we call it *Postscript*, sometimes *Operation Second Chance*. We re-create situations in which souls have lost themselves in the past, and we start a replay, turning them loose with free will and no memory of having done all this before. But in the replay we offer them just a little bit of a nudge at this or that critical if-node, and then we let them alone to see if they wake up and win instead of losing."

I considered that. I nodded once. But, hell, it wasn't real, it was theater! My mind smiled before I did.

"Shall we go to Hell, Althea?"

PAN SAGITTARIUS

IAN WALLACE

A BERKLEY MEDALLION BOOK
PUBLISHED BY
BERKLEY PUBLISHING CORPORATION

Published by arrangement with G.P. Putnam's Sons

G.P. Putnam's Sons
200 Madison Avenue
New York, N.Y. 10016

Library of Congress Catalog Card Number:
72-94258

SBN 425-02659-7

BERKLEY MEDALLION BOOKS are published by
Berkley Publishing Corporation
200 Madison Avenue
New York, N.Y. 10016

BERKLEY MEDALLION BOOKS ® TM 757, 375

Printed in the United States of America

Berkley Medallion Edition, September, 1974

CONTENTS

Conjointly, to
Pan, Althea, and Thoth
and to certain other fictional friends
from several planets and worlds:
Edom, Ave, Willy, Brownie, Lassiter,
Grayle, Gueraine, Pelleon, Merleon, Nineve,
Ben, and Meri Makrov,
Paige, O'Duffy, Hertha, Von Elt, Guyon,
Katharina, and Petruchio

May this my affectionate representation
of your selves and your honest concerns
not miscarry too far
and come out almost as fair as it was felt.

Then with a golden egg Donander made another world; and from the entrials of a spider he drew another; from the carrion of a dead cow he made a fifth world; and with the aid of a raven Donander made yet one more. . . . And throughout . . . these whiles Donander was pottering with his worlds, keeping them bright with thunderbolts and volcanic eruptions, diligently cleansing them of parasites with one or another pestilence, scouring them with whirlwinds, and perpetually washing them with cloudbursts and deluges.

—James Branch Cabell, *The Silver Stallion*

AUCTORIAL COMMENT

The author has old, old concerns with clinical psychology; and these concerns may be showing through in *Pan Sagittarius,* for sexuality clamant or latent is invariably a motif and sometimes the motif. But those who understand will swiftly see that the sexual motif is never sounded in the sense of Freud's mechanistic metaphysics. Consider the variations:

The frank sexuality in "Sagittarius in Scandia" is pleasure for its own sake as a pagan good, even though Althea seems a bit desperate and excessive about it (not for reasons of repression, but for reasons of Pan and prior privation), and even though Pan is using it with enjoyment to steer Althea, and even though Althea is using it with enjoyment to steer Pan. Sexuality is not visible at all in "Operation Second Chance," but who can doubt that directly or indirectly it has contributed to the troubles of the souls in question? Sexuality is a rampant motif in "A Certain Garden" —but it is open and natural in a simple primitive world, and the tragedy-threat coils around its puckering distortion by taboo. Sexuality as such does not motivate the hard racial rebellion of "Willy the Villain"; nevertheless, the rebellion is driving-male, race immaterial, and at the heart of degradation is sexual degradation that a naive-educated hero feels he must explore in order to understand the people. Disguised as something between lady worship and *amour*, a style-highlighted fever called *amourosis* threatens in "Caerleon" to destroy a noble dream. The thin, browbeaten heroism of "Makrov" is purely human, and I am one who refuses to shackle the broad warmth of family love and reverence within the category "sexuality"; yet perverse sexuality motivates Makrov's enemies, whereas by contrast, at one point the starkly sexual symbolism of soul love between Makrov and his wife is for me a near approach to what Heaven stands for. Lewis Paige in "The Bishop's Halo" is almost antiseptically asexual, and the same has to be said for the gauleiter in "Von Eltz in Vimy"; perhaps one has to be a technician to appreciate how deep-repressed sexuality indirectly expresses itself in obsessive-compulsive mentalities. Hertha, the wretchedly masochistic prostitute in "Adult, Western," addresses sexuality with a twisted directness: loves it, hates it, cries out to know what is so special about it. And even in the subhuman preorganic antics that are focused in "Creation of a Metagalaxy," Pan inescapably sees an inexact prelude to male female thrust-allure.

But the coin has another side. For Althea, sexuality is a value that she caresses with her left hand, while with her right she hard-reaches toward stars, and when there is conflict, the stars dominate. Problems far deeper than sexuality have thrust the souls of this novel into Hell. Until the serpent came, sexuality was merely one among the interests of those in the garden. All three of the leading men in "Willy the Villain" are idealists for causes beyond themselves, causes such that it is outrageously outstretching professionalese to assert that they are sex-connected. All the principals in "Caerleon" revere the dream and are piteously rended when they recognize that sexuality has trapped them; indeed, for a very long while Pelleon and Gueraine seek between them a dreamed beauty that is wholly asexual. For me, Makrov—making allowances for his soul-draining desuetude—treads the high roads. Even if Paige and Von Eltz *are* gripped in neuroses that science knows to have psychosexual roots, is it not human-prime that with all their conscious energies and wills they are reaching for what is lofty? Hertha is earthy, she is ordinary folks, trapped in her own environmental pressures, at once allured and repelled—but note: it is not the pleasures of sexuality that she questions; instead, what she questions is *why the soul-trap.* Leroy Guyon cannot be confined within *any* category. As for the preorganic centers of allure and thrust in "Creation of a Metagalaxy," perhaps they suggest a controlling theory to which Freud might pay less attention than Jung.

Although Pan in these pages is usually narrator of adventures whose foreground people are other people, Pan is always intimately and causally involved in the action. Meditation of this fact has evoked in me a good deal of speculation about Pan's outlook on life and on lives. Every adventure is revealing of him—is self-revealing by him—and yet, how much is revealed? To me, his author, at the end of it still he is ambiguous, I am still far short of his horizons.

Earth is not the locus of any of these adventures; but in several of them the locus is *Erth*—a planet in another metagalaxy, but a planet which is so much like our Earth that a whole essay (which here I eschew) would be needed to explain the subtle differences.

All characters and their names are fictions invented by the author. Any name-resemblance to the name of a real person would be mere coincidence; and any character-resemblance to a real individual would be equally inadvertent, except in the supporting cast of "Makrov" and in the stars of "A Certain Garden," "Caerleon," and "Von Eltz in Vimy" where some obvious historical or quasihistorical characters were partial models.

Nevertheless, all the major characters have become real in my private world; I like and empathize with all of them except the Fuhrer and Dubois, and even with these I can empathize. Consequently there is no satirical intent anywhere in this book, despite some straight-faced partial comedy in the first, second, third, fifth, seventh, eighth, and final adventures. And although the situations in all but the first adventure are meant to reflect (with distortions and reversals) human-universal situations, these my percepts must be viewed as personal-individual.

Ian Wallace

Earth, 1973

My dear twin brother,

I dare venture that you have once in a while let yourself worry about me during these two years of silence: not for long, though, since I am physically your duplicate and mentally almost so. Worrying, you would have said to yourself: "Pan is as safe as I would be, probably; he is silent for his own good reasons, probably: go to, I will not worry—probably." And you would have straightened your long hard body, and run a big hand back through your short auburn hair, and grinned with your wide mouth and sapphire eyes, and checked in a prayer-thought for me, and gone on about your business.

So hey, look! I am reporting! with tri-d multicolor thought-feeling flakes in which I recall for you in some detail ten outlandish adventures with a number of remarkable people and one embryonic system, on several planets and in two out-worldly nonplaces over a large range of millennium-epochs.

But, Brother—keep it all confidential, except for the one other person whom you know. Reading these flakes, you will see why.

It does now seem, doesn't it? that there *is* adequate reason for both of us to exist.

I know you're fine, I've checked. My best to you always.

PAN

Hell, 2509 AD

PART ONE

Sagittarius in Scandia

> So the two began the ascent of Vraidex, by the winding road upon which the dreams travel when they are sent down to men by the lord of the seven madnesses.
>
> —JAMES BRANCH CABELL, *Figures of Earth*

1

Since it was impossible for me to kill myself by ordinary human means, I got myself a 100-G scouter with a 1:100 inertial shield and cut loose for Sol at maximum drive with manual controls jammed: I'd be crisped long before I would hit star surface. My major problem, as I leaned back in the face of a mild apparent 1-G wind, was self-restraint: under fear-stress, I might automatically dissociate myself from my brain and wing it for some space-time security point, there to kidnap some body and make a new start at the expense of *his* soul. But it would be self-defeating: I had no business continuing to live, especially as a parasite. So last night I had made a point of debilitating my vigor with a covey of women and gallons of liquor; right now I was under heavy sedation, the scouter was guiding itself straight into the sun.

Unluckily I came out of sedation just as we were cutting Mercury-orbit: I was in an oven, and I hadn't been smart enough to expect this awakening and provide myself with extra dope. Agonized and terrified, grimly I went to work on my brain—setting stops, opening emotic switches to chop fear and dull pain, throwing a spiderweb of self-restraint around my escape-straining mind, widening every memory and motive that reinforced suicide: it was all I could do; again I leaned back, required myself to relax and go blank, endured growing heat: it would be only a matter of minutes before consciousness would go. . . .

Heat eased, unaccountably. I opened eyes, frowning. There was no G-wind. To be certain, I unjammed the manuals and cautiously rheostated out the inertial shield: no doubt about it, either I was motionless or I was in freefall—and to the latter, the progressive normalizing of heat gave the lie.

Cautiously I relaxed pain inhibitors: no real pain, although my skin was burned: well, that I could correct. Very gradually I closed my fear switch: my fear was only residual, not enough to drive my mind into silly behavior. Then I unspun my mind and opened viewports.

From what I could see outside, my scouter reposed in the center of a vast hotel lobby. And I was alone here.

Had I in panic done something ridiculous, translating not merely my mind but my body and my scouter vehicle somewherewhen?

Anyhow, suicide had obviously failed, although reasons for it continued clamant. Heigh-ho: let's see what the deal is, and then we'll try again. . . .

I stepped out of the scouter into the deserted lobby without even bothering to pretest whether the atmosphere would be oxygen or methane or nothing: either I would live or I would die, and the latter would be preferable.

The room was high-lofted rococo with opulent ceiling murals flanked by sculptured and gilded scollops; marble nymphs and satyrs graced wall niches; my feet sank into a deep-pile crimson carpet, I was tempted to take off my shoes. There was no furniture, there were no people . . . .

There were two pieces of furniture: a round heavy green-marble table flanked by a luscious armchair in forest-green plush. This table and this chair reposed thirty feet from broad steps that led up to a theatrical proscenium backed by a closed forest-green plush curtain. On this table, conveniently close to the chair, were an ashtray, a fat virginal cigar, matches, and a tall glass of what appeared to be frosted zac (but could not be zac in this evidently primitive time-era).

I turned to consider my scouter. It had vanished.

Shrugging, I went to the table, sat in the chair, lit the cigar, sipped the drink (which with difficulty, on a basis of uptime prowling experience, I identified as a Tom Collins), considered the proscenium.

The whole setup was twentieth century. Was it staged—or had I been swung six hundred years into my past—or both?

Perhaps ten minutes dawdled by; cigar and drink were half gone.

The curtain parted. The stage that it revealed was wide and deep; there was no backdrop, apparently the background was all the world—*some* world: the remote past of my own Erth, maybe? Centered on the stage was a broad low dais, and centered on the dais was a low throne, and seated on the throne was a dark-haired uncrowned woman who seemed uncommonly tall and slender; a man and a woman flanked her, standing below the dais; and other men and women arhythmically passed from wing to wing before her—paying her no notice.

The woman on the throne was looking at me.

I stood; she continued to look.

Leaving cigar and drink behind, slowly I mounted the steps to the stage: I would see what this might be, I would suicide later. . . .

She arose; and, after standing a moment on the dais regarding me, she descended and greeted me with both hands, while behind me a basso profundo enunciated: "The Honorable Miss Althea Candless, Chief of the Nordian Power Ministry: Mr. Pan Sagittarius." I didn't remember passing a man, but I didn't look back—it would have been impolite, and it was psychically impossible.

Still Miss Candless held my hands in her slim strong hands, standing back so that our arms were extended. She was as tall as I, grace to her two-inch heels, and so slender that she seemed almost thin (but this was mainly an effect of height); clearly she was self-conscious about her height, for her shoulders drooped slightly forward so that her quite respectable breasts were deemphasized; and yet she was inwardly and outwardly graceful, sheathed in a black gown, her black hair falling to her shoulders, her black eyes wide-set, her black eyebrows flat, her small-nostriled nose just a bit retroussé, long in lip and chin, her wide mouth semismiling. . . .

She said (and her voice was dusky also): "I am sorry to have interrupted your smoke and your drink." But she didn't suggest either completion or replacement. And she didn't mention having interrupted my dandy suicide.

I was reflecting that no matter how valid a decision for suicide may be, failure is like any other mors interruptus: there is always something else to be savored, if you aren't depressive—and depression had *not* been my motive. . . . I replied, essaying a smile: "I am grateful for the half-smoke and half-drink, and for the opportunity—"

Her smile flashed altogether wide: "Skip the graces, Mr. Sagittarius: think of me as a man, we have business."

Her left hand let go of my right, she swung me around beside her, she switched hands so that her left had my left, she hooked her right under my left arm, she moved me toward the rear openness, telling me confidentially: "Moskovia is about to blow Kebec loose from us—"

It was not going to be easy to think of her as a man. But as a human, male or female immaterial—*that* I could dig.

She steered me through the back of the stage and out into the busy city, tightly clutching my arm with both hands that were astonishingly strong. We were out on an energetic avenue in daylight, I recognized it as Fifth Avenue in the astonishing Nordian-Kebecois metropolis of Montvrai. "Here we catch a bus," she told me. Waiting with her, trying to make meaning-ends meet, I became conscious of two small glowering men behind us. A bus paused; we swung aboard, they followed; she slid into a double seat, I joined her; the small glowering men took a double seat not far behind us; the bus took off.

Still she held my left arm, she squeezed it in warning; I sat waiting, presumably she would be telling. The bus went and stopped and went and stopped; people descended, nobody boarded; presently we were alone except for the two small glowering men and the driver; rather surprisingly, the bus had swung onto the Skyland Freeway, had built up speed to sixty, was thrusting northward toward the mountains.

She squeezed twice: a signal to listen. Gazing out the window, she spoke low: "We are decoying those men back there, they are enemies. I do not know their tactical plans. But I know what they are up to strategically. If they make contact, pretend to be friendly. Now, please, engage me in small talk."

I said low, but penetratingly so *they* would just be able to hear: "I have gone a long way out of my way to meet the Honorable Althea Candless. My reason is a reason of personal admiration. Does Miss Candless care to comment?" And as I spoke, gradually it came clear in my own mind that I almost meant it: this made it easier to carry along. . . .

A notion hit me. Delicately I fingered the minds of the two glowerers behind us. It checked. In my sort of Gaulois, I suggested to Miss Candless: "Est-ce que vous parlez Gaulois?"

Her eyes widened. Then: "Oui. Pourquoi?"

"Parce-que ces gens la, ils ne comprennent pas Gaulois."

"Est-ce vrai? Comment vous savez ca?"

"Je sais ca. Aussi, ils sont Moskoviques."

"Eh." She slumped a little. "Alors, c'est confirmé."

"Si. Mais aussi alors, nous pourrons donc parler Gaulois. Ils seront soupconneux, confus; mais aussi, ils ne vont pas comprendre."

There was a little silence, during which my delicate mind-reach tasted their unrest. Then she remarked in Gaulais: "It is almost incredible that they would have sent agents to Kébec who do not speak Gaulois."

Already the window view was marvelous: mountain foothills were speeding by. I said quietly: "Suppose you tell me what is up."

Our physical relationship was curiously intimate: still her right hand gripped my arm, but also my right hand was on hers, and her left hand was on mine—and all this was disconcertingly pleasing.

She told me quietly in Gaulois: "Moskovia plans to tamper

with our hydroelectric power leads in such a way as to aggravate the Kébecois to the point of unanimous armed secession-and-aggression. Never mind how I have caught on to the general nature of the plot; it is sufficient for you to know that I know about it, and know little else about it. I want you to diagnose the plot and kill it."

"Your Nordian Bureau of Investigation can't handle this, Minister Candless?"

"There are sufficient reasons for bypassing that bureau, Mr. Sagittarius."

In the back of my mind was a small trouble, why *and how* she would have found me six centuries in her own future and reached out to deflect me inside of Mercury from a solar suicide in order to use me for this. But I squeezed her hand and told her: "You can count on me, Miss Candless. Now that you know these men are Moskovians, what do you think their plans may be?"

She pondered. She said presently: "Perhaps if we confront them and involve them in conversation, something may come through."

I warned: "Of course, they *may* be decoys—"

"You have learned somehow that they are Moskovians who do not understand Gaulois. Can you not use your methods to learn more?"

I frowned. "This is an ethical inhibition that I have. I will go so far as to taste an adversary's abilities and limitations; but I will not use this unfair method to probe his purposes and motives."

"Oh, la! You *are* delicately ethical! May I consequently assume that my own purposes and motives are safe from unfair scrutiny?"

Without speaking, I put the answer into her mind directly.

She slumped a little, relaxing. "Thank you. That was *most* convincing—"

Whereupon the bus took off from the freeway into the sky with the thrust of a four-engine jet; and in the sky, this remarkable bus leveled out and homed on the northland.

Still Althea sat relaxed beside me, her wide mouth semismiling. My right hand had an urgency to reach across her and grasp and caress her forward-thrust left shoulder. Repressing it, I suggested: "Perhaps my first step should be to challenge those guys back there."

She frowned. "Apart from the consideration that you would tip our hand, they might kill you."

I grinned at *that!* "I seem to recall, Miss Candless, that suicide is just the ticket for me." I went serious, puzzled suddenly: "How did you know? How did you interrupt? Why me?"

Her frown deepened. "Please do not ask such questions now. In due course, we will tell you—"

"We?"

Her frown seemed absolutely painful; convulsively she freed her hands from mine and clasped them knuckle-white in her lap. "I am Minister of Power. Obviously I am not entirely alone—"

I asserted: "I am going to challenge those two types."

She said low: "I have asked you to help. I must permit you to use your own methods."

I pondered. I left my seat (noticing through the window that we were air-flirting with snowcapped crests) and wove my way back up the aisle (in this rough-banging flight) toward the two small triggermen who were watching me tight-lipped. Dropping into the seat across the aisle from them, I lilted: "We seem to be almost alone as travel companions. I am Pan Sagittarius. Care to give me your names?"

Both of them looked Gallic. The one nearest me, whose thin mustache topped a full-lipped narrow mouth, answered in thick Anglian: "Pleased to make your acquaintance, Mr. Sagittarius. I am Stephen Foster; that is Winston Churchill."

I glanced at Churchill, whose nose and lip were long: he glowered at me. I said cheerfully: "It would be useless to deny that my companion is the Honorable Miss Althea Candless. Tell me, Mr. Foster: are you guarding her—or are you shadowing her?" Althea, I side-eye noticed, was back-watching us with some alarm.

Foster stroked one side of his mustache with an index finger; and then he replied: "I suggest, Mr. Sagittarius, that you mind your own business."

I leaned toward him. "Mr. Foster—if you were planning to sabotage the hydroelectric power lines in such a way as to turn the Kébecois violently against the rest of Nordia, what method would you use?"

His handgun snapped out, aimed at my heart.

I spread hands, smiling: "Excuse me, sir, for saying irritating things. Pray forget it." And I went back to Althea.

Settled beside her, I told her mind directly: "There is no doubt about it, Miss Candless—they are the ones."

Her mind responded: "Mr. Sagittarius, are you clinging to your ethos about tapping their minds?"

"I won't tap their minds—but I am willing to shoot them a shot of security and trust before I try to diddle them."

"Do that, Mr. Sagittarius. Do that."

The result of the sharp shot was that the four of us were now playing bridge around a big table centered in the bus as it statelily descended and effortlessly lit on the surface of a swift river perhaps a quarter-mile wide that flowed more or less centered in a gently rolling valley rimmed several miles away by mountains. The fixed bus seats had unaccountably vanished, having been replaced by nicely upholstered movable furniture. The driver, putting guidance on automatic, had left his post long enough to serve drinks, then had returned: from here on, drinks would be dummy-duty.

I was dummy, but we weren't ready. I stood thoughtfully in the stern, nursing my drink, alternately watching the faces of the players and the scene that drifted by at about (one estimated) ten knots as the bus-flyer-boat thrust smoothly upriver.

Althea was playing a slam bid in no trump. Her play was leisurely: not uncertain, always correct; not psychic, but inductively logical: when twice she finessed, each time she *knew* it would work to a probability of about 99 percent; it was not that her thought processes were slow—I dared finger her mind on this impersonal point; she was clicking like a binary calculator (quinary would be silly for bridge)—but rather that she *felt* leisurely, she was in no hurry. The Moskovians gloomed over their hands, played mechanically and correctly, seemed perfectly patient.

There were some elements of the situation that simply didn't add up. In the first place, this was no random bus that we had caught at a corner on Fifth Avenue, Montvrai: it was a rather highly adaptive bus. In the second place, Althea's complacency with the weirdities of bus performance practically constituted proof that this was *her* bus, that she was anticipating everything; on the other hand, the Moskovians who were presumably her shadowing enemies appeared in their gloomy way equally complacent and unsurprised. Again: I had shot security into their minds and engaged them in bridge obviously in the hope that they would inadvertently leak something of their intentions; and since I knew next to nothing about what was going on, I had left it to Althea to lead the conversation; but Althea had appeared perfectly happy with the bridge and with my company, and there had been no leading conversation. Perhaps, though, Althea was patiently feeding their security, just as she was patiently leading her cards (just now, the guys had their quota of one trick, she had eight): soon she might begin sliding in conversational come-ons. Another thought: what was *I* doing here? maybe not detective work at all; maybe, once she had the tactics figured, she planned to use me for the strong-arm stuff—although it *did* seem that she could have found a strong-arm with less trouble right here on Erth in her own time. . . .

She pulled the lead card for the thirteenth trick from dummy (South); West (Churchill) sloughed; but instead of dropping her card, Althea (North) debated with herself, slowly tapping the long pearl-manicured fingernails of her left hand with the card back. This hesitation could have nothing to do with play, there was only this one card to drop and we all knew what it had to be—a good ten of diamonds. I stared at the card back, and so did the Moskovians. Outskirts of a city were beginning to be evident along both riverbanks. . . .

Althea laid the card face down in front of her, tapped it for a moment with both hands, then intently inspected the faces of her two adversaries one by one. Insolently they returned her stare. She dropped her head, gazed at her card, and said with bell-clarity: "Tomorrow, I gather, the device will be positioned in the master synapse leading out of the generator plant beside Scandia Falls. If you will give me all the facts, the card I play will be the nine of diamonds, and East will turn out to have the ten. Look at your card, East: is it a worthy investment?"

But this was absolutely bizarre! I was riveted on the tableau. East (Foster) studied his card; then he muttered, "I *thought* it was a fixed deck—"

"The deck," declared Althea, "is not fixed. But you must take my word that I can fix it now. *Is* it a worthy investment?"

West stared at East; East stared at Althea's card back. East murmured: "What is your understanding of the bet, Miss Candless?"

"Fifty thousand on this hand."

My guts contracted: I did not remember nearly so much, and I had half of the bet automatically. . . .

Slowly East nodded. He told his card: "The device is pocket-size but transistor-complex and potent. It will affect the pulsations along the power leads in such a way that the secondary static fields will set the brains of Kébecois but no others into a passion of total activity against the Nordian state. Because the station at Scandia Falls is the primary for Kébec, its pulses will sympathetically communicate themselves to leads from all other sources into Kébec."

Althea frowned: "Not enough. *When* is it to be placed?"

Gazing at her, West grinned for the first time: the bus was pervaded by the pall of the grin. "We can lie about the time, Madame—and how will you know?"

Althea's eyes rose to mine; her brows were high, her lips were parted a little; between us there was some sort of subliminal communication. She replied slowly, keeping her eyes on mine: "Mr. Sagittarius will know whether you are lying."

My role was starting to come clear; I was in her service, she had to establish the ethics; but, God—twenty-five thousand? Suddenly I grinned: if I was in her service, I was on her expense account! Promptly I shot into West and East conviction that I *would* know; and I monitored both their minds to that limited extent. . . .

West and East were surveying each other: their mouths were persimmoned.

East agitated one brow. West lowered one brow.

East demanded: "Knowing the timing, will you try to stop the action?"

Althea responded coldly: "I am a loyal minister of Nordia."

Staring at his card, East asserted: "Give or take half an hour, two thirty A.M. local time."

"Why that timing?"

"The device is preset. It activates at one forty-five, it conks out unless triggered before three fifteen."

Instantly Althea exposed her card—the nine of diamonds.

Frowning heavily, East dropped the ten and took the trick.

Then he picked up the nine and the ten, inspected both sides, thumb-flicked the edges, handed them to West—who inspected, thumb-flicked, dropped the cards, gloomed.

I wasn't going to bother picking them up. I had caught cue from Althea and psychokinetically changed the spots.

Althea scribbled two IOU's and handed them to East and West.

We were full into the city, sailing smoothly under a bridge with more bridges ahead of us. It was a thick city, in places a towered city. I did not know of any such city this far north in Nordia. This paradoxical city was called Scandia. . . .

Althea engaged my eyes: hers were troubled. She said distinctly, ignoring the Two: "The driver will assign quarters here. *They* will be in one location, I in another, you in another; none of us will know where the others are, it is best that way. Pan, now you know all I know. Prevent it, Pan, prevent it—"

My quarters I found without much difficulty, following the driver's curt directions: a room near the top of the tallest hotel in this city named Scandia. And the hotel *was* tall, more than thirty stories. As I peered out my top-floor windows, it seemed to me that no building in Scandia except one was nearly as tall.

This window overlooked the river at a mile distance: that river cut the city into a major and a minor half—I was in Scandia Major. It was early evening, there was no smog; my vision followed the river upstream. In the distance I could see the falls: small in the distance—but, judging on my space-judgment, mightier than Yosemite and nearly as mighty as Vespucian Niagara. I could not hear the noise of this falls; I imagined hearing the noise of this falls. I let my auditory mind wander a few miles northward: I heard the noise of this falls.

Still I was almost totally confused. Miss Candless was the Nordian Power Minister. This was the twentieth century: somehow she had located me in the twenty-sixth and plucked me back from a suicide run to help her foil an international plot. Coolly she had dropped a fifty-thousand-dollar bet at cards in order to get at a truth—and her enemies just as coolly had *given* her this truth (and it *was* truth, I had verified the truth-attitude in their minds)—and she had wound it up by assigning me and the conspirators and herself to three sets of quarters (and the driver to a fourth?) with each party ignorant of the others' locations, expecting me somehow under these conditions to stop these characters before they could mind-bug all Kébec. . . .

Well, I had the facts about the locus and the timing. All I had to do was get out there and stop them. Just how I would stop them wasn't easy to imagine; but I suspected that I would have to throw ethics to the winds and use my mind-reach.

Not for the first time, it crossed my mind to doubt my centuries-old conviction that the past was unchangeable. Perhaps it depended on whether you were in uptime or in the real vital past. Often and often I had trod uptime, intimately I knew its symptoms and its behavior; well, here I was six centuries earlier than my own actuality—and yet every delicate sign confirmed that I was in germinal actuality, that *I* was affecting *these events,* that decisions and actions would have meaning for a future that was in my past. . . .

Obviously, though, the meaning for the future past would have to be limited. Presumably it would not, for example, be possible for me to change this past so drastically as to change recorded history. I recalled a clever explanation of the impossibility of time paradox in a twentieth-century science novel by Isaac Asimov: the tensions of time trends possess a high degree of inertia, they tend to restore themselves after transient detours. In history there was no record of any massive revolt by Kébec, although between Kébec and the rest of Nordia there had been centuries of tautening strain. Since presumably I had not been present in the original twentieth century, evidently this plot, if it had been plotted, had failed without my help. So all I really needed to do, now, was to go down to the hotel's opulent dining room and have me an opulent dinner and come back up here and go to sleep: the plot would fail anyway, somehow.

Wouldn't it?

One way or another, I had to follow this through. Despite the temptation to perform a pseudo-scientific experiment by remaining inactive and seeing what might happen, I had to confess that you can't experiment scientifically on history: it can't be laboratory-painless, and you have no chance for replication controls. . . .

I noticed hunger. It was about eight, in summer. Light was failing, but I could still see the falls. How much time to get there? Well, it was maybe twenty miles—but the real question was transportation. Could a guy snag a cab? or what else was there?

I shrugged: it was no problem—I could teleport. Just for kicks, I tried it, zeroing in on the Norman-Gothic roof of that high tower over by the river—the one that seemed second only in stature to my own hotel. A cinch: I was there. Poof: I was back in my room. All was well, then. I had lots of time for dinner. . . .

I frowned: it crossed my mind that even if transportation-time was no problem for me, it would be a problem for the Moskovians—or for Althea. There was no way out: I simply *had* to discover the realistic human possibilities—now, five and a half hours from H-Hour.

Jerking-to my necktie, and jacketing, and slapping pockets in a key-and-billfold check, I left the room and hit the primitive elevator.

This town of Scandia *was* thick, her downtown was intersecting canyons of stone and brick buildings—mostly five or ten stories, but some spiking up to twenty or higher. Decidedly I had not looked for such a city north of Montvrai—particularly, as I estimated on a time basis, five or six hundred miles north. Her population could be half a million. She was laid out like an Old World city; indeed, I could not find even a boulevard that was not interrupted in a few blocks by a dead end, with some building—usually a delightful building—plunked right down at street-head. I was looking for taxis, but first I had to learn to recognize them. After a few blocks of twilight prowling, I caught on: a taxi was an ordinary vehicle with three or four or five wheels, any color, any size or shape, but driven by a type wearing a képi.

Just about that time I hit an avenue that was *not* interrupted: it ran straightaway left and right, and only a few blocks to my left I could see what had to be a bridge from its superstructure. Well, why not contemplate the river? it gave me an excuse. . . . I hailed a cab and told the driver in Gaulois to take me to the bridge; en route, I asked him whether cabs could be hailed to go to the falls, and how late, and how long, and how much. He laconized: "Toute heure, pas loin, pas beaucoup—oops! nous sommes ici, M'sieu'—attention la tete!" and he swooped to the curb and stopped instantaneously.

When my head, catapulted over the top of his front seat and stopped only by my chest, found itself staring up into his hatchet face, I remembered that I had no Nordian money. When one is in that kind of trouble, one has to settle for second-best ethics: I shot him a shot of love, happiness, and personal appreciation; I descended; he waved and departed, his face a beatitude.

I stood on a sidewalk, facing the bridge and the river.

A mighty barge rode statelily by, inching up against the heavy current. For minutes I contemplated inch after inch of her black radiant-portholed length. When ultimately her tail sneered good-bye at me, I saw beneath her tail what had to be a two-prop water-churning. And that said a great deal about the power of Scandia Falls.

Beyond the bridge, it seemed, there was little to explore: the town fell away into outskirt squalor.

What kept coming over me was: how utterly realistic this town, where a town could not in this era possibly dwell!

That was when, as I watched the water, most of it patterned.

Part of the pattern was the way she played bridge.

Standing at mid-bridge, gripping the north rail, I diffused my visual concentration among the faraway invisible falls and the swift underneath water and the large and small craft that labored northward or scudded southward. And now I was not scrupling to put out sensors.

First I searched the city for the two Moskovians and the bus driver. They were nowhere in the city. Distance did not dull my sensors, although time did: I extended them to sweep a thirty-mile radius full circle, a radius extending far beyond the falls: within this radius, at least, simply they were nowhere.

I didn't bother to hunt mentally for Althea: intuitive logic located *her*. She wouldn't be in *my* hotel, but she would be high and grand. Now, here right beside the river lofted the splendid building that I had assayed as second only to mine in stature, the one I had hopped to and hopped back from: an elegant hotel with a Norman tower and much lower Norman wings. . . .

I slapped the bridge and grinned. Suicide could wait! One more adventure first. . . .

Entering the hotel lobby, I went to the desk and asked for Miss Candless. Up went the clerk's brows: "Inconnue ici, Monsieur—" I leaned toward him confidentially: "Precisely what I understand. What *is* her incognito?" Hard down came the brows: "Je ne comprends pas—" "Never mind," I told him. "Where are the room phones?" He chilly-pointed. I went to one, bypassed the computer, got a person, shot her with a *meaning*. A moment later, Althea lifted her phone and queried: "Oui?"

"Oui," I assured her. "Sagittarius here. Have you dined, or are you ready for dinner? either way, shall I come up?"

The momentary silence was touching. She said presently, low: "Shall I come as I am?"

"Evading speculation, I will only mention that I have in mind the dining room here."

Was that a low chuckle? Then: "How are *you*, Pan?"

"Very well, thank you."

"I mean, fool, what are you wearing?"

"What I have been wearing. What else is there?"

"Good. I will meet you at the dining room in a quarter-hour. Wearing what I have been wearing."

I went to the dining room, shot the maitre d' with love and happiness and appreciation, nailed down a bay-window table by the river.

Althea joined me. She was dressed just as all day—but somehow now it was fresh and evening piquant.

The dining room was dark-opulent, the table was broad, we sat side by side on a deep-cushioned wall bench with our backs to the center window of the bay: at her right was the southern river, at my left the northern river. Silently we martini'd; silently we mused over chilled vichyssoise and lettuce with roquefort and cold whitefish and Chablis and hot chateaubriand and chateauneuf-du-pape. Together, still silently, we contemplated the diversified flame colors that interflashed above the crepes suzette; even these emaciated pancakes we wolfed in silence until all was gone. Whereafter we meditated armagnac in deep goblets.

Althea broke silence, but low: "It is nearly eleven, Pan." With her right elbow on the table, she was letting her nostrils gently savor the brandy.

My brother, you know that I do not talk about women; but this is confidential between us, this you must know about. In what follows, never mind me: watch Althea.

I said low: "Where shall we talk philosophy?"

"I thought you might prefer to talk conspiracy. It seems to me that we established this afternoon a zero hour of two thirty this morning. That is a little over three and a half hours from now."

"Such a conversation, Althea, would be empty: when the time draws near, we will go there and foil it. More fruitful now would be philosophy—of one sort or another." And quietly I laid my right hand on the crest of her left thigh. And I became young, but I held my hand steady.

Her eyes never left mine, her brandy did not tremble. She told me: "I am here for business. *You* are here for business."

"For business, we must get to the falls. Do you know how long it takes?"

"I have a helicopter waiting. Fifteen minutes to the falls—and another half hour to the underground place where the business is."

"Good. Forty-five minutes. And I think you mentioned that it is only eleven—"

Now I felt her cool hand on my hand on her thigh. She told her brandy: "The only purpose of my hand there, Pan, is to control your hand. I rather hoped that you might be subtler."

"Subtlety is for leisure. We have under three hours. This fact your pleasant hand on my hand appears to be recognizing."

"You are direct. Or—is it indirect?"

"It is direct. Where do we talk one or another sort of philosophy?"

"My suite will do. Are we ready?"

"Yes—but first there is a concern with our waiter. I can make him happy with my mind—but can you perhaps make him happier with expense-account cash?"

Behind me, she closed the door to her suite; I waited there in the vestibule, there was a night-light glow; I turned to her, she looked up at me; her shoulders were forward and I clasped them.

She kicked off her shoes, thus dropping her eyes two inches below mine. She waited, looking up at me. It was the first time that her mouth had been small.

I told her honestly: "I love you. And there is time."

"I trust you, for some reason. And there is time."

"A man distrusts an avowal of trust. You trust me for what, Althea?"

"To be honest—and totally discreet. I am glad that you made this honest approach, Pan. Here I am—but there is no absolutely overwhelming hurry. Do you want a drink now?"

"Eventually. Not now. Do you?"

"No."

Gently I kissed the right side of her throat just where it flared above the clavicle; she quivered but said nothing. I told her: "Quite likely I shall some day report this to my brother. But no one else. And him you can trust—we have no other brothers."

"To know this is alarmingly arousing, it makes it in a sort of way two for one. Is he like you?"

"*Exactly* like me in body, almost exactly in mind."

"I think you'd better start kissing me now, on the lips. Take it slow, Pan: let our lips get to know each other, a little, then rather well. Wait until the time is right for both of us, before you let go. Can you do that, Pan? already I am noticing a certain preliminary turgescence—"

"Once I do let go, Althea—are there any ground rules?"

"Here I am not a minister of state, Pan—I am a woman. Improvise your own ground rules. Cancel your own ground rules. I believe that you love me a little, and I love you a little, and I trust you a lot—"

She clutched me around the torso, pressing her head against my chest. "Make love to me selfishly, and I will make love to you generously. Pan, Pan, my need is *so* great—"

My brother, how long has it been since *you* were in bed with a passion-hungry goddess throwing herself away for you?

We lay bare there. The night light was long gone.

Her face came slowly to mine: her lips were wan in window-filtered moonlight. "Excuse me for being punctilious at this juncture, but I do have a sense of time. Pan, it is nearly one thirty, the run will take forty-five minutes, we must dress and go now; already we may be too late to intercept, we can only remediate—" Her hand was on my chest, she was insisting: "Pan, we must *go!*"

My left hand caressed her left shoulder; my head was pillowed on my right arm, I was studying invisible ceiling. "How can it matter, Althea—since you have already murdered them?"

Slowly she rigidified. "*Murdered* them? murdered *whom?*"

"The two Moskovians and the bus driver."

"Are you *wild?*"

"They are nowhere within thirty miles of Scandia. So they are dead. So the Moskovians cannot plant the device. So why must we go?"

Her hand slid off my chest; she lay now on her back, lightly pressing five fingertips against five fingertips, examining her hands, peering at them through her ravine de la poitrine. Frowning, she asked her hands: "Now why would I murder them?"

"They know too much about you."

"Such as?"

"That they are not your persecutors but your stooges. That you are the one who has the device and will place it. That the Honorable Althea Candless is high on the Moskovian payroll. That you somehow brought me here because you were remorsefully ambivalent, hoping for a God-judgment: either I perceptively find out and stop you, or I would not find out and you would have to go through with it despite all you had done to get yourself stopped."

"That was very good thinking, Pan, since clearly you have not been spying on my mind."

"How do you know that I have not?"

"Because you think I murdered them."

"Not because my major guess is wrong?"

"It is wrong only in a peculiar way. How will you stop me?"

"I will not stop you."

"Then—I am to go through with it?"

"If you can." I ran a fingertip across the flatness of her belly.

Quivering, she clutched my hand with both hands, immobilizing it there; her face turned to my face; she looked down at me, then up at me, her expression terrible; she made a noise in her throat, and swung to me, and sprang upon me.

Clinging, she told my ear: "You have won, Pan. Already it is a quarter to three. They will kill me, but perhaps it will be quick."

"Can you leave the bed now, Althea?"

"I think—yes, now. In another half hour, no. Why?"

"Then you are free to place the device. And so they will not kill you, instead they will pay you."

She sat, gripping my shoulders at arms' length. "I told you, Pan, the device inactivates in half an hour—"

"How long to install it?"

"Ten minutes, once we reach the underground locus—"

"How long to dress?"

"Two minutes—"

"If you choose to dress, I will dress and take you there instantaneously."

"You are playing with me! After all this, you will not prevent—you will *help?*"

"What is your will, Althea?"

Leaning back against the bed head, she ran a hand back through her long hair, considering. Her body was appetizing-rangy; at the far ends of her long legs, the prows of her feet were mainely crossed . . . .

She leaped from the bed and went for her clothes. I went for mine.

Dressed, holding her bulky purse, she turned to me, and her eyes were secretive. "I thank you for some things, Pan. But not for others."

I took her in my arms, telling her: "We should be in close contact for this; and I must now read your mind a little, to get the locus right, but only for that. *Think* of the locus. Think first intellectually: the topography, the entrance, the approach, the underground coordinates. . . Good. Now, *visualize* all of it—"

Her free hand clutched my shoulder. "Malgre tout, je t'aime quand meme."

Instantly we were in a bright-lighted underground place filled in a hushed way with dynamo-susurrus: a vast clean, ultra-sanitary hollow, tiered with aluminum catwalks and reamed by thick varicolored pipe-type cables at a spiderwebbing of levels. No sign of inspectors or guards. I put out sensors (but carefully staying out of *her* mind): all humans within this catacomb were distant, mostly in one direction above; I surmised that this Minister of Power had advised them of an unescorted inspection between one and three o'clock this morning; they were all up waiting for her by the gate.

Much closer to us, my sensors were picking up something else. . . .

I checked my watch. "Better move, Althea. You have fifteen minutes."

She nodded slowly, three or four times. Lethargically she released me. She turned to the wall, ran both hands sensitively over a bare area, touched an invisible spring. A panel sank inward and slid aside, revealing, within a square-yard aperture, an intricate intermeshing of switches. Opening her purse, she produced a small pair of electrician's pliers and went delicately to work on eight minuscule connections at the two ends of a zinc box perhaps six inches by two by two. She was moving with leisurely smoothness; in three minutes she had removed the box and dropped it into her purse. She took half a minute to breathe heavily. Then she removed from her purse an identical box and began to wire it in. The leads from both boxes had jack-tips: splicing-and-soldering was obviated. . . .

I had watched her silently. I said now: "If you finish, you blow Nordia. If you don't finish, you die. Althea, this is fascinating."

She stopped and listened without turning while I spoke. When I finished, she went back at it. She completed the eight connections, checked each methodically with a tiny tap of the pliers, nodded, touched a spring, closed the panel: it was a blank wall again.

She checked her wristwatch, nodded, said, "Seven after three: made it," dropped pliers in purse, closed purse, folded hands on purse, looked up at me.

"No watchmen," I remarked.

"They are probably all up at the gate, waiting for me. I was expected between one and three o'clock for an unescorted inspection. Can you arrange now to take me straight to the exterior and let me now enter by the normal entrance and plead tardy?"

"I can. Now?"

"Pan, I find you a bit inexplicable. You understood me well enough to tip my wavering in the—shall we say, the virtuous direction? by a method that in your case I could not resist, and you could have kept it going, and you didn't have to tell me that you could make instantaneous delivery, and you didn't have to deliver me; and even so, at any time during the past quarter hour you could have stopped me by force or projective hypnosis or any old thing. But here I am, and I've done it."

"So I noticed, Althea."

"The device was connected in time, it is functional. Kébec will blow."

"Presumably."

"Pan, you share my responsibility."

"I don't think so, Althea. Morally I could not stop you. What I could do, what I tried to do, was to slow you down, to please your mood, to break your compulsive reverberating action circuit, even to bring you to the point where you were convinced that by your own choice it was already too late. But I could not morally deprive you of the final opportunity-confrontation. So I brought you here, but I left you no time to slip back into the reverberating circuit: you had to make what amounted to a fresh decision all anew, and act, practically on intuition. And so you did. It was your action, it was your will: you are responsible for the evil—or for the good."

Tilted slightly backward, she stared into my eyes. "How do you mean—*or for the good?*"

Gathering her into my arms, I teleported us to the exterior. We stood on a windy bare rock above the falls: the moon was full, the altitude high, the water incandescent silver.

"Sorry, Althea; I could not answer you right there, because your Moskovian chums had stationed spy cameras there to document whether you did switch the boxes—and some of them may be fairly good at lip reading."

My arm was about her shoulders, hers about my waist; we were gazing down into dark thundering depths. She uttered: "Cameras?"

"They have established that you did make the switch. You will not be killed, you will be paid—even if, through Moskovian technological stupidity, the device doesn't work."

"Technological stupidity?"

"Since their cameras have established that you did your part, they will have to blame their own technology if Kébec does not blow. And in truth, they *were* guilty of one small stupidity. They should have put a long scratch on the front of the new box—to match the long scratch on the front of the old box."

There was silence then. Abruptly her arm and hand tightened on my waist. "Are you suggesting that I may have committed a Freudian error?"

"I am saying that you made your decision. And it was yours."

She turned to me: "When did you see the new box, to notice that there was no scratch on it?"

"I didn't. But I saw a box with a scratch go into your purse, and a box with an identical scratch come out of your purse; and I am betting that the Moskovians didn't think of *that* subtle a match. Is it a sound bet, Althea?"

She looked down and nodded twice, fingering my lapel. She murmured: "You talk high about the morality of letting me face and make my own moral decision. But if I had decided wrong and blown Kébec—by your sufferance—how would *that* have squared with your morality?"

"Kebec wouldn't have blown. I mind-checked your new box, sight unseen. It won't work."

An instant longer she clutched my lapel. Then she twisted away from me, opened her purse, drew out a box, held it high in moonlight (I could see no scratch), and hurled it into the falls. The pliers followed; she threw very well. Turning back to me, she put her head far down, gripped my upper arms, pressed the top of her head against my chest, and gave herself over to sobbing.

I took her marvelous desirable-strong shoulders. "You can lead me now to the entrance, Althea, and we'll go through the mummery of your scheduled inspection. Then afterward—can you somehow arrange to send me back to my suicide?"

Her inaudible sobbing had quieted to the pace of one small convulsion per ten seconds.

It grew faintly audible. Sobbing was not what it was.

Up came her head, she was smiling brilliantly. "There will be no inspection, Pan," she told me, and her punctuation was chuckle-blurps. "And there will be no return to your suicide. I am not the one to tell you about all this—but I can give you a hint. I did not murder the three men. I merely sent them back to how they were before you arrived—which was nonexistent."

I stood digesting that—stood befuddled during three full minutes. Then: "God damn."

"Exactly. We considered that you were a candidate. We tested you. And you have passed. I have to bring you to our headquarters, which are located in Hell, so that maybe you will not too seriously mourn your twenty-sixth-century sunrun—"

"Headquarters, Althea? in Hell? What organization?"

"Sometimes we call if *Postscript*, sometimes *Operation Second Chance*. We re-create situations in which souls have lost themselves in the past, and we start a replay, turning them loose with free will and no memory of having done all this before. Sometimes there may be a phantom memory-flash, but they always brush this off as a mere déja vu. But in the replay we offer them just a little bit of a nudge at this or that critical if-node, and then we let them alone to see if they wake up and win instead of losing. There never was an Althea Candless of Nordia, Pan—but if there *had* been an Althea Candless of Nordia, and if she *had* got herself into this bind, and *if there had been no Pan*—"

"But her device would not work."

"We saw no reason to make it workable. But if a real Althea Candless had carried a *workable* device—"

"But even this time, Pan did nothing decisive—"

"That is the point: you contented yourself with nudging and leaving it ultimately to me."

I considered that. I nodded once. Had her device been workable, I would have known it; had she nevertheless attached the real device, I would have deactivated it; she would have lost—but not Nordia. But by virtue of my nudging, she had *not* chosen to attach the real device, and she had won. But, hell, it wasn't real, it was theater! With a real Althea, would my nudging have succeeded? Who'd have any way to know?

She added: "Pan—do you really *want* your suicide? You can have it back, if you want it."

My mind smiled before I did. "I will defer suicide; this is entirely my decision, for evil or for good. But I think you nudged a little."

"Complex internudge, my friend."
"That's the best kind. What shall I call you, now?"
"Althea is as good as any name I've had."
"Shall we go to Hell now, Althea?"
Again she was fooling with my lapel. "We are entitled to a delay en route. Can you bring off a return trip to the hotel, Pan? Scandia is an illusion, of course—but I haven't yet erased."

PART TWO

Operation Second Chance

> . . . this sea (in Hell) was composed of the blood that had been shed by piety in furthering the kingdom of the Prince of Peace, and was reputed to be the largest ocean in existence. And it explained the nonsensical saying which Jurgen had so often heard, as to Hell's being paved with good intentions. "For Epigenes of Rhodes is right, after all," said Jurgen, "in suggesting a misprint; and the word should be 'laved.' "
>
> JAMES BRANCH CABELL, *Jurgen*

2

When I had come before a mountain's base—
the ending of that steep and rugged valley
that lately so had struck my heart with fear. . . .
So did my soul, which still in terror fled,
turn back to contemplate with awe and fear
that pass which man had never left alive. . . .

These were the verses of Dante's *Inferno* that with difficulty and with some contextual license I teased out of the first canto for the sake of doing some kind of contextural justice to the fearsome-gigantic rock-wilderness that now in deep dusk I found myself semiburied in. The old Doré engravings, I reflected, were actually better than the Dante verses from a viewpoint of Gothic horror; but then, perhaps Dante had not been after Gothic horror, except perhaps in a few passages concerning the depths of Hell, as:

> Just so were stilled the jaws of Cerberus,
> that demon whose loud, raucous bark so stuns
> the spirits, that they wish that they were deaf.

or—

> Three hellish Furies, all besmeared with blood,
> with women's limbs, and aspect womanly.
> About their waists were greenest hydras girt;
> for hair, horned serpents in a seething mass
> hissed as they twined about their horrid brows.

or—

> One, seizing on Capocchio, fixed his teeth
> so firmly in his neck, he dragged him down,
> making his belly scrape along the bottom.

or—

> Two frozen in one hole, so close together
> that one was to the other like a hat.
> And even as bread for hunger is devoured,
> so did the upper one gnaw at his fellow,
> just where the head is fastened to the nape.
> Not otherwise did Tydeus eat away
> the temples, in his rage, of Melanippus,
> than this one gnawed his neighbor's skull and brain.

or, finally—

With all six eyes he wept, and from three chins
the tears and bloody foam were trickling down.
In every horrid mouth he crunched a sinner. . . .

Knowing that I was in fact going to real Hell, and with these sorts of images live in my mind—in themselves pallidly materialistic, less real than the supraimaginings invoked—I found it faintly bathetic to recognize in the crepuscule that in fact I walked in Zion National Park after visiting hours. I was indeed wandering up the trail-corridor in the Temple of Sinawava, between flowered rock walls that soared above the flowers to bare-stab the height of the night, beside the maidenly gurgling Virgin River whose full-moon madnesses had carved the canyon. I had nearly attained to the permissible end of the walking: a closing-in of rock with only a narrow cut beyond, a semi-dead-end placidly shallow-flooded by the Virgin: here by day children carelessly danced from step rock to step rock across fordable water high-walled by rock; here by night the half-moonlit water purled around the step rocks, the sound of the purling suggesting the riverlet's potential of lethal anger. . . .

And it was dark, except for the pale moonshine on the water. And ahead of me there was a slender pass, even darker, many miles deep with sheer walls, guarded by a sign warning visitors against penetrating this pass by reason of the peril of flash floods: you could not run up those walls.

I gazed at the sign. In my mind, it read: ALL HOPE ABANDON, YE WHO ENTER HERE. In my mind, it was guarded by a lion and by a leopard. . . .

I inquired of my tall, slender guide: "Are you a living man, or a specter from the shades? Were you perhaps of Lombard parents sprung? Were you the poet who sang the worthy son born to Anchises, who escaped from Troy after proud Ilion burned to ashes? Are you then Virgil—that great fountainhead whence such a flood of eloquence has flowed? My blood is trembling in my veins from fear!"

My guide, Althea, answered laconically: "I am Virgil no more than you are Dante, and your blood is trembling no more than I am male. But it ought to be trembling, because it is Hell that I am guiding you into—and not as a tourist, but as a damned soul."

She vanished through the forbidden rock gate.

I hesitated.

Blood *was* trembling in my veins.

I followed.

I stood in semidarkness in a hard noisy redflashing place. It was a semihigh place, as though I had descended underground in bedrock and stood now on an intermediate platform of rugged-riveted steel, with plate steel for three walls and floor and ceiling, and on the fourth side to my left redflashing down-below openness. The noises were clanging-explosive-loud, ear-drum-damaging, steel-mill-disruptive; the semiblinding red-flashes intermitted with the clanging, flash-clang, flash-clang. . . .

Althea said, below rather than above the clamor: "It is Hell's threshold. What is your wish, Pan?"

I replied: "To enter." And I felt it and meant it. But a clang blasted the word "enter," and I did not know whether it had been heard.

Althea said: "Descend." And the word coincided with a deafening clash complicated by wailing, and I knew that I heard not the word but the meaning.

Moving leftward, I descended a steel-stepped stair without rails, knowing that any wavering would send me plummeting into red-flaring noise-depths. There was high heat, it heightened, sound heightened, flash brightened, all of it should have tortured my eyes and ears and fears, instead I thrilled as I descended. . . .

The ninety-third step was missing. Beyond was only noiseglare.

I hesitated.

Althea said: "Step off."

I was suspended in noiseglare.

And then in silentglare. And then in silent nothing. . . .

I missed the noise and glare; I was heartbroken for the departed noise and glare. Soul in ashes, too late I knew why I had loved the noiseglare: it was total psychedelic responsibility, whereas this silent nothing was the *nausée* of total freedom.

Someone invisible (not Althea) said with a mental smirk: "That was the first test, Pan; and in a way you passed, and in another way you flunked. You passed because you dared it, and you flunked because you liked it. We await your suggestions."

Raising my mental chin a trifle, I responded: "Once there were four souls, a Catholic priest, an Episcopalian rector, a Jewish rabbi, and a Christian Science practitioner, who found themselves occupying the same flame in Hell. And the priest suggested—"

One commented: "We know the story. We await your suggestions."

I considered the silent nothingness that I floated in. It was not psychospace, it contained no pregnancy. Perhaps it was nonspace. I projected a requirement into it. There was no response. It was not even nonspace.

I was totally disconnected, not only from everything, but even from every real nothing. I had only the resources of my mind and body, out as far as my skin but no farther. And there was nothing for my mind or body to act upon or through.

I was utterly free; that is to say, I was utterly helpless. In my living, more than once I had felt utterly helpless because of the chaos of environing events—because whatever I might try, its effects would go wrong. This was worse: whatever I might try, there would be no effects whatsoever.

I said to nothing: "Althea brought me here assuring me that I had passed some kind of test that qualified me to join an enterprise called Operation Second Chance. Following her, I have entered Hell assuming that Hell would give me opportunity to do something worthy. Instead, it appears that in Hell I can do nothing whatsoever. A human needs relative freedom in order to act with meaning; but if he is perfectly free, he cannot act at all. I recognize that Hell is perfect freedom; and therefore I shall be perfectly passive—until Hell, of its own volition, offers me some sort of environmental countercontrol."

And I rested, prepared if necessary to pass eternity passive.

Countercontrol came: a voice lecturing. . . .

"Hell has four functions. It provides total punishment for those who have earned total punishment. It offers purging for those who have done generally well but specifically ill. It constitutes a secure place for devils who are sadistic enough to enjoy a variety of aesthetic delights at the expense of both sorts of soul. And it is a base for devils to go forth on command by the Bushy-Tailed Father, forth into worlds to make trouble for incarnate souls who combine the illusions of supposing that one can be virtuous and of imagining that one can chart his own course.

"I now focus particularly on Hell's fourth function. soul who disregards questions of virtue is immune to us in life but will see us in Hell. Any soul who supposes that he can chart his own course will be continually frustrated or ulcreated by us in his life and will probably see us in Hell. Any soul who denies that he can contribute any initiative toward the charting of his course will be disregarded by us in life but will fall into our hands in Hell. Finally, any soul who tries to be virtuous and also tries to chart his own course will be familiar with us in both places. Are you any of those sorts, Pan?"

"I am the last sort. I have known you here and there. Hello again!"

"Ah, there. We concern ourselves now with Hell's third function. Pan, it is not too late for you to throw in your lot with us: we have delicious cruelties that you have never dreamed of, and every cruelty is prudishly justified by knowledge that the victim has earned it—"

"Sir or madam, the prospect is entrancing for brief periods of vacation; but for permanent identity—no."

"Then we will turn to Hell's first function. Your own role in this function would be that of a victim suffering eternal punishment. But from your deposition a moment ago, we gather that you do not consider yourself totally depraved."

"Not totally, no."

"Well; unfortunately for us, we agree. So you do not qualify as a victim. So for you there is left only the second function of Hell, either as patient or as practitioner: purging for those who have done generally well but specifically ill."

"I thought that was for Purgatory."

"An artificial medieval realm-distinction, Pan: we double in purging, it is rather like KP, we prefer combat. And we have been angling for a suggestion from you as to how you need purging."

"But it is you who are the doctors—"

"If it is like that, Pan, your Dr. Freud has given us some marvelous guidelines for treating you. He is available here, by the way: do you call for his services?"

"Pray assign your own specialists. I neither call for him nor exclude him."

"All right. Him we do not recommend in your case, because we have the distinct impression that you have allowed no sin to be repressed into your unconscious, but instead you have made a point of remembering and frequently repenting and to the extent of your ability redressing every sin that you have recognized."

"Some I have not been able to redress; and some presumably I have not recognized. And so I am perfectly willing to undergo a while of purging, if that is your pleasure; but I should remind you that according to Althea—"

"You were brought here to purge others?"

"Well, the idea did not seem to be quite like that, but—"

Still I hung in void; and the face that now materialized before me plunged me momentarily into profound soul-shock. I was in Hell: this face was *benign,* in a saturnine sort of way. Let me limn it: long and slender, dark-haired, dark-eyed, long-nosed, wide-mouthed, chin neither weak nor assertive; smile-crinkles about the eyes, experience-furrows about the mouth—and the eyes and mouth were smiling. No body: just the head in nonspace. . . .

I blurted: "Thoth!"

The smile stayed, the brows went down. "Welcome, Pan: Althea's report was excellent, and your semifinal testing here has confirmed it. Relax: I am not the Bushy-Tailed Father, I do not even work for him, I maintain office here by his reluctant sufferance, and purging is not what I do. There is in fact a fifth function of Hell, although it is a thin start that I have given it. By way of explaining it, let me take you to a place of high interest—"

The countercontrol intensified: I was impelled into motion—downward.

Thoth took me so deep into black space that the streaming of the metagalaxies was like a shining snake slithering through indigo: a serpent having a fairly definite head and a fairly definite tail, with all ahead and behind and beyond raw space.

And I comprehended that I was surveying synoptically all that was real. All.

He brought me in closer to the tail, and faintly behind the tail of the streaming I descried phantom silver. He demanded: "What is it?"

I told him: "It is Antan, the frozen traces of the metagalaxies, the traces of *lives,* remote yesterday. It is permanent, from its birth omega-eternal, indestructible. Also it is not alive, although some of it is traces of lives living."

He responded: "You among few understand Antan; you among few have entered Antan; it is a major reason, although not the only reason, why Althea and I interrupted your suicide—"

We came in very close indeed, so that the radiance of the metagalaxies filled my space; we plunged back into the streaming, and gleaming superclusters flashed past—paradoxically gleaming for us outside themselves, although each of them was hugging all its light to itself.

We invaded a metagalactic skin: galaxies sped blurring past; and a third of the way in toward the center, we paused a distance behind the star-spiral that I knew as Sol Galaxy. Paced by the galaxy, we swung in its rearward; and for the first time, oddly I saw the forming of its antan—filamental silver wires spun out behind the galaxy as it swung around its metagalactic center, then weaving to join the thread-currents of other galaxies and metagalaxies, ultimately to wire out behind the total serpentine streaming.

Thoth required: "Explain it."

I told him, savoring what I said: "Each component filament is the fossil trace of a living atom. An atom dies when the lure of its nucleus turns inward upon itself, ceasing to allure the electrons: then the restive electrons depart, as they have always half-wanted to do, and the nucelus progressively and introvertedly differentiates itself into its component nuclear particles; and each irreducible particle shrinks in upon itself, tensive-coarctate. At last there is a blast, and the particles explode into fragments; but then each fragment, having surrendered all energy, subsides tiny-massive into itself, never thereafter to change or to act. Because each frozen fragment is more massive than anything vital, and denser and smaller than anything vital, than even the nucleus of a living hydrogen atom, it cannot thereafter be affected by any living particle, and it passes unnoticed through any living particle that accelerates intersectively with it. And because dying atoms generate new atoms, and these atoms perishing generate new atoms, the fossil particles come to form filaments, and these filaments are immovable imperishable thin wires; and these are what we now behold, pallidly reflecting starlight. They are Antan."

Thoth waited, seeming to want expansion.

I expanded: "In themselves, the filaments preserve frozen all the vents that ever occurred in the atoms they mothered. Each of these filaments is therefore an old-fashioned wire recording of all the events that ever affected any atom in its chain. The filaments of parallel atom series record the events of molecules; the spider cables of parallel molecular series record the events of mineral fragments or of living cells; a sufficiently complex system of filaments has recorded, unchangeably and forever, all the events of a human life."

"And do you know how to run these filaments, Pan?"

"When occasion has justified such an invasion of old privacy, Thoth, I have subjectively run these filaments as though I were the magnetic finger of a wire-recorder-reproducer. Whenever I run a system of filaments, I reexperience—with total fidelity of pain and pleasure, of sight and sense and meaning—the whole life of a man or woman. The life as it was lived cannot be changed, it never dies; but except as an invader of Antan may replay it, never again does it live. Should any philosopher be searching for an epistemic guarantor for his theory that the past is unchangeable, here it is."

"Then think of the pleasures for you, Pan, if we assign you to eternity in Antan with freedom of choice! Running the frozen filaments of Antan, you can be a savage young bull-man charging virgins; or Caesar, or better Antony, knowing Cleopatra; or Abelard knowing Héloise, perferably prior to a severance; or Don Juan knowing everybody. Should your fancy take a sadistic turn, you could be the Marquis de Sade himself—although this we do not recommend, his imaginings were better than his happenings, there were nobles under Caligula and Clovis who had more perverse fun—we can find them for you. Or should your thoughts go religio-philosophical, you could be Socrates, or Jeanne d'Arc, or Bruno—"

"As to all except the last three—I would not be damned for such fiendishness?"

"Only as you might damn yourself."

"I would not damn myself, Thoth, since the pleasures would be harmless, the harm being already done. But I would suffer for the harm already done. And there would be another embarrassing entailment. Always in the course of reliving any life, I would be doing so in the grounding of my own memories and identity and my own will-impulsion to make free choices—but I would be totally at the mercy of the past perceivings and willings of the person whom I would be haunting, and so I would be unable to change any event that ever actually happened, and this I would be continually experiencing as frustration."

The Thoth-head meditatively regarded me. And presently it observed: "You have gone far, Pan, with your researches. But in one man's lifetime, no matter how long it may be, one can never go far enough; indeed, during all time up to now, even potential omniscience has not arrived at actualizing omniscience. And so it appears that you have not yet stumbled upon the *if-nodes* of Atan."

Once he had explained them, and had shown me a few, I comprehended why—during a few of my uptime explorings—I had been uneased by the seeming of a paradox: two different versions of the same history, equally real. For a while I had suspected that this might be verification of old John Dewey's theory of a continuously changing history—but I had not been able to accept, concerning actuality, a hypothesis whose framework could only be epistemological. Then for a further while I had toyed with the concept of alternate probability-worlds; but soon I had concluded to give this hypothesis grounding only in downtime, not in uptime. So I had been left awash, concerning these experiences. But now that Thoth had shown me the perfectly simple solution, I wondered at my myopia. . . .

During the lifetime of an atom or a human, there are multiple moments when a balance can be tipped, or a decision can be made, one way or another, with no definitely identifiable system of mechanics to determine the tip or the choice. And as the actuality of the atom or the human reaches determination and freezes in Antan, the perseverating locus of indecision—a *state* in the atom, and in the human a lingering thought of what might have been—freezes with less immediacy, remains for a long duration indecisively germinal. Such a temporal locus in a filament, or such a system of interrelated loci in a filamental complex, is an *if-node*. And *here*, indefinitely into the future, that past *can* be—not changed, but *paralleled and superseded*. For cultivation of an if-node can make it burgeon into a new and parallel germinality; so that, in Antan at least, what might have been *can* (if you know how) exist eternally and unchangeably alongside of what was.

Conrad's Lord Jim, in an instant of weakness, *jumped*—and could not *un*jump, and passed a lifetime compensating for remorse. That was eternally so: any runner of Antan in any subsequent era would always find it frozen so. But if the soul of Lord Jim had been able to return with power to his own Antan-filament, and find that if-node, and *refrain* from jumping—and if (this is a crucial complication) all the people and all the environment associated or potentially to be associated with Lord Jim could at the same instant have had *their* if-nodes stimulated into burgeoning—Antan could have been multiplied by a germinal matrix of parallel tracks that *might* have been better for the people. But because these new tracks would always be growing beneath the surface of actuality, keeping pace with actuality but never overtaking it, the present could never be affected by this new past.

. . . Unless, of course, some power should *accelerate* these parallel germinalities. . . .

"Operation Second Chance," Thoth told me, "is founded on the proposition that one who repents ought to have opportunity to make redress. But no redress is complete unless it is entirely new history—entirely new biography. And no redress is meaningful unless it is a *different thought* on the part of the one who erred in the first place. Nor is any redress *life*-meaningful if it is undertaken after the individual has made the mistake and seen the consequences and second-guessed himself. No: to be *life*-meaningful, the so-called redress must be a *different action taken at an if-node,* taken by an individual who has no memory or clear foresight of what actually followed that if-node, but who like any other human being running with life must project or sensitively feel the *probable* consequences better than first he did, and therefore take action different from what he did, *without knowing* what first he did, and imagining that this decision has never been confronted by him before.

"We are a very young operation, Pan, and the members of our crew are few. We are based in Hell because this is where souls who fully repent tend to gravitate, eschewing glory prior to a purgatory that will involve not merely self-purging but redress. We locate such a soul. one who knows in a rough sort of way where-when and how he erred. We reinject that soul into his own Antan at some point prior to the if-node, and we allow him to rerun his own antan in current as he ran his life in the first place, with memories of all events before that point in time but no memories of what followed. And when he reaches the crucial if-node—"

I was frowning heavily in my profound concern. "If the soul reaches that if-node with all prior events and memories identical with what they were, and with environmental pressures and urges identical with what they were—how can he act differently, Thoth?"

He said: "We nudge."

I studied that. "You mean—you direct? you exert influence? But if the soul is now being helped by knowledgeable outside influence, how can his different action be counted as a credit?"

The Thoth-face grinned. "Pan, still you are wound in the human economy of debits and credits. You forget that as a result of the new action at the if-node, the soul *can* (if it works right) experience thereafter a whole real life of the good that might have been, and all the souls who were affected by this if-action can similarly be reinjected into their *new* past lives to experience in new reality the good that might have been; and when after their new deaths they contemplate with new enlightenment the new good that paralleled the old evil, knowing that the new good was created by a better decision of the old villain—" He stopped: enough had been said.

Gazing at him, I pressed: "But the external *nudge*—"

The Thoth-face frowned. "It is not a science, Pan. We are feeling our way. I assure you that you will be a pioneer, there are few guidelines that we can give you. If the nudge is *right,* it is this sort of nudge: it has the effect of removing blinders that circumstance has imposed upon the soul, so that of his own power and will he sees and feels more clearly; and it does so in such a way that he removes his own blinders. The nudge may properly be very slight, or very powerful; but always it must be just at the threshold-level of urging the soul to remove his own blinders—*never* at the compulsion-level of *requiring* him to remove his blinders. It is a treacherous business, Pan: the agent has to judge the nudge: if he undernudges, history is repeated and the soul-remorse is reinforced; if he overnudges, the better outcome is not the soul's doing—and eventually, the soul will know it."

My comprehension was a fist closing on my heart. I put it to Thoth: "You want *me* to be one of your agents?"

The face registered affirmation.

"I will have guidance?"

"Sometimes yes, sometimes no. If we fully understood this business, we would not require intelligent-sensitive agents. There will be cases where you will have a sharp briefing, and other cases where you will merely be dropped into a problematic area with the task of determining the problem for yourself, and still other cases where you will actually lose your own *identity* and *become* the man or woman (because you will be caught up in his brain) until, approaching the if-node, your own past clarity causes your present fogginess to feed the node into the brain. You will win some, you will lose some; you will overnudge, you will undernudge—and with luck, sometimes you will nudge just right.

"Candidly, Pan, as of now there are only three of us: Althea, a man named Vogeler, and me. Vogeler I doubt, a bit: there are indications of selfishness. Althea is—well, you have known her, rather well: feel no embarrassment about this, she and I know each other rather well; if I ever begin to doubt her, I will already be doubting myself—but she makes mistakes, and so do I. For my part, I take a few cases, but mainly I am wrapped up in study and planning. Call on Althea whenever you need a critique, Pan—but the critique must always be *after the fact:* you are on your own."

I contemplated the cobwebs of silvery filaments: the Antan of the universe.

I said low: "Why don't you drop me into the first one, and see how I bounce?"

PART THREE

A Certain Garden

Pan, legend hath it that on the planet Erth, Edom the first man and Ave the first woman dwelt in a garden that they and their descendants could have inhabited forever. But the devil, in the form of a serpent, tempted Ave into eating God-forbidden fruit, and she gave of it to Edom: whereafter they knew their nakedness and covered it, and God banished them from the garden. Like most folk legends, it disguises a real human happening, and the morality derived from it is not necessarily a God-given morality. So we are putting you into the old Antantrack shortly before the serpent turned up. Thus the first of your assignments will affect two who were reputedly the first of all humans. We will be fascinated to watch what you do with it.

3

I stood in a primeval garden, occupying an astral version of my own body—but this body was invisible. I had no instructions at all: I did not even know whom to haunt. And I saw nobody to haunt: the garden was lush, it was virginal, it was apparently unpeopled.

Except by yonder serpent.

Since the colorsinuosity of the seven-foot python was all the animal life in evidence, I gave it my full pleasured attention. And presently I comprehended, from certain telepathic emanations coming my way, that this python was rather more intelligently reactive than most snakes.

This python had, in fact, a human mind. And the quality of its mental intraput suggested that it had, superimposed on its snake brain, a human brain. An astral brain, presumably. In other words, the serpent was an intruder in this garden—or at least, its possessing mind was. It might be Thoth, checking me out. Or Althea. Or—who? Vogeler?

Carefully I disciplined my own mind and brain to keep their intraput internal, so the serpent would not detect my presence. Then I concentrated subjectively on the serpentine stream of consciousness. And gradually I gathered that this pythonoid human was astonishingly ambivalent.

The snake form, entirely physical and infinitely subtle, enabled its alien possessor to savor totally from tonguetouch to tailtip the divine sensuosity of the garden. It also generated in its possessing mind awkward conflicts of conscience —conflicts which presumably the snake's own mind did not share, although this minimal mind passed undetected by me.

The long slender brilliant-hued fine-scaly body was writhingly replete with kinaesthetic motion-rewards and everywhere sensitized with nerve endings of pleasure: the serpent brain deliciously interpreted every sensation into elaborate joy-without-consequence. As the python rippled through ferns or scraped across rocks, its body tasted different kinds of pleasure differentially from segment to segment. Concerning all these goodies, the snake's human guest-mind seemed undividedly happy.

But then the guest found himself leaping upon an unwary faun, wrapping it in coil upon coil, lovingly tightening his grip until the faun took thin-braying leave of life. The serpent brain urged its mind-guest to rejoice; but the astral-human brain that the guest had brought with him damned the sadism and pitied the victim.

When thereafter, in an unshaded sun-beaten place, the minded serpent lay torpidly soaking in divine warmth and tasting internally the faun molecules enriching all the cells of his body cell by cell, the snake brain soothed its guest with ultimate serenity while the human brain raised moral doubts. The guest-mind discomfortably sought reconciliation—and uneasily settled for a decision that killing-for-function was part of the cosmic design for subhuman nature, while the faun was probably a masochist. Presently, in this delicious torpor, the serpent brain began stealthily to take command: it was not that the guest's human intelligence lapsed—it was rather that the highly developed connate resources of the snake brain redirected his consciousness, lulling his superego. . . .

I test-challenged: "Are we a team here, Vogeler? My instructions don't include you." In fact, I had no instructions, and this guest-mind would not necessarily be Vogeler.

Sprung out of sensuous tranquillity, the serpent stiffened. Then the Vogeler-mind inquired: "Pardon? Oh—it's you, Pan, they told me about you." His countertelepathy seemed nettled. "Well, my instructions certainly don't include *you*—so probably you have misunderstood *your* instructions. What are they?"

I mind-grinned. "To be honest—I really don't have any. But here I am anyway, somehow. What are yours?"

"Mine are precise enough. Proceed to the planet Erth. Go to such-and-such a garden in the year 100004 B.C. and take the form of a serpent. Observe the man and the woman, and act as you see fit. End of my orders. And you have none. So you see, I am the one to be here; and clearly you are supposed to be elsewhere. I'm truly sympathetic, Pan—but it's your move."

All right: they had put me here without mentioning Vogeler, and him here without mentioning me. Was I somehow supposed to redeem Vogeler? it seemed improbable, and I chose to dismiss the idea that he was supposed to nudge me into self-redemption. Until I would know more, I shouldn't act: it might wreck something. Therefore I sat in the lush grass, hugged my invisible knees, and queried: "Mind if I observe?"

"Watch the master," Vogeler responded, "and stay out of it. Have you seen the woman, Pan?"

"What woman?"

"You *haven't* seen her? She'll be along presently. What a dish! Twenty miles ahead of any other dame in her clan—I think she's a mutation. Name's Avé. And wait till you see her man Edom! definitely a mutation, out of a neighboring clan. He stole her last week, they're honeymooning here—"

Foliage moved in a copse.

"Freeze!" warned Vogeler.

"Frozen," I assented, making sure of my own invisibility.

Avé emerged into the open.

The snake eyes of Vogeler didn't blink, but his tongue flickered. No mere human could comprehend this woman as the Vogeler-python now comprehended this woman. His man brain flashed him every signal that might be expected, save only warning signals: these are the province of the superego, and Vogeler's, having ingested the faun-problem, was now off duty. Meanwhile his snake brain added to the sexual signals a special crawling-curling-prowling appreciation of her contours, enriched by the snake's hyperdeveloped olfactory imagery. . . .

But the woman (who was naked, naturally) did not seem to be enjoying Paradise as Vogeler was enjoying it. Instead, she appeared concerned. Standing tense in the clearing, she kept looking back at the copse, as though some enemy might be following her—yet evidently someone who was not totally enemy: someone about whom she was ambivalent.

My interest sharpened: this woman was in some vague trouble. . . .

Her dear enemy crashed out of the copse into the clear, a noble hairy man, erect in every member. She cowered. He laughed and came on. Then with a leap he overcame her, and they grass-rolled in a snorting screaming comminglement of pain and pleasure. . . .

As it quieted, I was amused to observe that all of Vogeler's coils had straightened.

Disentangling himself, Edom sat for a while on the grass, legs asprawl, languidly scratching his haired hard belly, while moaning she rolled on her front.

She quieted and lay still.

He looked her way. "Swim?" he inquired in a happy baritone.

She shook her head no.

He reached over and slapped her hard, once on each buttock. "Stay there," he commanded. "I'll be back." Catapulting to his feet, he strode back into the copse, reaching up to snatch a bunch of grapes off a vine as he disappeared.

Still I saw no reason to intervene. I waited, observing.

The woman lay still.

Snake Vogeler slithered over to investigate. He knew that she would not be alarmed, since short pythons don't attack people; but he didn't want even to startle her. Approaching her from behind and below, Vogeler was momentarily tempted; but then he decided that she was in no shape to tolerate sensuous exploration, and instead he crept up beside her and flickered his tongue delicately in her ear.

Wearily she brushed it off.

He told her: "It isn't an ant, it is I."

She turned her head just enough so that her nose and mouth were no longer buried in grass, and she peered at him with one eye. "Hello, Snake," she said. "I didn't know you could talk."

He wasn't talking, of course; it was mind-to-mind stuff. There was a complication: she didn't have enough language even to say something as involved as "I didn't know you could talk." The *potential* for semantic complication was there—she was a mutation, fully *Homo sapiens sapiens*—but she had learned no more than her clan lingo. Her level—and the man's level—was of the order of: "Swim?" "No." "Stay there—I'll be back." Even the last was pushing the limit. Vogeler, however, knew that the semantic potential was latent: he had caught her wonder at his talking, and he had given her the words to express it. This conversation was going to be swiftly developmental.

He told her confidentially: "I can talk to *you*."

It pleased Avé, and she got up on an elbow and smiled and reached out to stroke Vogeler's head. He coiled lazily nearer, and her hand descended to caress his throat and back. "Pretty snake," she murmured. "Smooth. I like."

If he were to throw coils about her, she might struggle a little but would not seriously resist—not fearing harm, although really too weary for erotics. However, he refrained, allowing himself to be comforted by her stroking hand. He suggested: "Something is wrong. Tell me."

She frowned a little, continuing to stroke. "He's wearing me out," she confessed.

"Why don't you stop him?"

"I'm not supposed to."

"But if you could get him to hold off sometimes—"

She shook her head, still frowning. "He's too big and strong."

"How about the other women?"

"What other women? I'm his only woman so far."

"I mean, in the clan. Do the other women have the same trouble?"

She stared stupid, evidently not understanding.

He tried it again. "Do all women have to take what they get from their men—whatever the men want, whenever they want it?"

She grinned: "What other way is there? Snakes must be pretty dumb."

Vogeler's mind glanced at mine; I stayed impassive. He returned to Avé: "Does Edom treat you like this all the time?"

"Well, no. Sometimes he lets me alone for days. That's even worse. When I tell him I want him, he hits me."

"So it's only one way for you—is that it? Either he has all he wants of you, and you have to accept it—or he lets you alone, and when you want him he hits you."

"That's it," she nodded as soon as she had comprehended the long question.

"What else is there between you? Do you play games?"

"What are those?"

"Do you ever just talk?"

"What about?"

"Do you ever—like toss a nut back and forth to each other?"

"Oh, sure. Edom will holler, 'Throw me that nut!' And then he will crack it with his teeth and eat it."

"Don't you even hunt berries together?"

"I hunt berries. He hunts me."

The fullness of Vogeler's idea was beginning to enthrall him. He remarked: "It's hard for me to talk with you at this distance. Do you mind if I gather 'round you, a little?"

She smiled: "I think that would be very nice. You know, you *are* different from—*oo!*"

"How am I different?" he hissed—telling himself that his interest was not at all carnal: it was more snake-tactual, serpent-thermal; he had to play the role, didn't he?

"Well," she replied, "you *feel* different, of course, but—well, it's mainly that first you *asked*."

"Edom never asks?"

"Never. He just takes. He—ah-ah, *no,* Snake—*please*—"

"What's the matter?"

"I'm nervous, it's all. Some other time, when he's been leaving me alone."

"What if I just go ahead, whether you like it or not?"

Habitually helpless Ave wasn't really resisting, she couldn't resist, she was merely pleading. "Of course I can't stop you. But—you did *ask* to come over."

Sighing a little, Vogeler dropped mostly off, although his top coil continued to drape his head over her shoulder. "Then I will go intellectual," he told her, "and you must think along with me, while we get your problem solved."

"Huh?"

"If you pay attention, I can help you with Edom."

"How?"

"The whole key for you is to get Edom to where he *asks*—and to where he *will* take no for an answer. Tell me, Avé—if I teach you how to do this—how will you reward me?"

That one stunned me, a little. Did Operation Second Chance blink at kickbacks?

She dimpled, caressing the middle of the snake body that hung from her shoulder. "If you can teach me that, I will reward you any way you like."

It was a fascinating response for a naive, submissive woman who had never been allowed any *quid pro quo* experience. Inferentially, it was instinctive.

Leaving her entirely, Vogeler went a little way distant and erected hips head and front third high off the ground. "Follow me. Ave. There is a tree that I want to show you."

Invisible, I followed them. Increasingly I was worrying about something semiformless, vast, and ancient.

Vogeler scaled the tree pleasurably, spiraling up the slender stem as though he were a stairway on the Loire; and presently his head reappeared to her at the end of two feet of neck, peering down at her from the mesh of branches. Near his head swung appetizing fruit: its color was orange.

"First," he told her, "you must eat of the fruit of this tree. It is the best fruit you ever tasted." Carelessly Vogeler discounted the fact that he had no prior knowledge of this fruit:

they had put knowledge into him, evidently it was part of his mission.

Doubtfully she gazed upward. "We have always evaded this fruit. It is not to be eaten."

"How do you know it is not to be eaten?"

"We watch the other animals. We do not do anything that the other animals do not do. That way we show them that we are their brothers and sisters, after all. They do not eat this fruit—so we do not eat this fruit."

The point was well made, all right, and Vogeler totally grasped its implications. So superior was the brain of Man to the brain of any other animal, that Man's brain overrode all his instincts at will; and this meant that Man must continually be making decisions. But he looked at other animals, and he saw that they had few decisions to make: they *knew*. And so, for Man, it was the best part of wisdom to imitate the other animals, to follow their ways. . . .

Man felt inferior, actually! Indeed, when he killed another animal, he felt downright guilty, as though he had murdered his father. Man had magics to neutralize this guilt; but the magics only emphasized the fundamental inferiority.

Vogeler was about to defeat this inferiority; but before he could defeat it, he must join in. If Avé would not eat this fruit without animal authority, why then. . . .

"*Some* animal *must* eat it!" Vogeler insisted. "If no animal ate it, how would its seeds be spread?"

"All right, Snake, you tell me. What animal eats it?"

Vogeler didn't know, but Vogeler was crafy. He replied: "The cockatrice eats it."

"I have never seen a cockatrice eating it. What is a cockatrice?"

"A cockatrice is hard to describe, because it is invisible by day, and at night when it is visible it cannot be seen."

"Oh." Avé, hands clasped behind, rocked indecisive on heels and toes.

"Well?" Vogeler demanded. "Are you going to eat it, or not? Do you want me to help you, or not?"

"It will not kill me?"

"No."

"What will it do to me?"

"It will enlarge your perception."

"Edom might not like that."

"He will—because you are to talk him into eating it with you."

"Will that help me?"

"I will—when the eating is accompanied by the talking that I am going to give you. But you must eat a little of the fruit and enlarge your perception in order to understand the talking. Now listen carefully, Woman. I will nip off the stem: you catch the fruit when it falls. Eat just one bite—no more. Chew it carefully, so that the juice runs down your throat, then swallow it. Then I will tell you what to say to Edom. But before you say these things to Edom, get him to eat some of the fruit. You may take just one more bite in front of him, to convince him that it is good; but after that, give it to him. *Then* say these things to him. Do you understand?"

"That is all, Snake?"

"That is all."

"That will help me?"

"Positively."

"Give me the fruit."

He snapped with his sharp toothless beak. The fruit fell. She caught it. She hesitated. She bit and began to chew slowly. Her eyes widened. She chewed more rapidly, gazing at the serpent. Slowly she sank to her haunches, and swallowed slowly, and meditated.

Into her enlarging perception Vogeler poured his total store of twentieth-century semantics.

Upon this apperceptive mass he superimposed his prescription for freedom.

I witnessed aghast. Belatedly—beating my mental forehead for stupidity—I had comprehended what Vogeler was up to.

As Avé went predaciously away, as Vogeler slithered down the tree bole to follow her, my mind caught and held him. I was beginning to know what my own mission here had to be.

I demanded of Vogeler: "Are you really stupid enough, or villain enough, to start it all over again?"

The triteness of his innocent "What do you mean?" irritated me as much as the hypocrisy of it. We were mind to mind now, bodies abandoned, locked in a nonspace argument.

I insisted: "It ought to be perfectly clear to you. They sent you here to head off a primeval foul-up in a naive replay. Instead, you have just refouled the whole future of all mankind on Erth!"

"What makes you think that I have done damage? I played it the way I saw it, where Thoth placed me. I helped the woman."

"You helped her, Vogeler, with the same old help. And you have just lost them the garden all over again."

"You mean my conscience ought to be hurting me because I gave them forbidden fruit?"

"Don't try to evade me with conventional taboo symbolism. Nobody forbade that fruit except man's own fear of it. I know what it is, Vogeler, I caught the message from you: it is only a stimulant, a natural consciousness-expanding drug: the worst it can do is to make them drunk and leave them with hangovers; it does not have the brain- and gene-mutilating consequences of synthetic concentrates. The thing that counts, Vogeler, is why you are giving them that fruit, what you plan to have them do with it. You have given it so the woman will comprehend the words you have given her; and she will give it to the man so that Edom will be captivated by her suggestions. What counts is your words—and your words are devilish."

"I fail to see why devilish. The motivation of my words was generous. I was all wrapped up in the woman's problem. She is enslaved to the man. I cannot stand slavery, Pan. Can you?"

"Well, no—"

"So I taught her how to free herself, using three cantrips."

"Three, naturally."

"The first cantrip is not easy to talk about, because it concerns anatomical details with respect to which I have been bred in reticence—that is, not in their use, you understand, but in verbal discussion. And I think that it is probably correct, Pan, to be reticent about such talking, because intellectual discussion breeds an artificially objective attitude as touching matters, (as touching) which one should be purely subjective—"

"In short," bitterly I rejoined, "you told Avé to make Edom feel guilty about exposing organs whose exposure is animal-normal."

"But what can be wrong with that kind of advice, Pan?

Right now, because of his strength, the man has all the advantage, and so the women are enslaved. But with this new taboo-advantage, Avé will be able to equalize matters, a little. When Edom grows self-conscious about exposing himself, he will feel inhibited about Avé."

"She can also overequalize matters. She can emotionally castrate him."

"Thus, Pan, leading man through frustration and redirection and sublimation into the space age. Instead of being Freudian, why don't we go watch the first cantrip develop? And then I will explain the second and third cantrips to your mind which clearly requires advanced guidance—"

Edom and Avé sat idyllically on a rock beside Edom's favorite swimming hole, a lush beflowered viney affair, lines with bedrock, a few hundred yards in mean diameter, free form: it might have been artfully designed for the last word in rusticity. Where they sat, sun through leaves exquisitely flecked their sun-burnished nakedness with gently moving leaf shadows. Man squatted on the rock, legs apart, feet flat-splayed on grass; Woman perched on one of his thighs, her legs dangling between his legs, her toes touching grass: her right arm loose-affectionate about his neck, her left hand offering him the fruit; his left arm about her waist, his great left hand caressing her ribs beneath a breast, his right hand on her right thigh; his great white teeth showing through his black beard, ready to chomp on the fruit.

His head came forward, his jaws open; she drew the fruit away; his smile disappeared, but his teeth did not; he frowned at her, his grip on her rib cage and thigh tightening. He said: "Give."

She warned: "Remember what I said. Just one little bite. See if you get sick."

"Did *you* get sick?"

"No—"

"So *I* won't get sick."

Her right arm snaked on around his neck so that her hand clutched his beard to control him, and again her left hand proffered the orange fruit. He chomped. She pulled back. He chewed appreciatively, letting the sweet-pungent juice trickle down his gullet. He swallowed the pulp. He demanded: "More!"

She sprang away from him, holding the wounded fruit behind her. "Not yet. We wait a little while. See if you get sick."

He shook his head. "I feel good. Better and better. You want me to beat you?"

She shook her head emphatically. "Listen to Avé, now. I have to ask some questions."

"Why?"

"To see if you are drunk."

"I can tell if I'm drunk."

"Not with *this* fruit. I have to ask questions to know."

"Who told you to ask questions?"

"Snake did. He gave me the fruit."

"Snake is wise, I guess. What tree did this come from?"

She told him.

He got (somewhat unsteadily) to his feet. "Nobody supposed to eat this fruit!"

"Who said?"

"My people said! This fruit is taboo!"

"You *left* your people, remember? You said they were stupider than my people, even!"

He stared at her, confused. He ran a hand back through his long hair.

Deliberately she took a tiny bite of the fruit, chewed it, swallowed it. Then she asserted: "My people said the same thing—the tree is taboo. But Snake says the fruit is good. Snake is wise. But I have to ask questions to see if you get drunk—said Snake."

Frowning, eyes on fruit, he snapped: "Ask."

Woman demanded: "What is our totem?"

Man replied: "Atman."

"What does Atman call us?"

"He calls us Man."

"But you call me Woman."

"Just because you have a womb. But you are Man too. Avé. Soft Man, punk Man, but Man."

She winced but stayed with it. "Very good, my man Edom—I don't think you're drunk yet. Have one more bite. Just one. Then more questions."

Lunging, he seized her around the waist, grabbed the fruit, and sheared off a quarter of it. With difficulty she thrust him away. He stood chewing, savoring, swallowing. He glowered up at her: "I want all of it now."

"Not yet!" she begged, cowering. "Snake said! Not yet!"

"More questions?"

"That's right."

"Ask, then! Go, Woman!"

She frowned, trying to remember the next one. Behind her, Snake Vogeler hissed a prompt, while I shuddered. She demanded: "Are we friends with Snake?"

"Yes—"

"Friends with Lion? Friends with Antelope?"

"Friends with everybody. Of course."

"Are we as good as they are?"

Seated, he drew himself tall. "What do you mean? We are the best!"

"If we are the best, why are we always trying to do just the way they do?"

That one would have lost him totally had it not been for the mind-enlarging fruit; on the other hand, without the fruit she could not have asked it. He scratched his head, looking stupid: an impossibly culture-free test would have measured his IQ at 127 (as contrasted with his more primitive parents' approximation to 86), but he was a contented rustic bumpkin and had no incentive to be alert about abstractions. Presently he mumbled: "The other animals always know what to do. But we always have to decide. So we just do what they do, and then we don't have to decide."

"If they always know what to do, and we don't—why are we the best?"

"Dunno. We just are. *Look* at us!"

Resolutely fixing her gaze, she responded firmly: "I am looking at *you*."

He stared at her. Then he saw where on him she was looking. His head came up with a broad smile. "Good, yes? You like?"

Putting out her lower lip, she disciplined herself to move her head slowly back and forth in a deliberate hypocritical negation.

His face fell. He stood; and, slapping hands to hips, he looked down at himself. "What's wrong! I don't see anything wrong."

Continuing to stare, she asserted judiciously: "Antelope you hardly notice. Lion you hardly notice. Snake you can't even find. But *you*—"

"Well?"

"It gets in your way when you run. The brambles catch it."

His face flushed dark; and somehow his hanging hands had come together before him.

"In that way," she pressed, "they are better than you are."

He said low: "You really think so?"

"They good. You bad."

He was frowning deeply.

"And another thing," added Avé. "How often do *they* have to?"

"How often do *who* have to?"

"Our friends. Snake. Antelope. Lion. Even Peacock. All the ones that we are better than. How often do *they* have to?"

He spat. "Once a year. Twice a year. I dunno. When they get goin', though, boy, *do* they—"

It was a debate turning of the sort that tells a skilled tactician to introduce a red herring hurriedly. Said Avé: "You're getting sober. Finish the fruit."

While he was wolfing it with both hands, she needled: "Just think how it is, with these friends of ours that we are better than. They have fur and hair and scales and feathers, so nothing catches in brambles. They have their own times during the year to climb each other, and they don't have to do it any other time. How's the fruit?"

"Mmmmmmm-*m*!"

"And anther thing. Who does the choosing—he or she?"

"Mm?"

"With Antelope, who does the choosing—he or she?"

"Well—he does the jumping."

"I know—but which she does he jump, and when?"

"Got any more of that fruit?"

"You've had plenty. How about Peacock? Who does the choosing?"

"*He* does, naturally. He spreads his tail, and—"

"And one of the girls decides that she wants him."

"So?"

She spread hands. "You see why our people are afraid of that fruit? It's because it makes us think clearer. Here we've been going along imagining that we were better than our friends the other animals. But they don't catch in brambles, and they have time rules, and their women do the choosing. Their totems have given them these things. But what has *our* totem Atman given *us*? Woman abuse and season chaos and brambles!

"You know what, Edom? *They are better than we are!* They are good, and we are bad. We are bad, Edom—bad! *What are we going to do about it?*"

He was staring at her. He had thrown away the fruit core, and he stood with his hands hanging folded before him.

"It seems to me, Vogeler," I observed, "that we have been watching the effects, not only of your first cantrip, but also of your second and your third."

"They sort of flowed in together, Pan. But you see the consequences."

"You tell me."

"Credit me with no brillant predictions, Pan: this is nothing but remembrance of things past! It will begin simply: now that Woman has made Man feel sexually alienated from the other animals, he will try to find his way back to them with suitable atonements: he will be *hiding* his manhood that catches in brambles and gets in his way when he runs; very particularly he will be hiding it from Woman, who identified his shame; and also, to get back in the good graces of Antelope and Peacock, he will be *asking* Woman instead of demanding, with occasional lapses of course; and she will form a habit of refusing often enough to make this meaningful. Gradually she will build up her coyness into a mystique of the feminine: they are not generations away from creating an Erth totem, and the Erth goddess will follow. Meanwhile Man will feel guilt toward his totem, Atman, for denying what his totem had naturally conferred upon him: he will be unable to bear this totem conflict; he will therefore rationalize his denial of his totem as a command by his totem and later by his God, and he will seek other kinds of actions to feel guilty about—and he will find them.

"But it is not merely the forthcoming apparatus of sexual taboo that interests me: this is only the symbolically appropriate procreative core of what is to come. For the woman has implanted in the man a haunting thought that instead of being better than other animals, he is inferior to them; and this thought he will not tolerate. Therefore he will become a predator, proving his superiority by wearing their skins and drinking their blood—"

"He is a predator now, isn't he?"

"But only for food; but the woman and I together have forced his killing to become symbolic! Worse than that: she has taunted him by saying that part of the superiority of other animals is vested in the instincts that their totems have given them, the absolute rules they have to steer by; whereas the man and the woman have no inbuilt rules, because their vast brains can bypass every instinct that evolution has left them with. In those animal rules for Man reposed the soul of their garden; and this soul, Pan, I have destroyed. For Man will now rise to the challenge by inventing far more complicated taboo systems than any animal totem ever dreamed of; and he will guarantee the absoluteness of his taboo system and the superiority of his own totem, Atman, to the animal totems by asserting and believing that the taboos were given by his own totem, Atman,—or, later, by his God. And thus, within a few generations, mankind on Erth will be all wound up in an ornate artificial morality, exchanging this incubator garden for the cold real world of guilt and supernal fear and propitiation.

"And out of guilt and fear and propitiation, Man will generate a compensatory defiance that he will call self-confidence; and he will drive himself upward and onward to godhead and the stars.

"I did it, Pan. *Me!*"

My mind gazed at his mind, aghast at his *hybris* and his myopia—although of course I knew that the two go together; but this was a man who had been chosen by Thoth and Althea for Operation Second Chance! surely neither of these flaws had seriously troubled his past record! Of course, I too had been chosen, and with chagrin I remembered a couple of instances; nevertheless. . . .

Skip the *hybris*; consider only the myopia. Of course Vogeler knew that he was operating in Antan, seeking to nudge at an if-node in order to head off a mistake; and the mistake had been Avé's. How then could Vogeler—knowing the original story—have failed to see that the serpent whom he inhabited *had been here the first time and had done all the same things?* It was hard for me to imagine what supernal mind a hundred thousand years ago could have invested a snake with such far-seeing purpose: possibly the Bushy-Tailed Master: minds leave no traces in Antan, only bodies including brains leave traces. But I know Antan; and in my observing mind there was absolutely no question that originally the snake had done all the same things, that Vogeler had been merely running its fixed trace, that Vogeler's persuasion of will and initiative was wholly a Vogeler illusion.

He had, in fact, *overshot* the if-node, without even noticing it. The if-node had been the instant when the brain that controlled Vogeler (although he supposed that *he* was controlling *it*) had conceived the genial notion of enlarging the minds of the man and the woman with the psychedelic fruit and feeding them new ideas. But whoever the original serpent had been controlled by, he had fed them precisely the new ideas that Vogeler now refed them: the outcome had been no different—Vogeler had not even arrived at creating a parallel track in Antan. Simply, he was rerunning the past—and I was watching him do it. . . .

Should *I* have stepped in? they had dropped me here to do *something*. . . . Eh, but Vogeler too they had dropped here, and he had the con, and he had goofed it. Was I supposed to await a *later* if-node, maybe? But then I reminded myself that by the rules of Operation Second Chance I was on my own in these Antan sorties: there was nothing particular that I was *supposed* to do, other than watch for the chance and hope to catch it and use it. . . .

"Pan?"

I pulled myself back to the moment. "Vogeler?"

"I have a moral problem."

"Oh?"

"In full candor, I must confess that—my decision to help the woman was not—well—not entirely a selfless decision."

"Oh?"

"My snakiness appears to be inordinately sensual. I—well, she promised me—a reward, if it worked. I await your castigation."

"Until now, Vogeler, you have acted with total self-confidence. Why ask me?"

The voice was semihaughty. "Until now, Pan, my operation has been for the good of the woman and of mankind. But now reenters a question of personal interest, and committee work seems indicated. What is your opinion, Pan? may I properly claim my reward from the woman?"

Inwardly sighing, I advised him: "Take your reward, Vogeler. If you can, that is."

"If I *can*, that is?"

"There is a thing about primate females: it is a sex characteristic, whether women ever admit it or not. Women have a way of accepting the taboos around them, particularly those that they arrive at through their own preaching. Whether the customs of the country are Puritan or libertine, women embrace them with a whole heart. If a woman convinces a man that such-and-such is so, the woman will promptly *believe* that such-and-such is so. And this may affect your rewarding."

"I sense an internal contradiction. If all women accept existing taboos, how can any woman preach new taboos?"

"I will say it another way. Most women tend to accept existing taboos, Puritan or libertine. Some women, influenced perhaps by some serpent, preach new taboos. If they sell their new taboos, they themselves and all other women settle instantly into them."

"Even if you are right, Pan, I fail to see how this will affect my rewarding."

Silence.

"Pan?"

But I had retreated, hurting, into physical and mental invisibility.

Leaving Vogeler free to collect his reward from Avé by once again becoming the python in the garden.

Snake and Woman confronted each other in the copse. Avé was changed to this extent: her nether parts, as Milton Puritan-put it in his reticently pagan way, were hidden by an apron of leaves. Large rubbery leaves.

Snake Vogeler hissed: "How about it?"

"Not sure, my friend, not sure." Avé was frowning small. "These leaves tickle, is the thing."

"But is Edom bothering you anymore?"

"I can't tell, it's still the same day. He won't stop entirely, will he?"

Vogeler spoke with the Wisdom of the Serpent. "They will say of you that you violated God's law by eating of the fruit of knowledge of good and evil. But I am a pragmatist, and I would phrase it differently. For a pragmatist, 'knowledge' means 'warranted theory.' So actually, you and Edom, having eaten the fruit, are now *theorizing* for the first time about good and evil; and this theorizing, of course, terminates your innocence. So this jungle won't seem to be a garden anymore; but at least, Woman, you have entered upon your Domination of Man by Mystique."

Her brow was multiply wrinkled. "Stay on the subject, Snake. What did you mean about Edom not bothering me? He will *sometimes,* won't he?"

Vogeler sighed. "If you play it right, now you will be able to choose your own times for being bothered and otherwise dominated. As for you, Woman, the road is not going to be easy; but remember that you too are Man, you are on your way upward now, in time you will persuade the law that you are equal, you may even fall into the dismal trap of supposing that you are the same. You can use and elaborate your own mystique to keep him from using you all the time for and at his pleasure. Make it at least partly a matter of your own discretion, as the animal females do. Tie it in with religion—"

"Eh?"

"Totem propitiation."

"Oh."

"Be a weak and feeble vessel. When he approaches you, if you are not ready for him, weep and protest your weakness of your sickness, have a headache, remind him that he must keep himself superior to other animals. Set up some taboos around your menstrual times: that will give you several days a month when you don't have to worry at all. When you want to give in, make a great mystery of it, so that he will be grateful. And as he—with his great intellect made insatiably hungry by man-woman frustration—moves now vigorously into the new field of ethical theory, be very sure that he bases all his theory on sexual ethics—which you, of course, will establish. The fruit and I have made it all possible. Are you properly grateful?"

She purred: "Of course."

All seven feet of Vogeler were tumid. "Then," he hissed deep, "it is time to claim my reward."

He slithered toward her.

She sat rigid.

He wound his way luxuriously up a fine leg, over a knee, around a rounded thigh.

She said very low: "Listen, Snake. I am weak, I am sick, I have a headache, and I am superior to other animals. It is contrary to ethical theory for you to do this."

Vogeler scarcely heard her: already he was around her waist; his head was moving deliciously upward between her breasts, his lithe dry tongue lightning-busy. . . .

He was paralyzed by her shrill scream: "Edom! Help! EDOMMM!"

His upper three feet drew stiffly back; he stared at her contorted face. Scream after scream after scream. . . .

Crashing in the foliage.

Vogeler began to retreat.

Aproned Edom crashed into the clear.

Avé wailed: "Snake is attacking me!"

Emitting a roaring snarl, Edom grappled the Vogeler-serpent with both hands by the upper torso, tore him loose from Avé, flung him to the grass, and stomped on his head. Vogeler tried to flee. Edom kept bare-heeling his head. Half stunned, Vogeler whipped his tail around Edom's ankle and threw him; and Vogeler bit Edom's heel and got away into underbrush.

I heard the murmuring of a slightly sardonical voice that had to be Althea's voice: "So far, nothing is different from the first time. Take over, Pan. Vogeler, report to Headquarters."

I found Edom and Avé. The woman, lips pursed, was designing a nicer apron. The man was in swimming with all his clothes on.

I considered the nature of the problem, seeking the most promising long-range solution. The crux of the difficulty was sexual, and I thought maybe I knew why. Of the instincts that Man had left, some, like the survival instinct, were quite rigid, while others, like the social instinct, were highly malleable. But the most clamant-glamorous of all Man's instincts, and the one most precariously balanced on the threshold between rigidity and malleability, was the instinct for sexual aggression or receptivity. Consequently any theory of behavior inhibition that Man might form would center itself primitively on sexual behavior; and this had occured on Erth—twice, now—when some other serpent, and then

Vogeler, had deliberately utilized sexual behavior as a nucleus for theorizing about good and evil with their ultimate overtones of saintliness and guilt.

If this were a mistake, as I believed, then ironically neither serpent had needed to trouble himself about conferring this kind of theory; for, left to himself, Man—or, more probably, Woman—would eventually have arrived at that destination unaided. Consequently, if this were a mistake, I must now do something positive yet subtle to deflect this course of valuative events.

I must, in short, help them to project the nucleus of a value theory that was not in its foundation a theory of virtue versus sin. This theory must avoid repressive distortions, with their inevitable backlash of aggression and destruction and ultimate self-destruction; it must preserve the garden; yet somehow it must lead man onward to beauty and godhead and the stars.

What if I were to substitute, for the poles of good and evil, the rather different poles of beauty and ugliness?

In the long run, perhaps it would produce only complication: beauty would be good and saintly, ugliness would be evil and guilty, and the garden would soon be gone. Nevertheless, even the complication should slow down the progress of repressive distortion in its hurtful purity—and the qualitative meaning of the recoverable *foundation* would be altogether different. . . .

Edom, swimming fully clothed, cursed, tore off his clothing (which was a leaf apron), hurled it at Avé on the shore, and yelled: "Why am I wearing this nuisance? I can't even remember how you talked me into it—"

As Avé rose, shocked, to her feet, prepared to remind him, I saw that this pair of primeval lives was simply *loaded* with if-nodes: Edom's fruit-induced mental clarity had worn off, blurring his recall of the reasoning. Ave, of course, would remind him—she had more at stake, she had to remember. . . .

That was when I nudged her with an ineluctable urgency. And she hurried away to the secret place where she and Edom carefully magicked and buried their body discards in the fear that some enemy would find them and use them to steal their souls. . . .

Floating comfortably on his back, languidly spurting water upward from his mouth so that it splashed on his hairy chest,

Edom was too rapturously lethargic to be startled when the python that I now inhabited erected head and neck from the pond surface not a yard away and said: "Hi, Edom." He replied pleasantly: "Hi, Snake. I didn't know you could talk."

"I was watching your swimming."

"Pretty good, huh?"

"Just fair." I could get this idea across on the semantic level that Man had already attained: when oldsters were training youngsters to run and fight and throw stones, they *had* to develop adjectives for progress that was short of high proficiency.

And already I had activated an if-node. The old old track of the Edom and Avé story would continue eternally to filament changelessly; but parallel with it, I now had a new thing growing. . . .

Edom stopped floating, trod water, and turned to me full-face. "How do you mean, just fair?"

"Well, what I really mean is—clumsy. You ought to keep working at your swimming until it becomes graceful."

"Clumsy" Edom understood; but—"Until it becomes *what?*"

I responded, "Watch me"; and for a few moments I python-rippled through the water. Returning to Edom, I asserted: "That's graceful. See what I mean? You try it."

Valiantly Edom splashed about a bit, nearly drowned, floundered to pond's edge, and lay face down on the grass, recovering. My tongue sympathetically flicked his ear.

He turned to me: "You're right, I'm clumsy. How can I get graceful?"

"You are clumsy in lots of ways," I told him austerely. "You can't swim like Snake, you can't run and jump like Antelope. And your behavior with Avé—boy, is it clumsy!"

Edom did a push-up, eye to eye with my erected snake head. "What's clumsy about *that?*"

"Do you *really* want to learn to be graceful?"

"Can you teach me, Snake?"

"Follow me," I ordered. "There's a tree that I want to show you."

As the concept of *grace* would elaborate, and as Avé would catch it from Edom, interpersonal respect and desire to please would become entailed. And as the concept of *clumsiness* would elaborate—based, as it was, on something they already understood: clumsiness in learning to walk, for instance, a concept that was never absolute but merely degrees removed from grace—self-recognition that one was clumsy in some way might automatically engender not abiding self-gnawing guilt but urgent discontent accompanied by knowledge that one could with effort keep getting more graceful.

They might gird up their loins—but not with guilt, merely with humor, and not compulsively. They would evolve elaborate costuming—but for grace, not for flamboyant elaboration of a fundamental self-concealment.

Of all clumsiness, the clumsiest—as social consciousness would elaborate—would be intentional or inadvertent interference with another's progress toward grace: interference by killing or in any other way. Of all grace, the most graceful would be even a clumsy effort to help another along the way of grace that the other had chosen for himself.

It might stick from generation to generation—or it might degenerate into the old repressive taboo morality—or the eventuation might be somewhere between. But at least, it was a new start—a beginning with a different kind of mind-set. Its future would depend on the people.

PART FOUR

Willy the Villain

Pan, you are going to the planet Berlioz, and to its dominant nation Paladia, in an era when its dominant race was black. A subordinated white race was seeking equality, but the black masters were persistently holding them down. In one activity, pugilism, the whites were so often gaining superiority that the blacks were beginning to resent it in a symbolic way.

Two white brothers, Champion Brownie Brown (a White Power leader) and Challenger Willy Brown (publicly identified with racial integration), fought fifteen rounds for the world's championship, and Brownie won handily on points. Using his victory to claim national leadership of the revolutionary White Power Party, Brownie incited aggressive white support by singing that he had symbolically licked his brother the Champion of Appeasement. A direct outcome was a fiery white revolution which gutted the cities of Paladia, most particularly the city called Kashmir which had apparented the Brown brothers. Shortly afterward, Willy and

Brownie clashed in a saloon; Willy stabbed Brownie to death and later committed suicide.

Both souls are here in Hell: Brownie ulcerating himself with remorse for his Pyrrhic victory in the ring, Willy lacerating himself with regret for losing the first fight and for winning the second.

What can you do, Pan, about nudging them into some alternate track for their souls' sake?

4

Heavyset ash-blond 220-pound contender Willy the Villain Brown stood loose and ready, head and hands hanging, in ring center forehead to forehead with whip-lithe smooth-fair chestnut-haired 210-pound champion Brownie Brown while a bald beetle-browed stupid-studious black dwarf-referee haltingly gave them the instructions that both of them knew and told them to fight clean and sent them back to their corners. Just before they parted, Brownie slapped the backs of Willy's gloves and muttered: "Hit me good, brother—I'd love you to win, but I got no mercy." Willy just grunted and went away.

In round one, Willy shambled and poked and missed; Brownie danced like an angel, and occasionally he poked lightly and hit without hurting and danced away. It was how the aficionados (mostly black, of course) had figured the first round; and everybody except Willy—everybody including (secretly) Willy's white handlers and black manager—assumed that Brownie would carry his brother Willy for ten or twelve rounds, outpointing him steadily, and then would heavily outpoint him for the last three to five rounds, winning the bout handily without ruining Willy.

Consequently, everybody figured it for a dull fight. . . .

I was backtracking the boys in time. My mental dowsing rod had basement-floored me in a high-school classroom nearly ten years before—when Willy had been seventeen, when swift-minded sixteen-year-old Brownie had advanced to Willy's class.

It was an eleventh-grade civics class in Kashmir, one of the largest cities of Paladia, the dominant nation of the planet Berlioz. The ruling race in Paladia had always been black—since, that is, the blacks had immigrated to Paladia and practically exterminated the red aborigines; but the inward ghettos of their cities were packed with misery-ridden whites who once had been overseas-imported slaves but now were theoretically free-and-equal citizens. All the blacks were pure black, features-and-flesh—or, more properly, chocolate; their hair was usually neat black wool, their noses were mostly aristocratic-flat, their lips tended to run handsome-full (in contrast to white lips which were thin like monkey lips), their teeth were unbelieveably beautiful: they rode on millennia of pride in their beauty. The manners of their upper middle class were exquisite, of their upper class aristocratic-easy, of their middle and lower-middle classes nervous-correct; and if their lower classes were junky, they were a small, indolent minority. As for the whites, most of them had degenerately thin lips and sharp-chiseled features and stringy hair without a single baroque-handsome kink; but some were tawny or even brown with blurred features telltale of black blood, usually picked up by ancestral slave women under black masters. Upper- and middle-class whites were in their manners and mores indistinguishable from upper- and middle-class blacks; nevertheless they were shunned by most blacks, or patronized by tolerant blacks, and they were a thin minority. Most whites were impoverished lower class, a status that most middle-class blacks considered inevitable for whites because of hereditary white inferiority.

Some black anthropologists insisted that whites had evolved out of a lower and earlier anthropoid link than had blacks, although others insisted that it was only a matter of cultural disadvantage. Some religious blacks pointed to a Biblical basis for white inferiority. There were ultraconservative blacks who talked darkly about a *different species*, pointing (not with perfect consistency) to the alleged fact that most upper-middle and upper-class whites displayed complexion-and-feature evidence of black blood.

The teacher, Mr. Lassiter, was a tawny-skinned, golden-haired white man. He was meeting this class for the first day. He was young; and being a teacher, he was presumed to be upper-middle-class white—that is to say, a stooge for Blackie's power structure. He faced a class of thirty-four young men and women (Lassiter was not going to call them boys and girls), thirty-one of whom were white. Among the whites, ten had definitely aligned themselves with the burgeoning White Power movement, eleven were nonaligned but emotionally sympathetic with White Power, eight had no convictions at all except that they wanted life to be as uncomplicated as possible, and two regarded themselves as Paladians temporarily disenfranchised but eventually to become equals of blacks by working at it. Among the blacks, all three were lackadaisical. This high school was not located in what a middle-class black would call the best of all possible neighborhoods.

Having called roll laconically, restraining his impulses for sharp response to three or four scattered witty replies like "Yo!" or "Who dat want me?" Mr. Lassiter laid down his class book, came around in front of his desk, and leaned his buttocks easily back against its edge. He was skillful, all right, not green, and a natural teacher; he came from three years of experience in a fifty-fifty integrated middle-class high school.

Scanning each face as an individual while he spoke, Mr. Lassiter began: "Our topic this semester is Paladian history. The word *history* may bug some of you a little—it may hit you as a remote hard topic. It isn't. History is being alive. It is going through experiences. If you really *see* it, history is like remembering. You read about people a hundred years ago going through something—you imagine your*self* going through it, and it is a lot like *remembering* yourself going through it." Then he made his second tactical error: "How many of you find it interesting to remember things?"

Brownie Brown raised his hand high. Willy Brown, sitting next to him, muttered: "Put down your goddam hand." Brownie's hand went higher. Mr. Lassiter nodded at him politely: "You, sir. What is your name?"

Seraphically, tall rangy Brownie took the floor. His hazel eyes caught Lassiter's attention while Brownie's chestnut hair, as always, filled everybody's vision: most white in Paladia were blond-haired like Willy or golden-haired like Lassiter, and blue-eyed like Willy or green-eyed like Lassiter, these being the most common genetic characters in the continental area of Berlioz which had been the main source of the white slave market. And when black interbreeding showed its traces, the eye-hair coloring was often black. But—*brown?* that was a white race character, all right, but from a different quarter of Berlioz, and rare in Paladia. The eyes and hair had earned Brownie his nickname so early that he had all but forgotten his given name. They made him more than just a white man:

they made him a *special* white man. . . .

Now Brownie folded his big hands in front of his pubis, closing his hazel eyes but aiming them and their chestnut eyebrow arches at the ceiling, compressing his thin lips into a moue which made his long slim fair face extra-long; and Brownie declaimed: "I, sir, am Brownie Brown, sir. I just *love* to remember."

Somebody said: "Haw!" Lassiter, sensing trouble, brought down a golden eyebrow over a piercing green eye tawny-lidded; but he held patience enough to inqure mildly: "Why, Mr. Brown? Why do you like to remember things?"

Spreading his great arms wide, Brownie responded with the most angelic smile in God's Heaven: "Because it helps me to keep on hating Blackie."

Eight of the White Power crowd roared laughter (the other two were timid); all eleven nonaligned sympathizers joined in (they liked Brownie); reinforcing derision came from five of the convictionless, one of the pro-Paladians, and one of the blacks.

Lassiter stolidly withstood it, inwardly balancing tactical gambits to recoup this bad one, swiftly revising his three-year integrated-high-school outlook, finding his way as the laughter died and inevitably they awaited his reaction. He said to the class generally: "By the end of this course, that crack might not get a laugh; but we have a lot of background to develop before you see why." He had studiously avoided reminding them that he too was white. Then directly: "Mr. Brown—do you have anything *honest* to say about remembering?"

Brownie, making himself look shocked, protested: "But, Teach—that *was* honest!"

*Every*body laughed.

As it quieted, Lassiter said softly: "Sit down, Mr. Brown"—knowing as he said it that if Brownie should choose right now to make a leadership stand, it could end in physical contact.

Brownie spread his great arms broadly in a gesture of despair, and he sat. Chuckling. Lassiter got it, all right: this wasn't quite the ground of Brownie's choosing. Nevertheless he had temporary advantage: Brownie *had* yielded, if only provisionally; and the trick was going to be to keep Brownie's *right* ground from solidifying. He saw that Willy was glowering at Brownie. . . .

Folding his arms, Lassiter frowned at the floor, telling them: "I know you're testing me, every class tests every new teacher. But don't do it anymore, it hurts all of us. As a white, sometimes I get called Blanco, and I don't like it, but I am not going to get all hated-up because of it—instead, I am going to win equality, and I am going to help *you* try to win it too." He looked up and swept them with that individual-penetrating gaze: "Do *all* of you think I must be a stooge for Blackie's power structure?"

Temporarily, at least, it panicked them into silence.

"*I* like to remember," he told them steadily, "because remembering what I used to be tells me how much worse it was then. I remember when I was a dirty little blanco-kid wiping my ass on used corn cobs. I also remember when I won a scholarship given by a black association that wanted whites to pull themselves up by their own bootstraps, earning any help they got. I also remember the black majority on the faculty of this high school voting to have the faculty banquet at a white-owned restaurant because us white members would be turned away from a black-owned restautant. How do you dig *those* memories?"

He saw Willy and two or three others nodding slowly; most seemed sullen, which among whites meant nothing one way or another; Brownie frowned stormily at his desk, and most of the militants were watching Brownie.

Lassiter added: "I also remember another planet in this galaxy where the nation like Paladia was dominated by whites—and *they* enslaved *blacks*."

Beside Brownie, a henchman howled: "Thass a goddam lie!" Viciously Brownie kicked his ankle: already he understood timing. . . .

Remorselessly Lassiter pressed: "Likewise I remember that just south of Paladia there is an island where whites are the majority, and blacks are second-class citizens—"

He saw a hesitant hand go up, and he called it: "You, sir—please give me your name."

Willy hesitantly half stood, leaning on his desk. "Willy Brown. Sir, is that the island of Haibong?"

"That's right, Mr. Brown." Were they kin?

"Sir, my brother is in this class too, and I don't mind if you call me Willy to keep from getting mixed up." Turning on Brownie, he added in a threatening growl at his brother: "And Brownie won't mind if you call him Brownie—*will you, Brownie?*"

Brownie scowled down: his scowl was Adonis-handsome.

Lassiter had the right inspiration, which you don't always get. "Thank you, Mr. Brown, but I don't think it will be necessary. You'll know which one I mean if I'm looking at you. Of course, to be sure, you'll have to keep paying attention to me. Okay?"

Willy stared at him; Brownie's head came slowly up. Willy nodded once and sat. . . .

Nothing much happened in the second round of the championship fight, except a clear-cut revelation of the two contrasting styles. Brownie danced, occasionally throwing a left jab that invariably connected with Willy's forehead or cheek but stayed away from eyes and drew no blood. Willy shambled, using a standard guard, once in a while getting into range and leading with a left followed by a right cross according to the textbook—both always missed. Twice Willy got inside, and there was some body jarring—at this they were equals, but it was always Brownie who got away.

Invisible, I was tense. So was Lassiter, among the spectators. . . .

By the second week of the semester, Lassiter had the class manageably under his skilled spell, but Lassiter himself didn't like the feel of it: he knew that his imaginative concept of *history as remembering* wasn't getting through to them, and he knew why. At night he spent many hours talking with his wife about it; but she was really no help except as a sympathetic confidante, and she admitted it—she was third-generation urban middle-class white (which meant that her values were inhaled from the middle-class black culture that dated back at least a thousand years on two continents), and she recognized the culture gap between herself and the sorts of whites who were students of Lassiter's.

Seeking insights, he began to stay out at night, haunting lower-class white taverns, with his wife's worried consent: she accepted the night-owling and even the possible wenching-entailment, but the dangers for him bugged her. "Look, hun: keep your eye sharp for predatory men and unsanitary women. Promise?"

I followed him. . . .

Lassiter learned little. Sensing his social class, they avoided him.

Eventually, desperate, he allowed a whore to pick him up. I noted that Lassiter was discerning: avoiding the nubile youngsters, he surrendered to a well-groomed twenty-five-ish woman who was experienced enough to take care of herself yet not old enough to have grown careless.

As he started to leave the saloon with the woman, Lassiter felt a heavy hand on his arm. He turned: it was Willy. Shaking his head decisively, Willy said: "*Uh*-uh."

"Why not?" Lassiter demanded, flush-faced, while the woman stood angrily at bay. "You gonna talk about me, Willy?"

"Not me," said Willy, thoughtfully avoiding mention of Lassiter's name. "But don't go with her. Come with me."

The whore started to screech. A menacing crowd began to gather. Willy said: "Pay her off." Lassiter handed her a ten. She shrugged, took it, and melted into background. The crowd stayed but made no move.

Willy hooked Lassiter's arm and drew him outside. They walked rapidly a few minutes in silence; then Willy led him into another tavern. . . .

In a second-row seat that he couldn't afford, Lassiter watched the flurring third round in which, surprisingly, Willy tried to knock out Brownie. Five times Willy had Brownie on the ropes, three of these occasions in a corner; four more times Willy had Brownie tied up in bruising infighting. Over and over the crowd was on its feet.

It wasn't exactly that Brownie withstood it—rather, it was that Willy hardly touched him except during the infighting. At the ropes, a touch was all that the slaughtering ham-fist of Willy ended up conferring, because of a last instant Brownie evasion. . . .

"It's like this," Willy told Lassiter in a booth over beer. "*I* know you're a right guy, but *they* don't. I know that chick, she'da said she'd tell on you, dug your roll for blackmail, then blabbed anyway—an' you'da hadda dosa clap, man. Wrong chick, man. Hey, man—you *need* t'come down here after chicks? *You* need ta come *here?*" He was talking in the old slave-based blanco-lingo that was hardly Paladian; in school he did better, though you wouldn't call him a purist.

Lassiter decided to level with him—wasn't he allowing one of his own students to drink illegally with him? He said: "I do need to come here—but not for that."

"So why do you go for that?"

"Anything at all to get some insights. But scandal and clap my wife can do without—so thanks, Willy."

"You said *insights?*"

"Know what that is?"

"Not exactly." Willy had slipped into decently average Paladian.

For Lassiter the word labeled undefined comprehension, and he struggled for a simple definition. "Getting insight is getting to dig another guy's mind. Or your own. Follow?"

"All right—"

"I'm not getting anywhere with you classroom freaks. You don't trust me. You ought to, but you don't. So I figure I need some insights, so I can dig you, so you can dig me. I picked that chick because I figured I could pump her for some helpful atmosphere."

Willy's face spread in a rare grin. "She'da dug you—all the way!"

Lassiter smiled rueful-small. "Thanks, Willy. This ain't my dish."

Willy's face went ferocious. "Don't say ain't!"

Lassiter went sober. "My friends and I don't mind saying ain't—"

Glower: "This is different."

"Okay—"

Apologetic softening: "I don't mean you ain't a friend—"

"I know."

"You—do?"

"I mean—I think I dig."

Willy pouted at the table. Abruptly he slugged a ham-fist down upon it, spilling beer. He looked up and waved frantically for a barmaid, ordered more beer, and turned concerned to Lassiter: "You mean—you'd leave your park and prowl this crappy area for the sake of—"

Lassiter waited.

Willy went wondering. "You know, Mr. Lassiter—I think *I*

dig *you*! Sort of—" His face went vacuous, and he lurched at his new beer.

"I gotta tellya," Willy said presently, into jargon again. "Brownie an' me, we droppin' out."

"Why?" Lassiter's eyes narrowed.

"Nothin' t' do with you. School ain't for us. Brownie an' me, we been fightin' some. Brownie's a natural, an' I'm winnin' a few. We goin' pro."

Lassiter sipped. "Well, I have to admit it's a job opening for a white. Good luck, Willy. I don't recommend it, but I don't suppose I'll change your mind."

"Maybe I can change yours?"

"How do you mean?"

"If ya quit tryin' t' make good Paladians outa them freaks, maybe they'll settle down an' learn some history." Lassiter scratched the bridge of his nose.

"Look, Mr. Lassiter. Brownie hates your guts, but I dig you. You were a blanco like the rest of us, but you had good brains an' you worked hard, an' here you are, a class cat. You got reason t' be a good Paladian, even fightin' tha goddamn prejudice, because you're doin' all right. But tha rest of us got no reason. But a lot of us *do* want some education, not t' be good Paladians, but just t' get ahead a little maybe. You just teach history, forget that rememberin' bit: whadda we got t' remember, Lassiter? *whadda we got?* You just teach history, maybe half of us will learn somp'n about half of it, so you pass us with D's—okay: we got *somp'n* under our belts, an' maybe it will help us *get* t' be good Paladians if Blackie will give us half a chance. You dig *that?*"

Lassiter brooded, clasping his beer with both hands. "If we had some damn *other* way—once over lightly the way you said—then through it again, but a little deeper—"

"Hell, man, you couldn't keep their interest!"

Lassiter leaned forward. "Willy—do *you* dig the remembering?"

Willy glared at him. Willy nodded once. "Drink your beer," said Willy, "an' I'll steer you out of here and start you home."

The fourth and fifth rounds were more of the same—Brownie dancing and flicking, Willy the Villain shambling and boring and jabbing; the crowd was growing restive; one loudmouth got a laugh with "DIG THEM DANCING BROTHERS!"

I was haunting Lassiter—who was profoundly worried, rooting heavily for Willy yet dead sure that Willy would lose. . . .

Backtracking some more, I found in Lassiter a brilliant memory-trace of scared-courageous Lassiter skulking in a back row of a deep-ghetto white church where World Champion Brownie Brown was the Speaker of Honor; and Brownie was preaching a sermon. Minimizing the *Amens* and *Hallelujahs* from the passionate congregation, here is the gist of Brownie:

"You cats listen now! We white! They black! They yanked us out of our homeland and brought us over here into slavery! Then they said they were freeing us, but we weren't free at all—they just stopped giving us handouts! But they found out we had some political power, so they figured out some new handouts to keep us quiet—you know?"

"WE KNOW, BROWNIE! AMEN! HALLELUJAH!"

"So now they got stuff like equal opportunity which is horseshit, and Motheraid with the checks usually late and your mother has to be a whore to get it! Blackie owns all the good stores in Blanco-town and bleeds us black! So then a bunch of high yaller white Judases go 'round preaching to us about integration. *Integration*—what in hell *is* it? It's a scheme to make whites knuckle down to their black masters!

"That ain't what we're up to, brethren! *We got tradition!* We whites can make our *own* society here! Blackie brought us to Paladia—now Blackie can eat us! And we're going to sandpaper Blackie's black balls and burn his stores until he gives us what we *really* want—some *pure white states!* And when we *get* them states—

"WHITE IS BEAUTIFUL! WHITE IS BEAUTIFUL! *GOD IS WHITE—*"

Bedlam. Lassiter made himself small. . . .

But Willy the Villain, three rows from the back, stood up and made himself large. He bellowed deep: "Brother Brownie, do you dare let *me* talk a couple minutes?"

Brownie stared, gulped, stared, then grinned and hollered: "That's my kid brother, he's a lot whiter than I am. Ya wanna listen?"

The crowd sounded divided.

Brownie nodded at Willy, holding the grin. Willy shambled

down the aisle and up onto the platform. With a mockingly sweeping gesture, Brownie offered him the rostrum. Scorning it, Willy turned to the crowd:

"Y'all know me," he rumbled, his unmicrophoned voice easily penetrating to Lassiter at the rear. "I'm Willy the Villain. Brownie's the World's Champ, I'm the Number Three Challenger, I'm his brother. He thinks there's a Blackie, an' Blackie is a bastard. I don't. I don't think all blacks are alike, any more than I think all whites are alike. I think there are lots of blackies: some are bastards, some are good guys, most are nothin' special. And I think there are lots of us whiteys: some are bastards, some are good guys, most of us are nothin' special. How 'bout it?"

It drew some confused buzz. Willy lifted both hands for silence; Brownie studied him, his expression continuing to mock.

"Now listen," commanded Willy, "because this is important. A bastard is a bastard. Whether he's white or black, if he's a bastard he's gona kick the good guys an' the nothin' guys in the nuts. In this community, you know goddam well we got *lotsa* white bastards who are kickin' *all* of us in the nuts! You set up a white state, first thing you know it'll be run by white bastards who'll be kickin' the rest of us whites right—in—the—*nuts!*"

There was a kind of stupefied silence. Lassiter was gaping: Willy Brown had been a chronic flunker with an 84 IQ!

"So—*so*—so now let's get realistic!" Willy was trying to say something very deep very simple for a crowd of ground-under whites who apart from their socially degraded cultural impoverishment had wholly human potencies and aspirations.

"Yeah, we're second-class citizens; yeah, the blacks are on top; I ain't tryin' to blackwash history. But that's just how it is, *from history*. That's where we start from. I tell you what: we ain't lookin' for *white* leaders especially—we're lookin' for *good* leaders, white *or* black, who really dig the *whole* scene! I tell you what we're lookin' for among whites: we're lookin' for whites who have enough guts to *work* for equality or superiority—like my brother Brownie an' me, even if we do see the ways different, an' like a lot of you out there. I tell you what we're lookin' for among blacks: we're lookin' for blacks who'll give us an honest chance for good jobs an' accept us as honest competitors when we run for mayor an' sit comfortable at the next table to us in restaurants an' kid us for our whiteness while we kid 'em for their blackness an' not move out just because we move in—an' they don't have to give us their daughters! An' when we get all that, includin' a hell of a lot more whites who'll get the lead out o' their pants an' *work*—then you're gona see a *hell* of a Paladia!"

There was rumbling. And then Brownie, situated tactically by a mike, murmured into it so the whole hall heard: "Brother, ain't you gonna let the lazy black folks do a little work *too?*"

It turned the hall noisily against Willy. He made several ineffectual attempts to quiet them. Then angrily he strode to the rostrum and bellowed to his brother: "I'll take that mike now!" And he roared into it as gradually they semiquieted:

"Now listen you guys! I know another planet, and I know an island right on *this* planet, where *whites* rule the roost and *blacks* are second-class citizens! Where in hell are your *minds?* Can't you see that prejudice is *human,* black or white or red or yellow—and the guys with the short end of the stick always have to lick the prejudice by *proving* themselves? Oh, sure, we gotta have help—don't spit on the help, Blanco: we *gotta* have help—but don't you see that we *couldn't even be holding this meeting* if there weren't a hell of a lot of blacks who see it my way and are *trying to open doors for us to go through on our own power?*

"Blackie has a different background! Blackie *knows* he has to work! Four black guys out of five grow up *expecting* to work hard willing to work *hard,* knowing that it's the only way to get ahead. How many white guys do the same? Maybe *two* white guys out of five—because the rest of us figure we can't win anyway, an' we're past caring. Don't you dopes dig the point? How are you ever gonna knock down the black belief that whites are lazy, except by *working? working hard?* What we gotta do is tear into our own white people so that four out of five of *us expect* to work hard just like blacks—or maybe more, maybe nine out of ten whites! An' then, with a leadership of *good* whites an' *good* blacks, we gotta see to it that Blackie *recognizes* our work! I tell you guys an' chicks—when that happens, we'll have a twenty-percent white Congress in ten years an' a white President while a lot of us are still alive! An' all of us who works hard will be rakin' in good Paladian sugar! *Now how 'bout it?*"

Lassiter was in acute torment: courage and loyalty demanded that he get up and second Willy; discretion insisted that he was an alien among this category of his own race, that his support would only hurt Willy. Discretion kept him ulcerously in his seat.

Having withdrawn from the lectern to the middle of the platform, Brownie was doing a languid soft-shoe dance, paying no attention either to Willy or to the crowd.

The crowd went, finally, against Willy—bayingly, irrevocably.

Shrugging large, Willy departed. He never saw Lassiter.

In the ring, again Brownie was doing a languid soft-shoe, staying well away from Willy, who kept coming on. It was round six. The crowd was peppering the ring with snide comment. Brownie kept shouting happy answers to the crowd like "I'm a-wearyin' him!" They weren't convinced, and neither was Willy.

So far, the fight had stayed right on Antan-track. Brownie was going to win on points: he would progressively increase pressure during the coming rounds, but cautiously, so as not to be tagged again by a bullrush; meanwhile Willy, having worked off his anger in the early rounds, would rush Brownie from time to time but never lethally: for Willy, brotherhood counted.

Seeing what I had to do, I entered Willy's mind and activated an if-node—for Willy, for Brownie, for the arena crowd, for all Paladia. But it wasn't going to go quite right. . . .

All I did was to open up a system in Willy's brain, flooding his consciousness with angry recall of Brownie's perverse meaning for whites and for Paladia; and to fuel it, I stung Willy's suprarenals.

The change was swift. Willy closed on Brownie and tied him up. Willy was glaring up into Brownie's eyes; and Willy was muttering guttural: "You listen Bro—you hurtin' all of us—I gonna hurt you bad! You fight!" With that, Willy freed his right and jarred Brownie horrendously in the ribs; and I left him, to enter the brain of Lassiter at ringside.

Through Lassiter's eyes, immersed in crowd noise through Lassiter's ears, swept by Lassiter's endocrine emotion, I watched the fight go to hell. Angry hurt Brownie lost his head and mixed; Willy slugged back; and for a minute and a half they treated each other like punching bags. Between the bags at round end, however, there was a visible difference. Brownie, tired and breathing hard in his corner, had big welts on belly and ribs but not a mark on his face. Willy's face was almost pulpy.

I began to doubt the precision of my nudge, which had been intended to change history (on this parallel track, at least) by eventuating in a Willy-win. . . .

Willy sailed into ring center at the seventh-round bell. Brownie, again self-possessed, danced languidly in. Willy drove hard; Brownie tied him up; in the clinch, Willy jabbed joltingly at Brownie's ribs—but Brownie showed an astonishing ability to move his ribs away. I watched the referee closely: that one was tolerant, a laissez-faire man; he made no move to break the clinch, as long as fists were making contact. Brownie got leverage and thrust Willy away. Willy charged in again: Brownie, dancing back, laced Willy's face with half a dozen lefts and rights before the next clinch. Willy was bleeding heavily over the right eye.

Brownie broke loose. Willy bulled in, throwing a haymaker that caught Brownie on the chin point and sent him sprawling. The referee motioned Willy to his corner and started the count. Brownie took it to three and was on his feet, shaking his head, uncertainly dancing. The standing crowd was shouting—and nobody was mentioning brotherhood.

Now Brownie adopted an odd taunting tactic. He let his right arm fall so that it hung at his side; and he began dancing backward, poking with his left. Lassiter was yelling: "Easy, Willy! Cool, man! Watch him! Cool!" If Willy heard, it didn't register: he kept coming, while Brownie bicycled away. But abruptly Brownie planted his feet solid and crashed a left between Willy's eyes, shaking him. Brownie danced back; Willy, recovering, bored in; Brownie hit him between the eyes. It kept happening, like a stubborn bull being ended on by a two-by-four.

The bell rang. Brownie went to his corner. Willy stood there. A handler rushed out and took Willy to his corner. The referee seemed inattentive. A furious consultation developed among Willy's handlers while they worked over him: one angrily waved a towel, another patted his face; Willy opened his eyes and shook his head and closed them. . . .

And I knew what almost *had* to happen. Knew it with the dismay of realization that my failure was going to create cruelty and death. And I could not stop it: I was allowed one nudge, one only: after that, it had to be done by the souls themselves, or it was worthless.

But I might ameliorate the subjective tragedy. . . .

I began the swift minute between rounds by sampling Brownie's mind, and it was human Hell. Brotherhood with Willy had been Willy-beaten out of him: Brownie was power-drive-dynamized, vengeful-fury-inflamed: Willy was The Enemy to Be Annihilated. Toward this instant passional purpose, Brownie's control and concentration were total and implacable. Deep in his hindbrain I detected love lurking for Willy; but in Brownie's blood-activated forebrain, Willy glowered in the far corner there as entirely a dangerous-repulsive threat to Brownie-supremacy—a threat that had already hurt Brownie bitterly and *must be pulverized.*

Out of Brownie I scurried, in ten seconds flat; and I sought and found and entered Lassiter.

Having neutralized Lassiter's cerebral panic button, I telepathed within his brain: "Don't look around, Lassiter. My name is Pan, I'm a disembodied mind, I'm visiting in your brain, I'm a friend of Willy's. You aren't going nuts, you are entirely intelligent and conscious and sane, these things do occasionally happen to people. You and I both want to help Willy, and I am here to do it—but on the larger scene. Are you listening calmly? Don't speak—just think your answer."

Lassiter took it like a Solon. "I do think I'm nuts, Pan. It doesn't surprise me if my personality has split. If so, you are me anyhow, and I'm willing to listen to me. Go ahead."

I said: "I have to act very fast. Brownie is about to kill Willy, and that stupid referee won't stop him. I want to put Willy's mind into your brain so it won't experience its own killing. His mind will be groggy: you'll feel it there, but it won't have to bother you. Just sit quiet and let it be there, and I'll come back as soon as possible and take his mind somewhere else."

"Where will *you* be, Pan?"

"In Willy's brain-and-body."

"While Brownie kills him?"

"That's right."

"What do you gain?"

"No time to talk. Will you accept this?"

"What if—you can't get back to take Willy's mind away from me?"

"In that case, his mind will stay with you, and either both of you will go mad, or you will absorb his mind as part of yours. You have the stronger mind. Will you risk it?"

"It is my wife's risk too—"

"Can you speak for her?"

The bell rang.

Lassiter thought quietly: "Go, man."

Willy plodded out of his corner, dizzy, race-angry, seeing the updancing multiple image of his brother as a Judas-fiend whom he must kill before the fiend would kill their people.

The image monstered, filling his field, and a blow on the center of his forehead sent him stumbling backward.

He was too groggy to be surprised when a voice inside his head said: "Willy. Don't go to him. Stand still. Wait. When he comes to you, grab and hang on."

Willy stood stolid, numbly obedient.

The Brownie-image flared before him. Willy grabbed, hugged, held. The image tried to hit him, to shake him off; Willy held tight.

The inward voice said: "Listen, Willy. In a moment the ref will try to break you. Pay no attention. Keep holding. I'll tell you when to break."

Willy clung. Vaguely he felt slapping on his shoulder.

Voice: "He's trying to break you now. Listen, Willy. Brownie is going to kill you, and you can't stop him, and the ref is too stupid to stop him. I can make the ref stop the fight. Do you want me to make him stop it, so Brownie won't kill you?"

Willy's mind muff-muttered: "No. I'd lose. He'd win. Can't let him win. Better he kill me."

"Why?"

The referee was shouting, tugging: Brownie, both arms tied, was cursing, wrist-jabbing; Willy held his death grip. . . .

Willy's mind, into which I was pumping raw energy without directing the mind in any way, found an instant of clarity and asserted with dignity: "Brownie means White-on-

Top. I mean White *Equality*. If he wins and I lose, White-on-Top wins and white Equality loses, so white Paladians lose: that's how it looks to a lot of us white people, especially if I give up. That can't be. If White Equality loses to White-on-Top, black Paladians lose too—*all* Paladians lose, even White-on-Top loses. So I have to beat Brownie. But I *can't* beat Brownie. So next best would be if he would kill me. That wouldn't look very good for White-on-Top, would it?" Brief thought-pause; then: "Brownie's a great guy, he's deep, he could be good for all of us, he just all fired up—"

Mind-talk is swift: the clinch hadn't lasted fifteen seconds. At this instant, I wasn't sure that Willy was right about the killing, but he was perfectly predicting what had actually resulted from the losing. I decided:

"Brownie will kill your body, Willy, but I have to save your mind. I am going to take your mind and put it to bed in Lassiter's brain, and you can go to sleep there. I will stay here and take care of your body while Brownie kills it. Okay, Willy?"

Anguished protest: "But I *got* to stay with it—mind *and* body!"

Whirr of mental fuzz. Out of it: "Okay then—but you keep me fightin', hear?"

I sped the mind to Lassiter.

Taking hold of the bleeding brain, I drew myself into total control of its pain-throbbing sensory-motor-thought totality. I had become Willy.

I broke out of the clinch.

What I might expect during the remaining two minutes of the eighth round would be dangerously difficult and incredibly traumatic. My mind, like any mind, depended on having some kind of brain, even were that brain only the filamental totality of Antan; and all I had now, locked within Willy, was Willy's bleeding shocked brain; and I was involved in this battered brain so intimately that I felt as mine its every twist of agony, its confusion was my chaos. But I had to keep my head relatively clear so that Willy would be slain the tactical way. To do this, I might have to lose my own identity forever, tangled in a pulped brain mass that would rot without letting me free.

Resorting to a trick, I speeded up Willy's sensorium and his frontal and parietal responses so that everything Brownie might do would seem to be done in slow motion, as though underwater. Unhappily I could not touch Willy's midbrain or hindbrain: the Willy-body action was not speeded in any way—perceptually its motion too was slowed. But at least, now I had time to see and partially comprehend what would be coming. With the sensory slowing, the crowd noise went basso, a dull lethargic rocksurf-roaring.

Brownie, face berserk-twisted, was cat-moving backward from the clinch; no, he was a sinuous undersea eel. Willy-feet planted hard on the canvas, I swayed. I was no stranger to boxing, but my experience was amateur, and I was years away from it. I set myself the task of being pliant with respect to Willy's midbrain, letting it translate my cerebral commands into automatic-experienced action. So far, the midbrain seemed undamaged.

Having backed undulently almost all the way across the ring, Brownie had leisurely gathered himself into a catspring-pause and now was beginning to unfold and weave forward.

I got my Willy-body set.

Brownie filled my vision, slowly feinted, oozily started a right cross. I brought a lethargic sledgehammer right under the right cross and ultimately sank my fist an inch into Brownie's ribs just under the heart, so that Brownie winced and his right cross barely scraped my chin. I then realized that my victorious Willy-fist was now merely falling, that no automatic follow-through was going to come; and my groggy Willy-brain could not think of a thing for me to have Willy do next.

The left poke by Brownie started, telegraphing itself, coming around-and-through on a predictable route. Knowing I should be doing something about it, idiotically I studied the fist as it made its approach to me. It became all my world and mashed Willy's nose flat, clouding my visual field with Willy's tear. As the fist receded, I knew that another fist would be coming in from another direction, but that was all I understood, and I could see nothing. I waited, trying to get the Willy-body to respond; and presently Willy's hands did seem to be coming up a little; but just then the other fist crushed into my left temple, bashing brain against bone, starting another hemorrhage that still further clouded my comprehension. It did another thing: it broke down the speed-up of the sensorium; and I was hail-hit by a left-right-left-right temple battering that kept on and on while anguish multiplied and then ebbed and ultimately gave way to the seraphic soft pleasure of the repetitious beating and

Someone was stroking my face.

It was Althea.

I asked promptly: "What happened?"

"When?"

"In the fight. Just now."

"I stumbled over you here," declared Althea. "We didn't know where you'd checked your body, and we'd lost track of your mind. Brief me."

I did—quite calmly: why not? I was alive.

"All right," said Althea, helping me up. "That was a few hours ago our time, but eleven years ago their time; you'll remember we'd agreed to speed up the alternate track development if the track should look promising. So it might be worth our while if you would check it out, Pan—especially since none of the three souls has checked in."

I couldn't have agreed more fervently. Especially since I had failed in a detail of frightening significance. During eleven years, I had left the mind of Willy paired with the mind of Lassiter in the brain of Lassiter.

Rather as I had speeded up the Willy-sensorium, so we had speeded up the new germinal Antan-track. Normally a new shoot from an if-node meanders down through time at the same growth rate as the original track, so that the new burgeoning stays always the same interval short of the present; and usually it withers before if can create a time-paradox. But in the rare case where a new parallel track grows *faster* than its father, the new track may ultimately crash through into the germinal present. When this happens, there is a brief chaos during which the new track merges with the old in the current germination, with the new taking command because of its higher energy, but with the old inertially influencing the new; and when synthesis emerges from this brief chaos, memories and history resolve themselves into a single track because any other resolution would be insane;

and any phantom memories or paradoxical relics that controvert this resolved history are put down to the vagaries of the human mind. . . .

Eleven years later, track time! But it was *present germinality* that I now entered. . . .

I found Lassiter standing staring out an office window, hands clenched behind his back. The office was that of the Kashmir superintendent of schools. It was Lassiter's office. About to depart that office, hand hovering near the door activator, was a tall, stocky, sad-eyed man whom abruptly I recognized as Brownie Brown.

Brownie dropped his hand and turned: his movements and stature preserved the old pliancy, his eyes the old gleam, his face the old fair-white handsomeness that even blacks recognized. He said in a voice that was vibrant yet hesitant: "Must I conclude, Lassiter, that the first white school superintendent in Kashmir history will finally and definitely *not* endorse my campaign to be the first white mayor of Kashmir?"

Lassiter did not turn. After deliberation, he replied: "Mr. Brown, you continue to have my good wishes. During the past six or seven years you appear to have established yourself as the city's leader of moderate white militancy. Let me say it like this: a man having the identity that you now appear to have is the kind of man I would like to see as our mayor. But I repeat that the superintendent of schools cannot properly support or endorse any candidate."

Brownie advanced a few steps toward the superintendent's back. "Mr. Lassiter—I know how you feel about me personally, and I confess that you are right—as of *then*. How much do I *now* have to prove?"

Lassiter appeared to shrivel a little. "I'm not talking about that fight. It *seems* to have changed you. Personally I have faith that it *has* changed you. But I still cannot take the position—"

Up went Brownie's chin; and he told the window just above Lassiter's head: "Mr. Lassiter, I've said this to thousands and thousands: the White Power movement is measured by the kinds of white people who lead it, and the kind of bastard who killed Willy Brown was a leader in it, and *I am no longer that bastard!*"

Lassiter turned, and came to Brownie, and pressed Brownie's right hand in both of his own hands, while

Brownie's left hand covered Lassiter's hands. Lassiter told Brownie's eyes: "I believe you. I wish you well. In my heart I earnestly hope that you become mayor. But I can't endorse or oppose any candidate, because of my public role."

After a moment Brownie responded in a voice that was oddly not his own: "Okay. I dig. Thanks. I mean it."

He moved toward the door. He paused. He thrust a hand into a pants pocket, scowling at the floor. Slowly he raised his head and gazed earnestly at Lassiter, who gazed back just as intently.

Brownie said: "You've made your decision, and I know you won't change it no matter what I say. So I wanna say sumpn. I got a funny feelin' about you. A good kinda feelin'. Like you were my—older bro, or sumpn."

Instantly Lassiter ejected: "I feel it too. Like you were my—younger bro—or sumpn."

They held the gaze. Abruptly Brownie flashed the old derisive grin: "Just because *I* lapsed into a blanco-talk, *you* don't have to."

Lassiter told him soberly: "I didn't have to."

Brownie frowned down. He blurted: "This is nuts."

And he left.

Lassiter went back to the window.

I entered his brain, probing the prime locus of ego between telencephalon and diencephalon. Lassiter *was* serene, relatively speaking: that is to say, he seethed, but about others and not about himself; and there was absolutely no sign of psychic split—nor, in his fresh memory banks, any hint of less than reasonably serene love between his wife (the same wife) and himself.

No sign of Willy, either.

I considered the question. Presently I probed more deeply into the diencephalon. At length, almost at the very bottom of Lassiter's forebrain, I found the reason for the small intuitive hint of *caring* between Lassiter and Brownie. Telepathically there I comprehended Willy's mind in dormancy: fused so intimately with Lassiter's mind that Willy's identity was almost a meaningless idea, like the whisper of vermouth in a very dry martini.

It would be possible for me delicately to segregate Willy's mind from Lassiter's, convey Willy into Hell, rig there a surrogate brain for him, return him to intelligent astral consciousness purged of the old-track guilt by the new-track achievement, and in due course give Willy opportunity to choose his own future.

I decided to defer that procedure; and I checked through to Althea an advance note to reconsider the procedure when eventually Lassiter would die. Willy was dormant—but emanations from Willy were still contexturally powering Lassiter.

Wasn't Willy cosuperintendent of schools? Hadn't he helped Lassiter get here?

PART FIVE

Caerleon

In the year 2273 (Interplanetary Convention), on the planet Arcady (which was Nigel III), a chivalric sylvan-urban utopia called Caerleon was dynamited by the persuasion of a queen and a knight that consummation of *amourosis* (-amour inflamed by intersexual hypnosis takes precedence over all other values. The consequent destruction of Caerleon set back the progress of humane civilization on Nigel III by a thousand years. Perhaps from a celestial viewpoint it didn't matter much, since the star Nigel was only nineteen years from nova. Nevertheless, to three souls it did particularly matter: to Grayle, the cuckolded king who mourned his cuckoldry far less than he mourned the death of his dream; to Gueraine, his queen who friend-liked and respected King Grayle and mourned her inability to hold amourosis at arms' length; and to Pelleon, the Good Strong Knight whose surrender to amourosis wrecked the utopia that he had helped build and the king and queen whom he worshiped.

Pan, we are inserting into their Antan-tracks the souls of these three, in addition to the usual supporting cast of souls who won't mind the old-new adventure and who won't suffer unduly if the new-created track goes awry.

See what you can do, Pan. The key person is King Grayle. . . .

5

I selected a large island off the coast of the quasi-European continent, an island shaped irregularly like an hourglass, perhaps five hundred miles tall and having a mean breadth of about one hundred fifty miles (nearly double that width at the base, half that wide at the wasp-waist). Positioning myself ten miles above an uncertainly forested area somewhat below that waist, I backtimed cautiously until forests and meadows and ponds were all clearly delineated. Coming down to one-mile altitude, I found motion frozen: I was too far back into Antan; so I nosed delicately time-forward, coming ever closer to the planetary surface, until finally a minute examination of an energetic pismire at close range assured me that I was now fine-tuned to the era that I sought.

Clamping myself on this time-locus, I rose to a five-mile altitude and cruised the island, taking its measure at wide-angle perception. It seemed almost primitive, or more accurately premedieval—largely virginal, with small towns and villages scattered at great distances, generously beforested with mighty trees that resembled oaks, brilliantly meadowed, altogether a pleasant land. Most of the housing was thatched huts; rarely there were crude castles of timber and stone.

I was overpowered by my honest sense of *homing*. For I *was* coming home, my brother: *we* were born and bred in this land, it was the year of our conception that I was entering.

Wry Thoth, bland Althea, what caprice humored you into sending *me* on *this* errand? For the Queen Gueraine of this land had been my mother, and the King Grayle of this land I considered my father; but as for the knight whom as a child I had called Uncle Pelleon. . . .

Humorlessly I asked myself, Brother, whether I was about to nudge these three onto an alternate track that would not include *us*.

Seen from above, the castle was low and spacious—not cold-hard or technologically high, like the late-medieval fortresses that had made the word *castle* a stereotype on Erth, but built mostly of wood with a good deal of rough stone exterior facing, spreading and beautiful. (*We* had played here. . . .)

The castle dwelt within a free-form triple moat of clear water harboring carp, bridged forward and postern by noble bridges that looked as though they had never been raised. Seen from above, this Castle Caerless was mainly a broad courtyard with an arched and shaded promenade all around the interior; in court and promenade, lords and ladies lounged. The exterior of this promenade, facing outward toward walls and moat, was stone-defended and practically windowless; but the interior was cordial.

Castle Caerless had also a number of two- and three-story buildings that were sparsely windowed in a slit-defensive way; and the large main structure was topped by a square five-story turret with a crenellated crest: this tower overtopped the forward drawbridge threateningly. And yet, even this early-type fortress had its luxuriant charms: see there, a woman with long blond hair hung out of a second-story window. . . .

Hovering in air ten yards before the face of this woman, I lost my heart. And I knew that my desire-love was incestuous. And then, rethinking, I comprehended that it was *not* incestuous, not in the soul. Once my mother had been like this; but even as a child I had not known her like this, for a young mother is not young to her child. And when I had grown into the age of desire, she had been much older and we had grown remote from each other: no thought of desire for her then—or afterward, in retrospect. Now, a full man, I came upon a young woman who was arrestingly beautiful, and I desired her; and if my knowledge of her motherhood to me, indeed my misty remembering of careless-loving childhood intimacy, piquantly flavored spontaneous desire, this irrelevancy was to be dismissed. Put it that instantly I understood how it must be with Pelleon. . . .

She leaned elbows on the sill of the open window (whose tiny disk panes marvelously were colored glass). She was no more than twenty; her face was smooth long-oval, her eyes wide apart and serene blue, her nose a Dresden trifle, her mouth middling-wide and middling-full, her hair a long-flowing flaxen wonder, her throat long and fair, her breasts firm and deep. . . .

Behind me there was cheering; but before I turned, I appraised the expression on Gueraine's face. She was intent on near-distance below. She was looking at whatever was causing the cheering.

It was time for me to turn. . . .

The roads around Castle Caerless were a labyrinth of ways that snaked among bold little salients of the surrounding forest. Along one of these ways, now disappearing, now reappearing, jaunted an armed warrior on a huge crazy steed that I well remembered. People were scatteredly cheering the warrior in front of the castle. Not all the people were commoners: there were knights in the crowd, and there seemed no curb on their enthusiasm either.

I floated over to the approaching knight. His black steed faintly resembled a tyrannosaur, lumbering along on two great ground-devouring hind legs, balancing itself with a massive-restless tail, pawing air with two ridiculously tiny-futile hands; but it was entirely mammalian, something between an ungulate and marsupial: a *graul.* (Behind the knight, a squire rode a four-legged assish thing.) In all other respects, though, the knight was what might be expected by anybody sophisticated enough to expect that fifth-century knights on Erth would be more primitive than the late-medieval archetype immortalized by Geoffrey of Monmouth and Sir Thomas Mallory. This knight was bareheaded, and his black hair was restless-unruly. He wore no iron at all—only very heavy leather—except that his leathern gauntlets were viciously iron-spiked about the knuckles. A great round hardwood shield, cross-bound and knobbed with iron, hung to the left of his equipage that fell a great deal short of being a saddle. He did carry a hardwood lance socketed in a rest on the right flank of his graul; and this lance had an iron beak, it was not for idle jousting; but it was little more than two yards long, designed for mounted infighting or perhaps for throwing. . . .

From his manner of riding, I recognized him with difficulty as Pelleon—whose memory-image for me was fiftyish, gray-haired, gentle. But this was the early-thirty Pelleon whom I had never know. He rode with grace. His face was young—
had never known. He rode with grace. His face was young—

And it was an earnest-courteous face, hard-merciful. This was a powerful knight who would win and win and would never stoop to crudity or false play. This was a man who *always* won, *honestly*.

I followed whither his great deep gray eyes gazed.

His eyes were on the Lady Gueraine, who leaned from the window.

Waving to the people with a kind of cordial abstraction, Pelleon crossed the bridge (with me just behind him) and put his graul into a curious dancing curvet at a point of vantage just beneath the queen's window. Standing in his stirrups (which were no more than loops of braided thong), he let his left hand fall to the haft of his sword; and he inclined his head low, with his thick black hair falling over his forehead; and his mind said, "My Gueraine," while her lips replied silently, "Pelleon."

He raised his head, then, and engaged her eyes; and the love that passed between them was unmistakable and deep. The people gawked; the random knights came to something like attention out of pure respect. Why were they not concealing this love? I comprehended: Pelleon and Grayle meant it for holy lady worship, and the people took it for that, and quite probably King Grayle took it for that, so there was no need for concealment and indeed every chivalrous reason for publicity.

Gueraine gently broke their trance by drawing together the glassed window shutters, disappearing. The astonishingly handsome-powerful-intense young Pelleon gazed a few moments longer—penetrating, I was sure, the shutters. Then he dropped his head and rode slowly away, while the people began to cheer again.

He did not, however, get far. A husky scowling blond-mustachioed knight reached up to grasp his stirrup (for the bridle hung high) and horned at Pelleon: "I said it publicly in thine absence, and I say it now publicly in thy presence: thou'rt making a whore of our king's worshipful queen!"

The people made shocked noises and crowded around. They were now fairly into the broad fair court. I noticed, looking over the heads, an unpretentious lean redhead in shirtsleeves and loose long woolen trousers leaning against a thin square pillar, one arm twined high about the pillar, watching; instantly I had a vague *feeling* about this nondescript watcher, but the feeling did not rise to the level of intelligence. . . .

Easing his lance into a lateral rest, Pelleon folded arms and looked lazy down. "I love thy foul mind, Scans, but not when our worshipful queen is in it. For in my mind she is not whored, but worshiped."

The square challenging chin went higher. "Worshiped she may be in thy mind, but whored she is in thy bed."

Pelleon lost languor and stiffened alert. The shirt-sleeved watcher on the distant veranda hung his other arm high around the pillar and leaned forward.

Now the voice of Pelleon came low, even, unstrained. "Thou knowest, Scans, that if I kick thy throat, thou'rt a dead man."

"Thou'rt not too noble to whore the queen, Pelleon, but nevertheless thou'rt too noble to kick my throat."

Another stillness. Then Pelleon: "Remove thy fist from my stirrup so I can get down on equal ground with thee."

Scans moved back, keeping his head high. Except for a poniard, he was unarmed, unprotected; Pelleon was leatherned and sworded.

Dropping to the ground, Pelleon signaled to his squire. The man came forward and helped him off with his gauntlets and leather jacket and boots and pants, leaving him barefoot and wearing only worsted underpants that came down to just above his knees. Standing loose-armed before Scans, Pelleon said softly: 'Draw thy poniard and attack."

Scans, who was as large a man as Pelleon, drew his poniard and dropped it on the ground. He said: "Thou'rt whoring her."

Pelleon stepped in, and his bare fist crushed the teeth of Scans.

Letting go the pillar, the distant redhead—whose hair was not really red, but ruddy-brown—shook his bowed head mournfully, turned his back, and disappeared into the villa.

While two helped Scans away, Pelleon looked calmly about at the people. "I serve my king," he said, "and I worship my queen, and my saintly queen worships her king."

He waited.

They cheered.

He moved away, leading his graul by a high stirrup.

I followed Ruddyhair. *Thrillingly I knew now who he was!* The king, my presumptive father—the red-auburn fellow—was seated on a great armchair-throne in a private room, gnawing on a knuckle. As a youth, this Grayle had been miraculously designated king of a small province in an incident involving a sword and a stone, and he had been reluctant, but he had thereafter organized knights and expanded his dominion to all the Island of Caerleon. In battle, no single champion had been more worshipful. Kings had crossed the sea to join him. One of them was Pelleon.

In my childhood, I had seen the king, my probable father, as a giant. In our final encounter, I had seen him with the eyes of childhood. Now, in my maturity (a rather considerable maturity, if years are what count), I contemplated this mighty champion of arms in his early thirties. With luck he might weigh 140 pounds. Pelleon, by contrast, must be pushing 180 without any fat anywhere.

The posture of skinny King Grayle was all ungainly. He leaned forward in hard thought, chewing a knuckle, the other hand (long, long) draped over a chair arm; the elbow that belonged to the worried knuckle was propped on a bony bare knee whose sandaled foot pressed a foot rest, while the other leg stretched random-out to drag a heel on the floor. The face on Grayle was long-slender, the eyes were blue-deep, the brows were hard-down, the forehead was high-creased, the nose was long-pinched, the mouth was wide-thin-puzzled, the chin was unimportant.

This was King Grayle, who in a scant fifteen years had possessed and unified and now wholly dominated the Island of Caerleon. The ingredients of his dominion were one part force of arms, one part force of will, one part intelligent persuasiveness, one part devotion to friendship and justice.

Instantly I felt a thing against entering the brain of Grayle. Instead, having delicately fingered his memory banks to bring off a swift and discreet but adequate sampling of his life continuity, I materialized on a nearby chair in the likeness of Grayle's long-dead father, King Otter.

Faintly distracted by my materialization, Grayle glanced up, nodded, said, "Ah, Father," and went back into thought.

"I don't know how thou knowest me," I protested, "since never didst thou see me in my living since thou wert at pap."

"One grasps these things," Grayle murmured. "Excuse me a

moment, I am almost on to something—" He thought hard a little longer. He shook his head impatiently. He looked up as though seeing me for the first time. "I crave thy pardon, Father. Welcome to my poor palace."

"Thou hast done well with this poor palace," I asserted. "I remember when I used its beginnings for a summer house, it could barely stable two graul. I am proud of thee."

Grayle's blue eyes suddenly shone. "*Art* thou? I think of thee often, my father. I am only building on thy foundation. I could never have done what thou didst, and thou couldst have done far more than I have done hadst *thou* been a-building on *my* poor foundation—"

"Cut it," I suggested boldly. "The Kazans have thrown out those thees and thous, and I think you ken Kazan." I was referring to the dominant civilization of this planet Arcady: the name of that sophisticated empire was Kaza, and it maintained tenuous relations with Caerleon after once having dominated Caerleon.

The pensive thin mouth suddenly flashed teeth in a wide grin. "Ohé, you *are* my father—or a monstrous good scalawag! Let us then talk Kazan-sophisticated. Where did *you* learn it? in Hell?"

In Hell I *might* have learned it; in fact, I had learned it right here on Arcady; either idea was too complicated for expression. "That," I remarked, "I'll pass. You must pick me up on your program here, Son. I know about you conquering Caerleon and all; but I am damned if I know why Caerleon is so primitive while Kaza is so advanced."

His brows came down. "You won't criticize?"

I grinned. "Not as a father. As an equal, King Grayle. And as between peers, if I weren't critical, you wouldn't like me."

His grin came back, easy, easy. "Yes, it is my father that you are."

I went serious. "No, I am not."

The Grayle smile wavered. "You are not?"

"I do not like hypocrisy, and I discard it. I used this disguise to enter your confidence. I now respect you, and I will have your confidence man to man or I will not have it."

The thin mouth hardened. "Assume your true form." It was a crisp command, I felt subordinate to it.

Transmuting myself to my Pan-body, I stood discomfortably before Grayle in what had to be the most anomalous situation in my memory. From having been his father, I had become his presumptive son, before him visibly in my truth: red hair, blue eyes, all of it—different only in age (the apparent difference between eighteen and thirty-six) from the way he had last seen me. And I worried that he would recognize me. And this worry was utterly ludicrous—because when he had last seen me was nineteen years *later* than this date when now I challenged him; and on this date I had not yet been conceived.

And of course he stared at me without recognition as I told him: "My name is Pan. In a twisted way, it is true that I am a man long dead. Otherwise, all was false."

Grayle's mouth did not change. "To make an understatement, I am disappointed that you are not really my father. I would like to have said to him the things I have said to you. Do you have access to him?"

"I will seek access."

"When you find him, report this."

"If I find him, I will."

"Good. Continue now with your self-clarification." The face was still hard; and now I thoroughly comprehended the human intensity that had driven Grayle past his own physical inferiority to become a winning champion.

I temporized; "It would not be possible for me to appear in my natural ghost-guise to a king of the Kazans—they have abolished all supernatural beliefs, they would conclude either that I was a deceiver or that they were mad. Here on this island Caerleon, though, it seems that I can appear frankly as a ghost and be believed by the king. And yet the king is wise. Pray begin by telling me about this, why it is."

The mouth was a shade less grim. "Explain first the nature of your interest."

"You have problems. I do not offer you any magical aid, it would be unfair. But I give you opportunity to talk them out with someone whom you can trust because he will talk to nobody else."

"Prove that you are supernatural."

I disappeared and reappeared.

"Very good," Grayle commented, a touch of whimsy on his mouth corners. "Are you from the devil? Understand, I would not respect you the less, only—"

"I am not from the devil."

"From whom, then?"
I was hard on the candor-kick. "From someone whose name you know, in a mythological sort of way. From Thoth."
Electrifyingly Grayle rose to his feet. "From Thoth."
"Did I say something interesting?"
Grayle went back into a crouch on his throne, fingering his chin. "You have not told me, Pan, the planet of your origin. Are you perhaps from Erth?"
"What would a king of Caerleon know about Erth—or any other planet—or about Thoth?"
Grayle brooded upon me. He said: "About forty years ago our planet Arcady was visited by Erthmen. I'm told that it was a bit of a shock wherever their spaceship touched down. We have no such technology on Arcady; and they left us no technologists, only missionaries—"
"Missionaries?"
"I should tell you that I know more about this than do most kings on Arcady because of the wisdom and personal candor of the missionary we got, who later became my teacher. His name was Merleon. Their ship, said Merleon, had been funded and dispatched by an Erth cult calling itself the New Serapis—"
I nodded: by now the New Serapis was one of the most influential cults on Erth, but I was frequenting Grayle three centuries earlier. "They are new," I remarked, "but already they are very wealthy, able to purchase and fund a number of starships for interplanetary conversions. But I didn't know any of them had come to Nigel III—" I hadn't known it—but now I was remembering some things, particularly about this Merleon. . . .
Grayle queried: "Nigel III?"
"Arcady. Your planet. It's the third out from your sun Nigel."
"Our star, you mean—Merleon told me privately about that. Anyhow, his ship wondrously touched down at various lands on our Arcady, in Kaza of course, and once near here in the heart of Caerleon; and everywhere it stopped, the ship left one or two or half a dozen missionary-scientists whose task was to propagate knowledge among the elite of each land, enriching its culture without disturbing its culture. And then the ship disappeared, never to be seen again. I suppose it went home."

"Leaving them all here?"

"Yes."

"I'd think the people of Arcady would kill them!"

"A few did get it, I understand, but mostly they were too interesting and valuable and cunning to get themselves killed. And besides, the new religion they brought was so reassuring to humble people, while at the same time so useful to kings, that their propagation of it was a prime point of their universal value. For instance, you mentioned Thoth—"

I leaned forward.

Grayle frowned. "I can't go right to that, I have to give you background. These missionaries taught that men, or *croyds* in our tongue, were created by the great god Atom." (My brother, are you attentive?) "But Atom was an artist; and before he arrived at thinking up men, he invented more primitive experimental models of intelligent life—like fish, and serpents, and shrews, and apes, and even some crude man-things—until at last he perfected our model which is called *croyd.* And then, having perfected men, Atom went the next step forward and created the gods who are extra-perfect men; and the purpose of gods is to serve men at their own pleasure while enjoying themselves; and the purpose of men is to worship gods while enjoying themselves. Is it not seductive?"

Warily I ventured: "You aren't being skeptical?"

"Not at all," declared Grayle, his mouth corners quirking upward a bit. "But I am trying to get around to Thoth."

"Sorry. Carry on."

"It seems that within the religion of the New Serapis a king can choose any god he may wish to be the patron of his people; and customarily then that god's consort-goddess becomes the matron for the women. As one might expect, the emperor of the proud Kazans chose Horus for their god and Isis for their goddess. To complete one's identification with one's god, it is customary for each people to add its own divine subspecies name to our common *croyd*-designation; and so the species-subspecies name of the Kazans is *croyd Horus*—"

"While the Caerleons are *croyd Thoth?*"

The Grayle grin broke open again. "Since you cannot read my mind, you are as swift as I might wish. Or *can* you read my mind?"

"I am not reading your mind. Tell me about Thoth."

"Our missionary Merleon—"

"He is alive?"

"Barely. May I continue?"

"Pray do. Apologies."

"He told my father King Otter that Thoth is the subtlest of all the gods, one who uses his head as well as his heart. And this concept my father liked passing well, although in practice he used his head or he used his heart but not both together; and so do I like it, and my own practice is what it may be. And so we are *croyd Thoth.*" He paused, frowning a little. "That is, most of us are."

"Pelleon is not. And neither is Queen Gueraine."

Grayle was on his feet, just like that—light-footed, lithe-armed, dangerous.

I said quietly: "I am from Thoth." And I disappeared and reappeared.

Reassured, Grayle sank back, his mouth rueful. "You have touched," he admitted, "on a very sore point. May we talk about it? I have not talked about it with anyone, Merleon being the way he is—"

There came a stately rap on a portal: one, two, three. Grayle glanced at me: I disappeared. "Come in," said Grayle.

A varlet entered through the distant door. "Sire, it is the seigneur Pelleon."

"Send him in, and gladly."

The varlet departed. Pelleon entered, clad now in courtly clothing. Advancing lithe-rapid to the throne, he knelt on one knee at the feet of his liege, kissing Grayle's great ring.

Grayle said with a smile that was somewhere between friendship and love: "Get up, my brother, and embrace me." And they both arose and embraced.

"Pray seat thee," invited Grayle, waving at my apparently empty chair—which I hurriedly vacated.

Pelleon disposed himself therein with the unstudied grace of a panther. "Sire, I have come to report."

"Report, then. It is a good excuse for talking."

"Sire, I went at thy command to the dungeon of the seigneur Gelt of Galt, and I informed him that he must pay his taxes or show cause why not to thee through me. And he waxed wroth, and he caused two varlets to take me by the arms with intent to cast me into jail. So after that, poor fellows, I made the point again full gently to Seigneur Gelt. Whereupon four knights attended by ten men-at-arms entered and set upon me. To make it short, I have brought back with me the assurance of the seigneur Gelt of Galt that his taxes will be forwarded to thee within a fortnight; his sword is in my room as pledge. And I pray that my next mission may be more challenging."

"Thou tell'st it crisply, as always," commented Grayle, scratching the top of his head with a forefinger. "Our chroniclers will be hard put to it to amass famous tales of thee."

"Sire, I put faith in their low talents."

"I have no immediate mission for thee, but I will think of something." The king leaned forward a little: "Dost fret to learn that thou must linger here?"

Pelleon flushed, but he replied steadily: "I praise my lord Thoth and my king Grayle that I shall be permitted to pleasure me here with thee and with my lady the queen." He paused. He cleared his throat. He flushed more deeply and was silent.

Grayle leaned back on his throne, plucking at his lower lip. He murmured: "Merleon used to tell me about something he called Freudian slips of the tongue—"

Stiffening, Pelleon said solidly: "I think that for the first time I must lay the issue on the table in order to kill it. Thou knowest that I worship the queen. And that is all."

Grayle, coming to some kind of resolve, faced Pelleon earnestly. "My brother, we love each other, and we love the queen; but most of all, we love our Council Table and our dream and our land which together we have unified under Thoth."

Pelleon, fervently: "On the matter of the unification—mostly thou, not I."

"I on the initiating and the attaining, but thou and I on the establishing and expanding and securing."

"Thou'rt right that I love the things you mentioned in the priorities you noted."

"The other things more than the queen thou worshipst?"

Pelleon held the king's eyes. "I do not see a choice. But if there were a choice—more than the queen."

"Now listen, Pelleon. I know that thou are a *croyd Horus*; and my lady queen, whose mother was a *croyd Isis*, has never fully reconciled herself to Thoth or to his consort-goddess Maath. Art thou sure that thou comprehendest the potency of this mixed-up god brew?"

Jaw taut, Pelleon asserted: "I have adopted Thoth, and I am loyal to him because he is the god of my king."

Grayle straightened, laid his hands upon his thighs, and regarded the massive distant doorway. "Then," he said, "let us put it more directly. I respect the lady-worship that thou accordest my queen. And candidly, Pelleon, if it were more than that, privately I would stay blind, for a man is a man and a woman is a woman and I am often away at wars, and besides, she does not really love me, she only likes me well. What I may feel for her is here inconsequential. But equally inconsequential is what I have just said." His soul burned in the fierce eyes that he turned on Pelleon: "What is consequential is our kingdom and our people and our dream, and these are all one, wherefore the copula is one. And *thou shalt not* jeopardize this dream!"

They held hard gaze together.

Pelleon declared with ardor: "Grayle, never have I touched her or offered to touch her; never has she invited or encouraged me."

A few moments later Grayle leaned back, closing his eyes. "Pelleon," he said quietly. "I believe thee. Just remember two things. First, if that ever changes, it will become known, and our people are fetish-minded, and our dream will perish with the fetish of the queenly saintliness—and our dream *must not* perish."

His eyes came open, they were full on Pelleon. "And second—if the first is not enough—if that ever changes, no matter how secretly, it *will* become known, and our Gueraine will perish hideously at the hands of the people who serve the old cruel law."

The silence was very long.

Pelleon cleared his throat, raised his chin, and stated simply: "It will not happen, my brother."

Imperiously Grayle stood. "As a croyd, I am not selfish and I believe in the consummation of true love. But as *this king*, I command thee to be wary of the god-mix!"

With natural dignity, Pelleon stood and told him: "I will be wary of the god-mix."

They compelled each other. . . .

King Grayle's face went into an easy smile, and he came forward to embrace his adopted brother.

Pelleon embraced him. I knew that soul-noble Pelleon was totally sincere in this.

Pelleon gravely departed.

I tossed toward Thoth a recommendation that Grayle be truly my father. But on the other hand, if my father were Pelleon. . . .

Heavily said Grayle: "I do not believe him."

Half-heartedly I defended Pelleon: "He was entirely sincere."

"Of course, because he believes himself. But love is love, and he is of Horus, and she is of Isis."

Grayle's fist began a slow, rhythmic beat on a throne arm, and aloud he meditated:

"If I command him to desist, or send him away, he will obey—and both of them will die of heartbreak, and I love them both.

"If I *warn* him to desist—but I *have* just warned him to desist; but he is evasive with himself, and in fact he will not desist because he cannot—this is greater than he, and that is very great.

"If I fight him, either he kills me, which ends my dream, or I kill him, which ends my love and theirs.

"I can neither divorce her nor clamp a chastity belt about her loins, for either would dishonor her, and either would be known.

"If I let it go to consummation, it will be discovered and I will have to burn her. Or if I bless it publicly, I will be ridiculed for a royal cuckold and my dream will die. If I were a small man, I could simply bless it; but I am a king, and my dream would die.

"And as for trying to persuade or command *her*—" The fist stopped beating, the hand spread hard-hopelessly.

"Do you see, Pan? It is a totally enthralled situation. No trio was ever trapped so neatly, or with such vast consequences hanging by—well, by the trivial testicles and ovaries that command a man and woman beyond their spiritual power to bypass.

"Pan, I confess I do not understand this—mean, I do not think I could be trapped by such a compulsion in myself if I knew the terror of the consequences. I am no saint, I have strayed among beds—and the consequences of one of these pleasurings may turn out tragic—but never have I gone straying when I *knew* that the long-range outcomes would be bad. But *he* knows, and *she* knows—and yet they *will*, they *will*—" His fist resumed the beat.

I queried: "Have you consulted your mentor Merleon on this?"

He laughed without mirth. "My revered mentor is caught in the same sort of trap—and in his sixties! For years he has been a besotted love-prisoner of a nymph called Ninevé, she keeps him in her ornate cavern along with a variety of loves of all ages, she visits each of them at her pleasure and she keeps them enthralled with her eyes between visits. Pan, what *is* this blood-bubbly that soars to high heaven and yet demands such clownish behavior for its consummation?" It was not rhetorical; he was pleading for reply.

I frowned somber. Presently I ventured: "Objectively it is comical, but it is not meant to be objective. For two alone and in the dark, without mirrors, it is totally subjective, and it is high."

"*Why* high? Why is it subjectively high even when the cool-thought consequences are foolish or even disastrous?"

"Do you really want my analysis?"

"I asked."

"The erotic need is in the glands, mediated by the brain. The erotic desire is in the mind, controlled by the brain. The high love is in the mind purely, but the mind of necessity refers it to the brain for interpretation; and the part of the brain that supplies the most clamant meaning is the part that mediates the glandular need. And so the kingdom fell."

Meditative silence.

Grayle ventured: "Does all that make it bad or stupid?"

"Often bad. Often stupid. Often neither."

Meditative silence.

"Queer brains we have," Grayle murmured. "And if all this be so, why do these same croyd-minds damn to the fire a woman caught like any of them in such a cross-fire?"

"Because, as a matter of self-preservative pride in one's own mind-will, few humans will let themselves believe that they would be caught in this ornate trap; and therefore anyone whom they see so caught is damned as somehow subhuman."

"They will not *let themselves* believe that they can be caught?"

"You don't believe it of yourself. You said so."

The smile-quirk came. "Touché. But on the other hand, *I* do not damn *them*."

"That is because you are *really* a Thoth. But—can you save Gueraine and Pelleon?"

"No."

"Have you prayed to Thoth?"

"Only for clarification. Not for intercession."

"Why not for intercession?"

Grayle sat erect. "Thoth put me here in this place to do my best unaided. I would serve him ill were I to call him to my aid. More, I would be taking unfair advantage of other croyds who are not so aided. I must be a man of Thoth in my own right."

I meditated the interesting argument. There had been a time when I too would have advanced it.

I said softly: "You really do believe in Thoth, don't you."

Grayle frowned down. "To oversimplify, while being ultimately truthful—aye."

I suggested: "It looks to me as though being an independent man in *this* quicksand will preserve your pride at the cost of destroying two loves and a dream."

During many minutes the king quietly gnawed his knuckles.

And then Grayle said, not looking up: "Thou art from Thoth. Teach me."

Already Grayle was on a germinal track, and a souled one. Automatically, all whom he might ever touch or influence thereafter were entering or would enter upon alternate tracks at their own next if-nodes. For most of them, though, the new tracks would perfectly parallel the old tracks; for some, the new would perfectly duplicate the old for a while, until the crisis would come; and even then, psychic inertia would inhibit breakaway. . . .

Thus—just as long before, only new for them because their souls had been injected into their tracks—young Pelleon encountered young Queen Gueraine in a small private garden that only she frequented, except when he also frequented it. There was a low old chapel in this garden.

They stood five paces apart. He gazed at her white forehead, her eyes being lowered. He said: "My lady, I have been too long away from thee."

After a moment, low she returned: "Aye."

He stood gawky, arms hanging. She too went awkward.

He cleared throat and said: "Thou knowest that I worship thee."

"Aye."

He wet his lips. He said then: "A worshipful knight should hide no thought from his queen."

"Aye." Her eyes came up a little, dwelling on his jaw.

He got his mouth open to say the next thing. He closed his mouth. Suddenly his chin hit his chest and he groaned: "Oh, my God." Up came his chin, and he darted foward and seized her hand in both his hands.

Then her alarmed eyes met his. Not moving her hand, she protested: "My lord Pelleon!"

Sinking to both knees, he pressed his lips to the back of her hand.

She stood trembling, gazing down upon him.

Moving swiftly to him, she slipped a hand behind his neck and drew his head against her belly.

Long they stayed, not moving.

He told her belly brokenly: "Long have I worshiped thee. But I love thee."

Blessedly his ears just heard the whispered answer.

Silence. Horus and Isis do not reason: rather, they know.

To her knees she went and pressed her lips against his.

After long embrace, they hugged them one to the other, and she told his ear: "Grayle will be away tonight. I will be in the Chapel of Maath."

I watched the hidden varlet slip away to report to Scans.

I went away too.

The cavern of Ninevé was deep-hidden in the old-oak forest, and its entrance was barred by an immovable rock. Penetrating this rock, I wound down chthonic corridors until ultimately I came to the cell that housed Merleon.

I found the old priest of the New Serapis limp in an armchair. No sign of Ninevé.

In the mind of Merleon I spoke quietly. "Not to shock you, sir, I will tell you that I am a spirit of the air; and since we spirits are familiar to you, thus you will take me easy."

Merleon, eyes closed, answered: "I think you are lying. Either you are my delusion, or else you are an alien mind occupying my brain. I warn you away from my pyriform cortex; it's wide open and pretty wild."

"Just now," I commented, inspecting it, "wide open it is, but pretty mild—pooped, I would say. How did you ever get trapped into this?"

"Into Ninevé? Well, at first that seemed to take some doing; but now I realize that she—"

"This adventure, I mean. The whole Arcady thing. And why did you pick Caerleon for your territory?"

"Young man's adventure," Merleon reminisced. "I was sold on the New Serapis, it combined all the best of modern science with a psychically updated version of what used to be crudely called magic, all framed-and-decorated by the aesthetically fascinating god symbols of old Kamat. So naturally at eighteen I jumped at the chance to help convert a planet. As for Caerleon, I didn't exactly pick it. I had asked for Kaza, but at my age I had no seniority; so they gave me a choice between Angouliers across the sea, there—Pelleon's land—and this Caerleon. Well: I was not only a Serapian zealot but also an Arthurian romantic; and here was a chance for synthesis—so here I am."

"In the Cavern of Ninevé."

"I like it here—about every third night."

"I congratulate you, sir, at your age. Why you so often?"

"The others have vigor. I have imagination."

"I note that here you are addressing yourself rigorously to the eroticortical aspects of love, without troubling yourself about romantic idealism."

"It is a perfectly Arthurian approach: remember your Mallory. However, sir—did I catch your name, if you have one?"

"Pan."

"*Sir* Pan?"

"Pan."

"However, Pan—I presume that your wry remark about me veiled an allusion to Gueraine and Pelleon."

"Exactly."

"They do contrast with Ninevé and Merleon, don't they?"

"They do."

"It's a shame for Grayle, too. Were I with him, probably I could. . . . But I'm not with him. And I could be, any time I might choose. But I'm not."

"Why not?"

"I don't choose."

"Why not?"

"For decades I worked hard serving Grayle and his father Otter before him. Now I've retired at stud. Sooner or later a king has to be his own man. Let Grayle solve it."

"He can't."

"Then he shouldn't be king."

"It is because he is king that he can't."

"Say the rest of it. It is because he is king *and what* that he can't?"

I pondered his searching question. "I see your point. If he were all king, just plain king like his father and most other kings, he would have Pelleon killed and be done with it. And if Gueraine then should go astraying with another knight, he'd kill Gueraine and be *all* done with it."

"Precisely, Pan."

"But Grayle is a king in a much larger sense, and you are partly responsible because you taught him what *Thoth* means."

Merleon's eyes opened a little: they were rheumy. "Perhaps I taught him too well. I have taught him into unbeatable trouble."

"So why don't you go back there and teach him *out* of this trouble?"

The eyes closed, the rheum stayed. "I am human. I cannot teach him out of this one."

I said tart: "You are human wreckage. What kind of a priest *are* you?"

"Irrelevant question. I was a very good kind of priest. I am a priest no longer."

I mused, then dared a challenge. "Gueraine has given Pelleon rendezvous for tonight in the Chapel of Maath. And Scans knows about it."

There was a great deal of mental silence, but the old eyes were wide open. Presently, speculatively: "Since you are able to enter minds, *you* are able to do something about this, Pan.

The fate of Grayle's dream turns on the outcome."

"I have the start of an idea. But it would be better if Merleon were to execute it."

"Merleon stays here with Ninevé."

"Then I must edit a little. Merleon remains here if he chooses; but my combinaison involves Ninevé, and afterward she will have no time for Merleon."

After more silence, Merleon suddenly struggled himself up to something more closely resembling a sitting position. Eyes wide-open-staring at a rugged-mossy rock wall, he grated: "I think you know what it is you have me by."

"Drive into it affirmatively, man! Wouldn't you like to be a priest again—a priest of Thoth again?"

The staring eyes came around to me who, materialized now, stood challenging Merleon. There was wonder in the old voice: "You think I could?"

"I think you could."

He squeezed the eyes tight shut. He muttered: "You know, Pan—now that I have seen you, I have a silly sense that if this were happening nineteen years later, I would recognize you."

Young Pelleon came cloaked by night to the small Chapel of Maath. Shadowed by ancient mighty trees, the low old-stone shrine huddled ivy-shrouded, moss-ruinous, having dwelt here for centuries before the coming of Thoth and Maath, sheltering a pagan altar whose goddess was discarded and forgotten. Grayle had wished to rebuild the chapel, honoring Maath, the new goddess; but Gueraine had prevailed against this design, pleading the cause of archaic beauty, inwardly unready to accept Maath and yearning after the gone divinity.

Tree-hidden, Pelleon stood gravely contemplating this place of consecrated assignation. It would be wrong to say that Pelleon was thinking, or wrestling with conscience, or presavoring a triumph of blood passion: Grayle was not in Pelleon's mind, but far distant from his mind and from this place; it did not trouble Pelleon that he had made promise to Grayle never to touch Gueraine, for at that time he had believed himself, and now that memory was lava-buried by this passion. Rather, Pelleon was filled with glowing holiness: long had he worshiped the goddess Gueraine, now she was opening herself to him in total surrender of her divine being: his soul and his body were one, her soul and her flesh were one: this was fulfillment.

Now Pelleon advanced to the rite of consummation. Clutching his cloak about him to avoid the brambles that crowded the crumbling tiny doorway, he stooped and entered. Having passed through a dark vestibule, he came fully into the dim-candled atrium.

She awaited him, wholly receptive.

He stood palsied, unbelieving, seeking to convey his mind to her—his mind richly glorified now by her acceptance of his love, as before his mind had been ascetically glorified by her acceptance of his worship.

She laid finger to lips and nodded slowly, wisely.

Discarding his cloak, he came to her in three paces and embraced her—tenderly for a while, then passionally, then terribly but leaped away as the chapel walls emitted armed men and recognized the burning eyes of Scans whose mouth was muffled by a scarf and crouched, and caught up his sword from the altar whereon he had laid it, but they did not advance, and the eyes of Scans betrayed his disconcertment as he stared at the woman, and Scans bowed low and managed to utter intelligibly through his ruined mouth and muffling scarf: "Your pardons, my lord Pelleon, my lady Ninevé. I mistook the situation. Soldiers, we withdraw and forget what we have seen." And he turned swiftly and led the way out through the low door, and the men-at-arms followed until all of them were gone.

And Pelleon was alone with his lady.

Still crouching, clinging to his sword, Pelleon stared at her. "He called thee Ninevé. My Gueraine, how could he have mistaken thy fair hair for the darkness of Ninevé? for he recognized *me*, and the candles clearly light thee, every feature is Gueraine—"

She came to him, putting her hands on his shoulders, gazing up into his eyes. "There is a thing that thou didst not know. Merleon is at work for us."

He ran a hand back through his hair. "Merleon? but how could he—" His eyes widened: "Enchantment, eh? He charmed them into looking at thee and seeing Ninevé!" Driving a hard grin onto his face, he seized her shoulder with his free hand. "So then thou art safe with me, Gueraine—forever, if Merleon chooses to keep guarding us forever—"

He paused. The grin died. He said: "Only—"

Her fingers touched his face. "*Only*, my love?"

His left hand gripped her right wrist and brought the palm off her hand to his lips; and then in a fey way he prowled off, drawing her by the wrist after him, still holding his sword; and he sat on a wooden wallside pew, drawing her down beside him. He muttered: "And yet, if Merleon had not been here to cast this enchantment, we would have been discovered, thou wouldst have burned, we would have killed the dream. And another time, if Merleon should not be here to guard thee—discovery, thy burning, the death of the dream. For there is Scans and Scans, and when there is not Scans there is some other treacherous knight or jealous lady, and Grayle was right, there is no worship in this because of the universal prurience that poisons all the worship inherent in this—"

He turned his great agonized face to the lady. "I love thee, Gueraine—and yet it seems I cannot love thee. I must go, and I cannot go. I wish to seek battle and give myself cheaply to death, but that would be disloyal to Grayle. But if I stay and do not die, surely I will dishonor thee, and it will be known."

In a dark corner of the vestibule, Gueraine, peering with pain through a stone curtain at the two on the pew, said quietly to the man who stood beside her: "I can stand no more of this. Release the enchantment, Merleon."

"Aye," the man assented; and he thrust a wand through the curtain and waved it peculiarly. Thereby Merleon withdrew his projective hypnosis from the mind of Pelleon.

Gazing at his lady, Pelleon saw her blond hair turn black and her face alter subtly: her eyes were dark and closer together and somewhat slanted, her nose was longer, her lips fuller, her skin darker, her face more slender.

Being fey, Ninevé felt the change in his mind; and as his own expression went shocked, she laid a long hand on his big hand on her small wrist and told him quietly: "I *am* Ninevé, and that is how Merleon has helped us. Thou hast they sword in thy hand: kill me."

"Aye," breathed Gueraine in the shadows.

Face darkening, Pelleon began to raise the sword. Ninevé,

already partially disrobed, closed her eyes and threw back her head, exposing to his hand the length of her beautiful neck and the rise-and-pit of her bosom.

Sword fairly aloft, Pelleon bent above her throat, and his voice came in a thrilling alcove-penetrating murmur. "I worship Gueraine as I worship the goddess Isis and the goddess Maath, and there will be no hour of my living when my worship of her will not burn higher in my spirit than any transient passion; and in every moment of my worship I will be desiring her. But I will not dishonor my goddess, and I will not shame my god and my king. Tell me, nymph, what shall I do: slay thee, or use thee to slake my unholiness? for if I do not use thee, then will I be using another to keep me holy for Gueraine."

Ninevé clarioned, breathing hard: "Long ago I offered up my pride on the altar of Isis. Either do the second, or I shall welcome the first."

Gueraine entered the atrium. Seeing her, Pelleon leaped to his feet, arms hanging, sword at trail, but feet together and shoulders back. She came and stood before him, outwardly composed, looking gravely up into his face.

He asked low: "What shall I do with the nymph, Madam?"

She answered low: "Use her, Pelleon—but not here in our chapel. I would gladly burn for thee, and indeed I do burn for thee, but neither of us would kill the dream, and Merleon and Scans have proved that indeed we would have done this. So do thou slake thy burning with Ninevé who excels at the art of slakery, and I will make shift with Grayle while dreaming of thee. For were we to come together now, and stay together even undiscovered, in time it would grow tawdry-secret, and the worship would be gone—and I would wish to keep thy worship."

I knew that eye-to-eye soul interchange can be real. Unseen, I experienced this reality.

Then Pelleon drew up his sword whose name was *Invincible,* holding it with both hands by the sharp two-edged blade with the curiously serpentine Serapian haft-and-guard before his face; and Pelleon kissed the three sacred serpents where they intertwined, and held the sword to Gueraine, and she laid lips upon it. When at length she stepped back, he turned and went to the altar and laid the sword thereon; and he turned again to face her, arms half outspread, hands bleeding from the sword edges.

"I will leave the sword here," he told her. "I have another sword, his name is *Dauntless,* he is younger brother to *Invincible.*"

She told him: "I will see that *Invincible* remains there. For a time may come when we can enter this chapel together and reclaim him. But our time now is wrong by years, and that is all our trouble."

He bowed his head and was still.

Gueraine turned to Ninevé who had not moved from her head-back self-abandonment. Gueraine spoke sharply: "Divert him but do not ruin him. He is worth more than both of us and all the men in this kingdom."

She paused. She turned to Pelleon. "Except, perhaps, Grayle."

His jaw rose. "Grayle is worth more than all of us and all the men in this kingdom. Lady, I say that, worshiping thee as my goddess."

Her head went down. "Go now with Ninevé."

Flowing to her feet, the nymph departed.

Pelleon turned a final time to Gueraine.

Laying her left hand on his left forearm, she turned her back to him, telling the floor: "It is unwise for us to kiss. But remember this parting as though we kissed."

Arm encircling her right shoulder, he laid his right hand on her hand on his arm, and strength flowed into her.

And Pelleon departed.

Gueraine stood by the altar breathing hard through her open mouth, struggling for reason.

As the tall male figure emerged from the vestibule and came toward her, she looked up at him, desperate and appealing. "Merleon! Thou has intervened to save Pelleon and me; perhaps we were nothing to thee, perhaps it was only Grayle's dream that mattered to thee; nevertheless by thy sorcery thou hast saved all of us. But I die now, Merleon, I die burning—and I pray thee, enchant me into serenity, make me sexless and cool!"

Standing a little way distant, he surveyed her, saying nothing.

From the mind of Gueraine, Merleon, still alcove-lurking,

withdrew his projective hypnosis; but not without implanting a faint vestigial suggestion that would perish in time as an alien vestige but only after her own mind would have intuitively adopted it, seeing its worth.

Before her eyes, the seeming of Merleon subtly altered, smallening.

"Grayle?" she uttered. But the cold shock thawed in her soul by reason of radiant warmth stealing in. Sinking to her knees, she murmured: "Then, after all, thou'rt Thoth."

He said gruffly: "I am not Thoth. I am Grayle. But I love thee. And I understand about Pelleon, and I continue to love both of you. Tell me therefore whether it is better for me to leave thee alone or to stay and help ease thy torment."

Great things sped through her mind. How he had conquered those stronger than himself through force of will. How he had brought together all Caerleon through force of mind—aided, but only aided, by force of arms. His kindness. His brilliance. His dream. And then, how tonight he had found supernal power to take the likeness of Merleon, and intercept her en route to this rendezvous, and enchant the eyes of Scans and the eyes of Pelleon and her own eyes. . . .

But Pelleon he was not.

But, all in all, he was greater than Pelleon.

But Pelleon he was not. . . .

But long ago, he had chosen her; and he had cherished her, cherished her now; and Pelleon still he cherished. . . .

She bowed her head before the transfiguration, crossing her arms on her breasts. She whispered: "Thou'rt Thoth, my Grayle. Here in thy Chapel of Maath, canst take me to be Maath? Right gladly would I be Maath for thee—"

Merleon and I telephoned ourselves out of there.

Under stars:

"Well done, Merleon."

"Well done, Pan."

"I did nothing, Merleon. Except to shake you loose from Ninevé, of course; but other than that, I did nothing; you did all of it."

"That is why I said well done. Thanks to you, I am entirely in self-command, I am again a whole Priest of Thoth; and I am therefore qualified to evaluate what you have done. You had at your disposal all powers of effective interference. You restricted yourself to awakening and springing Merleon. Following your leadership, Merleon restricted himself to creating a handful of trivial deceptions. But in finality, it was the people who made their own decisions and found their own ways out of an utterly impossible impasse. That is why I say, Pan: for self-control—well done."

I coughed: "It was nothing, really." I wasn't entirely being self-deprecatory: rather, I was thinking about a Nigel-nova which in a scant nineteen years would negate a star-system holocaust all the gains for Grayle's long-range dream.

Perhaps, though, the nova would not negate the gains for three people. . . . No, four people. . . . Or five? or *six?*

It was on the tips of my lips to tell Merleon who I was. Or who I *thought* I was—asking him, a pro colleague, who *he* thought I might be.

I desisted: it would be too much interference, just as warning Merleon about the nova would have been an absolutely obscene interference. But suppose I *should* reveal my identity-ambiguity to Merleon? I fell into imagining the dialog:

What do you think, Merleon? Recall that I was spawned on another Antan-track. Which of them fathered me, do you think?

The only way to know, Pan, would be to run that track.

This I refuse to do.

I understand; and I am glad, because my own original future would be on it. But I am noticing, Pan, that your hair is auburn like Grayle's and your eyes are blue like Grayle's.

My mother's race is such that I could have these features from her.

And your will is indomitable like Grayle's.

Or like Pelleon's; and I am tall like Pelleon.

But like Grayle you are thoughtful, and like Grayle you subtly nudge; and these are traits that Pelleon would have to study in faint hope of understanding them—

Merleon coughed. "I dislike interrupting a train of thought—"

I brought myself violently back to this present. "I was only wondering, Merleon—what will you do now?"

"Why, I will stick around," quoth Merleon. "For when you and I quit the chapel, all signs pointed to the need for a prince's tutor in approximately nine months. I am thinking about it already, Pan: I am toying with the notion of using basically Rousseauvian methods, modified by certain Serapian psycho-physical theories—

"—Pan?"

PART SIX

Makrov

In the year 1945, on the planet Mojud, a Fust-enslaved Lord-person named Makrov was spirited by Nazis onto a Presidential warship that lay off the coast of Vania; and there he destroyed the chiefs of three allied anti-Nazi states by violently exploding himself with a microbomb concealed in his stomach. Even though the Makrov-soul realizes that he was operating under threat to his wife and children, and that he was drugged, he does not forgive himself for his suicidal treason to the world in general and to his Lord-people in particular. Pan, can you nudge him in a replay?,

6

"By a peculiar concatenation of circumstances," said the Fuhrer, "the finger of fate is on *you,* Herr Makrov."

The skinny prisoner sat in the armless chair, shivering a little. There is a mystique about power: the Fuhrer had it, and Makrov felt it in his nearly fleshless bones. He did not answer: he waited.

From my vantage point in the brain of a Fuhrer-henchman, I watched the Fuhrer with an interest which, despite my duty, considerably overweighed my interest in this poor Makrov, who was in fact my assignment. Although I had psychoscreens up to minimize influences from the henchman-brain that I occupied, my host's ambivalent love-hatred for his short, dark, apoplectically hypnotic leader made it hard for me to stay dispassionate.

Subliminally I was interpreting the situation in context with its global background. My assignment had targeted me on Holofernes, an applaneted star in the Large Magellanic Cloud. This planet, Holofernes II, called itself Mojud, and it was aflame with war. The aggressor nation was Fust; its three chief antagonists were Vania, Columbia, and Pirov. My assignment was in Fust—in the Fustian capital—in the office of the Fuhrer—in the presence of this emaciated prisoner named Makrov who *seemed* unimportant.

With distaste, the Fuhrer was telling Makrov: "I will not hide my disgust at having to confide in you, to lecture you, to depend on you. Your stinking race that calls itself the *Lord-people* is a cancer imbedded in our noble Fustian race. You are one of those whom I mean to extirpate—totally, even the memory of you. When you do for me what you *will* do for me, I will not thank you for it, because doing it will be in your own self-interest. Your personal reward will be that I will have you exterminated promptly and painlessly under conditions of pleasure—instead of—what you know, what you have anticipated. Your larger reward will be that I will remove from misery those whom you profess to love: your wife, who is of our pure race, and your children who are therefore half-pure. Well? what do you say?"

Makrov touched thin lips with a dry pale tongue and, after several attempts, replied hoarsely: "I do not know what to say. I do not know what this is all about. They took me out of the concentration camp and brought me here. That is all I know."

Sampling the brain of my host, the Fuhrer's henchman, I grasped that my host knew a good deal more, being one of five in the Fuhrer's inner group. However, I was mainly listening to the Fuhrer—who now ruled Fust, one of the two most potent nations on Mojud, and who had involved his planet in a world war that was bidding fair to end in the rule of all Mojud by Fust and its leader.

"Well?" barked the Fuhrer at the end of his bombastic proposition. Stiffly he paced in short turnings, a hand slapping a hand behind his back, while he awaited Makrov's reply.

Makrov's weak voice dazedly emerged from his dry throat. "May I say it again, in my own way?" Reply would be condescension: the Fuhrer kept pacing. Makrov ventured: "You have learned that my wife is first cousin to the Chancellor of your enemy Vania. The Chancellor is about to participate in a summit meeting at sea with his allies the President of Columbia and the Chairman of Pirov. Your Intelligence has already used its counterespionage to get word to the Chancellor that his dear cousin and her children and husband are set to be spirited out of Fust into Vania; that her husband—me, that is—is unusually well informed about Fustian war plans; and that the summit meeting would profit from having me present for questioning. You will send me and my family to Vania, and you will get me into that summit meeting. I will be a bomb; and I will explode, killing the three national leaders."

"Correct. Well?"

"Why is it that you need my consent?"

"There are three possible ways to detonate you at the right instant. One is to time the bomb, but the timing would be far too uncertain. A second is to detonate the bomb by remote control; but our chances of getting an agent with you into the meeting to bring off this detonating are small, and he would probably be searched and his equipment discovered. This leaves the third alternative: you must detonate yourself. For this, obviously, we need your consent."

"Who would want to explode himself?"

"It will be pleasant rather than painful. You will have a capsule concealed beneath your tongue. At the right instant, you will chew into the capsule, and five seconds later you will explode. Meanwhile, however, the ingredients of the capsule will plunge you into an orgy of pleasure beyond your wildest dreams, an orgy that will subjectively continue for many hours; at its terminus, you will drop deliriously exhausted into unconsciousness, during which you will explode without ever knowing about it."

"The Fuhrer makes it sound inviting. And if I refuse?"

"Your wife and children will continue to languish in misery; and you will die as you would otherwise have died—and this is not the way that I would choose to die."

Makrov brooded.

"Your consent," yapped the Fuhrer, "must be total and sincere! No hidden resolution to warn anybody, or to fail to go through with it at the last! If either happens, we will surely get your family back here out of Vania—and they will die as you would have died!"

After long hesitation, Makrov closed eyes and uttered: "I want to see my family first."

The Fuhrer looked directly at my brain-host—that is to say, at me.

My henchman-host told Makrov acidly: "Request granted. However, you will be accompanied by select armed guards who know about this planning. If either of them detects that you are communicating any of this, we will kill your children, and you and your wife will be brought back for prolonged torment."

Still unready to enter the brain of Makrov, I made a series of transfers that left me finally in the brain of one of Makrov's guards in a command car that was bumping the party of three down a back road through a wilderness of bomb desolation. I tried to read Makrov's mind on his face. Makrov's emaciation revealed nothing but apathy.

What kept me out of his brain was the very slight danger that there I might involuntarily affect the course of his thought and action; and until I would understand the subjective situation better, I dared not risk this.

Having passed through a dirty little village and negotiated a barren terrain, our command car approached and stopped at the door of a ramshackle hut which apparently presided over a small, wasted truck farm. The guards bounced out over the side of the car, and the guard whose brain was currently hosting me took Makrov roughly by a skinny bicep and half helped, half dragged him over. Guards were posted at this door, which had suddenly become valuable to the state of Fust. Intricate watch-words were interchanged; ID papers were displayed. At length Makrov and his guards were allowed to enter.

Pausing just inside the door behind Makrov, with the other guard behind, I-in-my-host saw beyond the stooped shoulders of Makrov a piteous tableau. A woman stood bent-legged, embracing two small children. Her blond hair looked bleached (Makrov's was balding-dark), and so did her pale-blue eyes; her dress was cheap-clean and ragged; she had scarcely any shoulders or breasts, and her bare arms were wasted. She stared at Makrov, trembling a little, saying nothing, clutching the children.

"Get behind her," said the other guard. My host stationed himself behind the woman; and now my visual field was almost hers—dark-balding emaciated haunt-eyed Makrov half-cringing before his suffering wife and starved children.

The tableau held.

Makrov tried to say her name: "Meri—" No sound came, but his lips said it.

Her voice was cracked. "It is you, Ben. They have brought you, so it must be bad. But it is good."

The little girl set up a wailing; the slightly older boy hugged his mother's leg, staring at the father-stranger.

His mother hugged them, and her voice came a little Stronger; "It is your father, children. Of course you have almost forgotten—but it is not his fault, and we love him."

Makrov, gazing at them, suffered.

Suddenly Meri freed herself of the children and hurried to her husband. They embraced, sobbing. She thrust him away, turned, held his hand, and beckoned the children. They came hesitant. Makrov dropped to his knees and held out his arms. Frightened, they stood. Gently Meri shepherded them in. He embraced them. Then all four were sobbing.

My host-guard cleared his throat. The other guard was frozen in a feet-apart stance, watching objectively, a hand on his pistol.

Hugging the children, Makrov raised a wet face to his wife. He told her: "We have to talk."

Taking each child by a hand, gently she raised them to their feet. "Go out and play," she said.

But now they did not want to go.

But she made them go. And then she turned to her husband, glancing at the guards. "Come sit on the bed," she suggested. "We'll talk there, and we won't care about these listening swine, they can't understand our kind of talk anyway."

My host gripped his pistol, and the other guard's gun came half out of its holster; but my host snapped: "Cool it. We can't act unless he does something wrong."

So I had been saved any immediate need to act. My host-guard followed them to the door of the hovel and lounged in the doorway while they sat on the bed and talked, ignoring him.

Makrov: "I love you."

Meri: "I love you."

"I love the children and you."

"I love them and you, Ben. But mostly you."

"You mustn't say that, Meri. They are more important than we."

"Is that what your Lord teaches?"

"Not necessarily. What does your Master teach?"

"Theirs is the kingdom of Heaven."

"There. You see, Meri?"

"Nevertheless I love you most. I would give them for you. You do not have to feel the same way. If you would give me for them, I would understand. But that is how I feel about you."

"I feel that way about you, too. But I think it must be wrong."

"Probably it is all right in feeling, but it would be wrong in action—do you think?"

"You mean, we can love each other most, but in a pinch we have to be ready to give each other up for them?"

"What do you think, Ben?"

"That is what I think."

"This is a funny way to be talking, when we come together after two years."

"Yes. I would rather kiss you. But there *they* are." He nodded at the guards.

"They wouldn't—"

"No. They wouldn't leave."

"Maybe it's just as well. I have no lips anymore—or anything else."

"Neither have I."

Pause. The sense of the pause was that these were trifles.

"I've hardly seen the children, Meri. We sent them away to play. I think that's funny, too."

"Everything is funny, Ben. That's a hell of a word."

"You never used to swear."

"Funny is a hell of a word."

"Yes."

Long silence, during which Meri's thin hands massaged his bony hands, and they suffered, and the guards tried not to fidget. Then:

"Ben—"

"Meri?"

"I'm stewing a rutabaga. Do you—"

He shook his head.

"Ben—"

"Meri?"

"They brought you here for something. What?" She was tense, and the guards tensed: I felt my host stiffen and mentally prepare himself for swift pistol draw.

After thought, during which he looked about him slowly and vaguely, Makrov stared at my host, telling Meri: "You were taught, Meri, that your Master's Father put us into this world for testing. I was taught that this world is probably all there is, and that in it our Lord God expects us to be virtuous. So I look around, and here we are, a couple of innocents, philosopher-farmer and farmer's daughter, dusted-off and screwed into dry dirt because of the purposes of great men that we cannot touch or influence. And it crosses my mind that most of us are like this. You have it harder than most members of your pure race, because you are the wife of an impure man; but even among those of your pure race, most of them are bad off, maybe not so bad as you, maybe worse. Many of them are dying in the war, taking orders from corporals. These two guys right here, they are fat and sassy, but even they are—"

He cut it off and by habit shrank back (against his wife) as the second guard advanced threateningly on Makrov. I was at the point of intervening—but my host took intitative to bark: "NO, Fritz!" I got the mental message: the guards were to intervene only if Makrov should begin to hint at the Secret.

Meri was hugging Ben hard to her, shushing him. He struggled with her weakly; she let him be; he got himself upright and glared at the second guard, but common sense told Makrov to let it go.

Looking then at Meri, he continued, valorously brushing

off the interruption: "I am not talking only about our own country. I think it is so everywhere. Even in the southeast, many of my own people are shrinking from hostile men of their own race but of different nationalties, and then counterkilling in self-defense; and their dead enemies understand no better than my people do. It is the leaders, Meri; and if we become enthusiastic, it is because they enflame us; and if we suffer, it is because they use us. So—"

The extreme dryness of his throat had almost cut off his voice. She was hugging him again, but she was not trying to stop him—sensing, I grasped with a sudden sharp shot of sympathy, that this talking was a must for her man who could not expect to go on living anyway.

Having got saliva into his throat, Makrov struggled on—working with his enfeebled brain, as now I electrically comprehended, to *find out* something from Meri *without revealing* anything to her:

"I am too weak to propose solutions. They say that in the far west there are peoples who can really influence their leaders, and it may be so; but I bet their influence is only relatively better and their knowledge only a little better; and I bet that when they choose their leaders, they have only a few leader-chosen candidates to choose from. And maybe this is just how it is with people in the world. And this is why I am saying what I am saying, Meri—wait, I've almost forgotten what I was getting at—"

He struggled with his thought as he had struggled with his voice. Then he clutched her shoulders, looking with his popeyes into her faded eyes, and he said fiercely: "If my Lord God is right, that there is no future and we must be virtuous here for Him, then He allows us precious little chance to be virtuous! And if your Master is right, that this world is His Father's testing for hereafter, then this is a cruel testing by a God who is supposed to be a loving Heavenly Father! Meri—*tell me how it is!*"

She stared at him, stricken, clutching his arms as he gripped her shoulders. And I *knew* that *she* knew that this was a great deal more personal than a mere discussion of theology.

The silence was very long. This turn of the discussion was boring both guards: the second guard had actually turned his head away, brooding with a foot on a stool; and for the first time I had to exercise subtle influence in order to keep my host's eyes on the tortured couple so I could watch.

Meri quietly said: "Hold me, Ben." After an instant he released his grasp on her shoulders to enfold her in his arms, and she pressed her head against his chest, and Ben laid his lips on the back of her neck, and I watched her thinking.

I knew how it was!

Perhaps *now* was when I should intervene?

I forced myself to remain passive in the guard's brain. They *must* play it out *themselves*.

Then why was I here? *When* would I act?

Meri was talking low, it was hard to hear: "I think your God is right, and I think my God is right. I don't know whether they are the same God; I think they are, but I am too stupid to know. But I think they are both right."

"I am a philosopher. Tell me *how* they can both be right."

"I think that this *is* a testing for hereafter. And I also think that in this testing we must behave *as though it were all*. My religion stresses the hope. Your religion stresses the strength of hopeless loyalty. It is all one. Let us not talk about our Gods, let us talk about our prophets. If *our* prophets are right, then we must behave as *your* prophets say in order to earn the blessed hereafter. If *your* prophets are right, and there is no hereafter, then my hope will help me behave as your prophets tell me I must behave."

He said harshly: "You reduce it to a question of educational psychology."

With her mouth on his wrist, she said simply: "I reduce it to a question of hope and virtue. I think we must be courageous."

"And suffer?"

"Yes, if we cannot virtuously help it."

He wet his lips and asked *the* question, coming as close as he dared to the real issue. "What if you knew that I had knowingly acted in such a way as to intensify your suffering—and the misery of our children?"

In a kind of sluggish double-take, the second guard's attention went back to them.

She asked low: "Do you love us?"

"Yes."

"Do you love God?"

"Whatever God is—yes, I love God."
"Then you have your decisions to make. Be virtuous."
They stayed that way quietly for a while. And then the hour was done.

After that the guards command-carried Makrov back to the capital; and Makrov knew just as well as I that Makrov's wife and children would be following. I longed to enter his brain, to gauge him subjectively in this piteous crisis; but still something was warning me out, so I stayed out.

Instead, I abandoned Makrov to stay in my guard-host as both guards went in to report to the Fuhrer's deputy. This was the same man whom I had occupied during the first Fuhrer-interview with Makrov: this man was small and stooped, skinny and dark, and one leg was crooked, and he was a saturnine genius.

He said: "Tell me."

My host reported: "Nothing. They exchanged sentiments. They talked religion."

The dark man squinted. "*How* did they talk religion?"

The guard stiffened; he was select, no fool, a college graduate, a trusted confidential lieutenant in this enterprise; and now, grasping that he may have muffed something, he went to work on memory reconstruction. With hardly any perceptible hesitation he stated: "They were concerned about the ironies of their respective religious teachings. He thought that one of their gods must be wrong, because one taught that there was no hereafter and yet life was unjust, while the other taught that life is a testing for hereafter but it was an unjustly rough testing. She said that they must behave as though both gods were right—that they must be virtuous no matter what. He seemed to accept this."

"That was all?"

"That was all. But it was very subversive."

The dark man turned his questioning gaze to the second guard—who assented, not really remembering much.

For several minutes the dark man paced. Then he told the guards: "I shall think about this. Meanwhile, have the process proceed. Dismissed."

The guards saluted and left—but not before I had transferred to the brain of the dark man, to read his inwardness.

Reduce it to essentials:

She concluded, and he accepted: play it with both gods. That would mean:

If life is unjust, and there is no rewarding hereafter, be virtuous anyway.

If life is unjust, and there is no rewarding hereafter, be virtuous.

Hence: whether life is just or unjust, whether there is rewarding or no rewarding—no matter what, be virtuous.

What does that mean for Makrov?

The common golden rule for their two religions: love God, and love neighbor as self.

Wife and children are more than neighbors to him. Or even if they are only *neighbors to him—love them as self, not more than self.*

Key point, though: love God.

What does their god stand for?

But it is two *gods. But they agreed to respect both. So I have to know what* both *gods stand for.*

One way, his wife and children would count most, together with himself.

Another way, his wife and children would count most, more *than himself.*

A *third way. . . .*

A phone rang, and he answered it. Barking voice: "Is all moving forward in the Makrov affair?"

"Affirmative, Fuhrer."

"Good. Out." Click.

Where was I?

Loused-up thinking. Too many phones. Too much Fuhrer. Too much war. Did I pick the wrong horse?

Forget it. Stay with the Fuhrer-horse. Where was I? God, though, the Fuhrer is nuts. . . .

Wonder what Priest and what Teacher I could talk to, in the hope of exegizing this Makrov-esoteric. . . .

By an adroit series of brain transfers. I managed to keep myself always in one of the Fuhrer's minions most closely associated with the clinical details of Makrov's psychosurgical adaptation, taking occasional side trips to follow what was being done with Meri and the children. It had all been meticulously articulated under personal direction by the dark man who limped.

Makrov's abdomen was not opened, for this would have weakened him too much: instead, the procedure involved advanced techniques for working by remote control, visually and manually, inside the stomach from the esophagus. A thin section of the stomach lining was folded back; the tiny bomb was inserted and stitched firm; then the lining section stitched over the bomb to guarantee solid anchorage. From this bomb, hair-fine antennae, instantly and specifically responsive to the acid that would be contained in the capsule to be placed under Makrov's tongue, protruded to undulate gently in enzyme flow.

With Meri and the children, similar procedures were followed, utilizing his diabolical variant: the explosive charge in each bomb was tiny, barely sufficient to break a little vessel containing a virulent strain of cancer-inducing protein ironically developed among prisoners at Makrov's concentration camp. The antennae were responsive not to acid but to high-frequency microwaves that could be produced by small equipment carried by selectmen among the Fuhrer's agents.

They were sure that the bomb in Makrov would work. They were not sure about the little cancer bombs in Meri and the children: this uncertainty was a source of mild amusement; the thing was regarded as a scientific experiment; and the current betting odds were long that the Meribombs and kinderbombs would be used, just for discovery's sake, even if Makrov did bring off his assignment. All that was essential here was to make sure that Makrov *believed* the little bombs would work. And so they saw to it that Makrov witnessed the surgeries on his family before he was taken in for his own operation.

While the four patients were recovering, they were kept under sedation to facilitate hypnopaedia. Meri and the children were taught a simple lesson, mainly truth skillfully blurred: Makrov had been taken away from them two years earlier, they did not know whither, they supposed to a concentration camp; they had not seen him since, until their reunion in enemy Vania (scheduled for three days hence); they had been miserable; recently they had been under guard, but the guards had turned out to be Vanian agents rather than native Fustian troopers, and they had been told a week ago of their impending reunion in Vania.

Makrov's lesson was far more complex, departing much farther from truth. He had indeed been taken to a concentration camp, but incredibly he had escaped—so the hypnopaedic story went. For the past year he had been working as an underground anti-Fuhrer agent in bureaus at the very highest level in War Planning. Utilizing advanced bugging techniques that the underground had developed, Makrov (so he was taught) had been able to listen through walls; his custodial duties after high-level conferences had brought him into the conference rooms, and there an occasional obscurely marked map or a carelessly discarded sheet of carbon paper had regularly filled out the lacunae in what he had been wall-hearing. Against this background, Makrov was sleep-taught an involved, entirely plausible, and totally false version of the major war strategy that was to open up in a fortnight.

It was not intended that Makrov give himself time to tell this full story to the summit rulers. It was intended that he first chew on his little capsule. The story was insurance: he might have to start the story to gain their attention; he might be cross-questioned ahead of the summit conference as a precondition to being received at the conference; he certainly needed something plausible to tell his family—Meri and her high-ranking Vanian father—at the reunion in Vania.

Hypnopaedia for Makrov was accompanied by a specialized intravenous feeding. It physically built him up to an appearance of health which, although substandard for a storm trooper, was standard for a poor although highly trusted custodian and miles above concentration-camp standard.

Toward the end of the process, the dark limper turned up and conferred darkly with the presiding psychiatrist—into whose brain instantly I got.

"I have a hunch," the limper was saying, "and I do not know how to express this hunch, but I know what must be done about it. You must implant in the minds of Makrov and his family a total inhibition against talking among themselves about religion. And if possible, you must go farther with Makrov: in him you must implant a total inhibition against even *thinking* about religion. Can you do this?"

My new host was doubtful—and I was not intervening.

"With his family I can do it," the psychiatrist intervened; "but with Makrov, it is like this. He seems simple, but his simplicity has a complex intellectual-emotional basis. He is used to developing selected inhibitions for himself, on intellectual grounding. If we were to implant anti-intellectual inhibition in him, his whole habit pattern would force him to fight it; and in the process, he could easily go psychotic—an outcome which would hardly foster the success of his assigned mission."

The limper studied hard, glancing several times at his wristwatch. Presently he looked up. "In that case, I have another tactic for Makrov. He is in conflict about his wife's god who teaches that life is a testing for hereafter and his own god who teaches that there is no hereafter and yet one must be virtuous. He feels that the first god seems wrong, because while considering Himself merciful He makes the testing too bitter; but at the same time Makrov feels that the second god seems wrong, because He demands virtue without future in a world which is unjust. Now tell me, Herr Doktor: if you were in this kind of conflict, what kind of synthesis would you arrive at?"

Promptly the psychiatrist replied: "I would become an atheist."

"Exactly. And, as an atheist, if you loved your wife and children, what would you do if presented with the following dilemma: to murder three world leaders in a suicide action and thereby save your family; or to save the leaders and possibly yourself, thereby condemning your family to prolonged and miserable deaths?"

"Sir, I know that your question was not serious; because if it were serious, it would not be worth asking."

"Exactly. Tell me, Doctor—in the mathematics of psychology, is this conclusion mathematically certain?"

"In the psychomechanics of a moderately strong ego which has deliberately built and therefore respects its own superego, this conclusion is the necessary resultant of the vectors entailed."

"Then—overlooking your mix of psychologies—use what I have told you, and make him an atheist. Just incidentally, that will *certainly* keep him from *wanting* to talk religion with his family!"

There were four train transfers interspersed by three truck trips, all most private and undercover, entailing five changes of guard, mostly by night over a period of three days. It was all executed amid most extraordinary silence: the family interchanged few words, and few were exchanged with guards. At first, both children clung to their mother, who however pressed herself against Ben Makrov; somewhat later, the little girl clung to her father; later still, both children clung to their father, while their mother clung to all three.

By now, I *was* in Makrov. But I was finding little in the Makrov-mind except stuporous apathy. Still I had no notion what I must do with this man.

On the second night, while we jounced in a freight car on straw, there came a time when the children were asleep, and Meri crept close to Ben. His arm tightened about her thin shoulders. Presently his hand thrust a sleeve of her dirndl off her shoulder. At this instant, I disconnected; and I passed the rest of the night quietly musing with the aid of Makrov's frontal brain area, pleased that the man and his wife seemed to be coming to life a little, distressed about the death which had been planted in them and in their children.

The last stage of the journey involved a compact limousine nosing through the foggy night-streets of Vania's capital. The passengers were discharged at the servants' entrance of a large old town house. A cadaverous nightcapped man whom Makrov scarcely remembered embraced Meri, his daughter, passed her to the nightgowned witchwife behind him, and shook hands with Makrov, uttering fuzzy throaty quarter-phrases. The children hung back: Makrov shepherded them in, and the door was closed hastily. A few moments later, Herr and Frau Makrov found themselves in parlor chairs, being plied with port, while the exhausted children drowsed feet to feet on a sofa.

Somewhat afterward, inhabiting Makrov I found myself in bed with Meri—in a great plush bed, in privacy. I was inclined to disconnect; but then I decided that this husband-wife relationship must be comprehended, now on the night which was at once its blessed reassertion and the eve of its possibly catacylsmic dissolution; and so I stayed in subjective rapport.

For a little while they lay somberly together, her hand in

his, their shoulders touching. Then her bare feet came over and intertwined with his big feet. All four feet were bony. Like this they reclined for a while somberly, looking at the darkly invisible ceiling.

Makrov said: "I think we need to be naked."

Instantly Meri shed her nightgown; rather more deliberately, Makrov got rid of his pajamas. Then again they lay back together on the bunched-up pillows, hand in hand, feet intertwining, naked together, gazing upward.

It was to be their last night together. Makrov knew this. Meri did not. Makrov could say nothing that might hint it. I could not clearly make out what kind of thing Makrov's mind was framing: it was far more complex than flesh desire.

Releasing her hand, his hand slid behind her back, ran down her flank, grasped a protruding ilium. It squeezed the ilium, hugging her to him. Meri was totally submissive, ready to respond to his mood whatever it might be.

He told her: "I want to talk. All night. But I think they have done something to our minds, and so there is nothing that we can talk about."

"You do not have to talk, Ben. We know."

He frowned. "*What* do we know?"

"We know *us*."

His frown deepened. "This is the thing, Meri. Tonight I want to know you intimately and totally. But I do not know any way to do this except by talking. I could caress you and come into you, and presently I will, but after we subside it will only be body to body and nerve to nerve, and not at all the soul-in-soul knowledge that we need now."

"But this we *have*. We have lived together. We *know*."

"Do we? We know signs. But have our souls intermingled as our bodies have? A man needs more of a woman than just living with her."

"A man *like you*, Ben. A man *like you* needs more than just living with her. A woman like me does not. Just living with you is knowing your soul directly."

His hand tightened on her hip. "Do you know my soul well enough to know its ugliness? Do you know that I have an urge to overwhelm you, to outrage you? Does *that* seem like me?"

"Yes. It is all right."

"Why?"

"It is what I want too."

"*Why?*"

"If you were a sperm and I were an egg, you would viciously drive your whole self into me and annihilate yourself in the process of making me live. If your soul could come into my soul, again it would be like that. When your body comes into my body, if we put our whole souls into the thrill of the meaning, it is a little like that."

"But not enough like that."

"It is the nearest we adults can come to that. You told me yourself: nature considers us only as vehicles for the sperm and the egg that *can* wholly know each other—but without any dream. So we are impoverished—but we do our best, and we do have the dream. Here I am, Ben. I love you no matter what."

I disconnected.

As the chugging launch brought Makrov across rough water to the battle wagon where the summit meeting was transpiring, I lost Makrov in my own subjective thrall. *I, Pan,* was being brought here: the waves were tossing *me*, the battle wagon was growing monstrous in front of *me*. . . .

The climb up the ladder was heroically wearying.

Heavily shepherded, I trudged many miles of hard steel deck.

Again I mounted an endless ladder.

I stood on a vast poop deck amid a vast crowd. Most of them were seated. I stood among my guards in the rear. Up front, not clearly descriable, the three heads of state sat on a slightly raised dais, surrounded by high-level aides, talking together, listening to testimony.

I felt the bomb ticking inside me, although I knew it did not tick. I felt the capsule throbbing beneath my tongue, although I knew it did not throb.

Somebody muttered to me: "The agenda are clicking right along—inside of ten minutes, you'll be on."

I was jolted back into my own identity when my host, Makrov, replied: "I'd like to see them clearly. Can you get me any closer?"

As someone took Makrov's arm and steered him-and-me in,

he and I simultaneously realized that the exchange had been in Fustian. But here in Vania! The implication was clear: a Fustian agent *had* got through; and if an agent of the Fuhrer could get through to this superguarded ship rendezvous, why then with respect to Makrov's family if he were to fail. . . .

The three chiefs of state were now clearly visible: cherubic Vania center, suave but aging Columbia to his left, iron-hard Pirov to his right. They were listening to not-quite-audible testimony by a diplomat whose back was correct. Makrov saw no point in trying to hear; he would be signaled; and now, *in quite possibly the last nine minutes of his existence,* he had things to think about.

. . . Of his existence! Nothing after! For now he accepted quite calmly his new atheism, wondering indeed why this perfectly logical conclusion had always been rejected by him before. True, his own religion had never encouraged ideas of life after death, although some Teachers hinted vaguely at the possibility; but life with Meri, who believed in it, had tended to sway him—and the notion is attractive to any self-respecting human ego. Now, in his atheism, the prospect had to be irrevocably dismissed. And that left him *eight* minutes of existence, for he was surely going through with it.

He excluded speculation about the experience of ceasing-to-exist: they had already told him how it would be, and now he would simply wait and see. He was inhabiting a kind of dead emotional calm. There were many reasons for this. The two gods—or the two disputing sets of prophets of one god—had canceled each other out, and there was no god left and nothing to dispute about. The hell of two years in a concentration camp had taught him apathy even before he had been plucked out of the camp: death, probably horrible, had never been distant from him. Besides, his mind was made up; and worry is unsuitable in a settled state of affairs, especially during one's last *seven* minutes.

Perhaps it would be suitable to review the ethical considerations that had settled him surely. Was it futile to consider ethics in a context of atheism? Makrov had never thought so, having known many thoughtful atheists and agnostics. If a man did not have rules to live by, especially in a society of other men, his life was meaningless. But in the context of atheism—which, coupled with the epistemic isolation of the egocentric predicament, left one not only devoid of an authoritative source of ethical dictation, but also without necessary confidence in any human credo—one was free, condemned indeed to freedom, for complete ethical self-determination. Some atheists, it was true, believed in a transcendental interhuman commune; but this belief, Makrov thought, was of their individual devising. The Fuhrer believed that the stars had predestined *him* to rule the world at any necessary price of cruelty and slaughter: well, that was *his* ethos; and although Makrov's was different, Makrov had to admit that the Fuhrer's was atheistically tenable.

Meanwhile—during his last *six* minutes—Makrov felt strengthened in his own ethos, with no god conflict to disrupt it. This ethos was, curiously, the Golden Rule that brought harmony between the oddly beautiful faith of his Meri and his own discarded faith which had initiated the teaching: love God with all your heart and soul and mind and strength, and love your neighbor as yourself. Approaching this rule atheistically, Makrov felt that he had made only minor semantic modifications. With respect to the first part, he had substituted *life-purpose* for "God." And with respect to the second part—admitting that every human is one's neighbor, at the same time comprehending now that tragedy and shipwreck are in one way or another the lot of every human—he had decided that one must simply assign priorities to one's neighbor-love.

Generally, Makrov loved all humans in an intellectual sort of way: assassination of these three chiefs of state who were humans would shorten the war and therefore help all humans, even though all humans would then dwell in Fuhrer-bondage. Being patriotic, Fustian Makrov loved all Fustians better than all humans: this assassination would help Fustians more. But most of all, he loved Meri and the children; and for them, this assassination—to defuse the little cancer bombs in their bellies—was peremptory! He discounted the point that one was supposed to love neighbor *as* self (not more than self); for since his own self-destruction was essential to those he loved most, self-saving would have been no service to himself.

"About *five* minutes," the Fustian agent murmured at his ear. "Are you ready?"

Makrov merely nodded, scarcely noticing. For his thought

was moving on to an odd irony in the situation. In his atheism, he had abandoned Meri's Master and his own Lord. But by the same token, his self-annihilating assassination-act would condemn both the Lord-people and the Master-people to destruction; for these three chiefs of state, these archenemies of the Furher, represented the Master-people, and the Fuhrer was sworn to destroy all Lord-people. And so, in a way, when Makrov would chew upon the capsule about *four* minutes from now, he would be celebrating his new atheism in an act of Valhalla symbolism. He began to feel a bit heady about this though; and as his euphoria mounted, I shuddered, still not in the least knowing what to do about it or why I was here at all.

Makrov glowed. His fists began to clench and unclench. Religion was the opiate of the people. In his heroic act of self-sacrifice, he was going to show the world the Truth! Two million Lord-people in Fust, ten million Lord-people the world over, would suffer and die with him to demonstrate this truth! All the billion Master-people would be enslaved for the purpose of *learning* this truth. There is no God! There is no God! *There is no God!* Surely, surely, at the instant of his self-immolation, Makrov in his Glory for Truth would be raised high in the pantheon of the Fuhrer's Valhalla for his sublime. . . .

Correct-Back the diplomat finished and stepped down. "Not more than *three* minutes," asserted the shepherd of Makrov. "You're next."

The Fustian agent did not find it peculiar that Makrov was beginning to tremble; only, the Fustian agent was imagining the wrong reason why.

Makrov was trembling because the bottom had dropped out of his euphoria when he had heard himself fiercely hoping for apotheosis in Valhalla as his reward for annihilating twelve millon Master- and Lord-people and enslaving a billion Master-people. For if there were no God, then there was no Valhalla: the purity of his atheism had been indicted by his very joy at its triumphant celebration.

A good atheist is not triumphant! A good atheist has *humility*. . . .

Humility in his knowledge that despite this world's chances and risks he has chanced to be born and has chanced to survive. Humility because by chance he has been chosen to settle the fate of a world. Humility in the realization that in a self-annihilative act he will be permitted to save the lives of those he loves most. Humility in the comprehension that those he loves most are being saved at the price of twelve million lives and a billion enslavements, and that in saving those he loves one is saving the peace of the world. . . .

The trembling increased. (Somewhat troubled by it, the Fustian agent grasped his arm, squeezed it, murmured: "In *two* minutes or less, it will all be done—")

In a world without a god to observe the act and at best praise and at least forgive, what is the value of killing and enslaving?

The value is the continued living of one's beloved family.

They *will* be safe—won't they?

What if he pushes the button on them anyway?

Abruptly Makrov's trembling ceased, reassuring the Fustian agent as the *final minute* began. The agent should not have felt reassured. Makrov was on the verge of going into paralytic shock. He had just comprehended that, in the absence of a God, he had no object for prayer that Meri and the children would be safe!

"Apparently you will be all right," the agent whispered. "Look alive, now. I have orders to save myself." He squeezed Makrov's arm a final time and departed.

Makrov did not feel the squeeze. As the chargé d'affaires up front consulted the agenda and muttered about it with his three grand chiefs, Makrov began to grow skin-cold as profound psychosomatic shock-depression settled in to squeeze capillaries and withdraw his blood to his central somatics. . . .

I comprehended that this involuntary physical disorganization could clamp his jaws on the little capsule—indeed, probably *had*, on the original Antan-track that had not as yet been breached.

Suddenly I knew one thing to do—now, after all this time of knowing nothing to do about Makrov. I could return Makrov to self-mastery! Whatever Makrov might then decide to do, he had to decide and do it for himself.

Instantly I acted on his autonomics. Adrenalin flowed from his suprarenals. Capillaries dilated, and Makrov's heart began to accelerate, and Makrov's brain cleared to a level of unprecedented clarity.

The chargé d'affaires was demanding: "If the man Makrov is here, will he come forward please?"

Tremendously conscious of the capsule under his tongue, Makrov slowly and firmly walked forward.

He was rehearing Meri's words. "I think your God is right, and I think my God is right. . . . I think that this *is* a testing for hereafter. And I also think that in this testing we must behave *as though it were all.* My religion stresses the *hope.* Your religion stresses the strength of hopeless loyalty. It is all one. Let us not talk about our Gods, let us talk about our prophets. If *our* prophets are right, then we must behave as *your* prophets say in order to earn the blessed hereafter. If *your* prophets are right, and there is no hereafter, *then my hope will help me to behave as your prophets say I must behave.*"

The Vanian Chancellor said to him pleasantly in Fustian: "Herr Makrov, we understand that you can tell us a great deal about Fustian war strategy. Let me present my colleagues and myself." He introduced the two other great men and himself informally, and he added: "Tell us in your own way—but if you can manage to pause at the end of each sentence while our interpreters operate—"

The desperate Makrov suddenly saw a clear way to run to the rail and jump overboard and chew on his capsule at swimming distance from the ship.

For the first and only time on this mission, I intervened with directional persuasion. I caused the following explicit thought to arise in Makrov's mind—a thought that was thoroughly a Makrov-thought, not Pan-injected, merely Pan-released from the turbidness of his trauma so it could surface. *Meri and the children will die, won't they? and I will be well out of it, won't I?*

Angrily he answered himself: *But they will die anyway —lingeringly, hideously! That I cannot live to face, knowing that I did it!*

—And then, before I could think of a counter, Makrov had his own counter. . . .

The Chancellor pressed: "Well, Herr Makrov?"

Swiftly Makrov reached finger and thumb into his mouth, produced the capsule, thrust it toward the Chancellor, and blurted: "Here!"

* * *

Eternity would not erase from my mind the memory of Makrov's counter.

Makrov had simply reminded himself: *While they are dying lingeringly and hideously because of me, I have to be alive with them to love them.*

PART SEVEN

The Bishop's Halo

On the planet Erth in its twentieth century A.D., an obsessive-compulsive young scientist named Lewis Paige met with an occult phenomena-complex that he could neither understand nor test. After another twenty years of a moderately successful and apparently normal scientific career, inexplicably one evening, and without leaving a note, Dr. Paige fired a shotgun into his own mouth. Naturally his soul is here, eternally eating itself out because (1) he could not think of a theory or test, (2) he did not have the courage of honesty to publish his failure with the paradox in the hope that other scientists might resolve it, (3) he could not successfully command his own brain to stay alive and beat his neurosis.

After you've looked him over, Pan, make your own judgment whether to try nudging him into some alternate track. His coarctation was such that we would predict failure on *any* track. If you do try, and if you fail—or if you decide not to try—we will have to undertake an excruciating form of direct therapy on the soul, with no guarantee of success.

7

Having located the system of Antan-tracks called Lewis Paige, I elected to enter his brain immediately and run, not *with* Paige, but subjectively *as* Paige. Of course we had reinvested these old tracks with his living soul, it was here in him near me, but he knew of my presence no more than he knew that he was reenacting his own past. At no time-point in Antan can an Antan-brain house any memories of what was to happen at a later point in time: thus our two souls in this single body each lived its own bodied life as though it were thrusting with discretionary will into the futuring present. . . .

As young Lewis Paige, I was an engineer of sound mind and body, and my powers of observation were actue. Yet never in my travels had I seen anyone in the same class with Bishop O'Duffy. The bishop was long and spindly, with an arthritic bend at the midriff; his face was long and gray; a fringe of gray hair encircled a shiny pate, which might have been tonsured but wasn't; he was dressed always in a near approach to sackcloth, and he wore a turnabout collar. So far, so common; it was not the appearance of the bishop that awed me (who, being Paige, was unwilling to be awed), but the man's manner.

Saintly? courtly? on the whole, it was a combination of the two, with an inexplicable infusion of the occult. As Paige, I had no patience with mysticism; but I was forced to admit to myself that the essence was there, simply pouring from O'Duffy. "Some illusion," I reflected. "A conditioned response." But whatever I might call it, I felt it.

(Be clear that I had jettisoned my Pan-identity; for this while, I was Lewis Paige wholly, with only his memories and attitudes. But I had risked this self-abandonment with considerable confidence that the approach of a really viable if-node would alarm-clock me into self awakening. . . .)

Not that the bishop in any way affected a manner. Rather the contrary. Naively benignant. I was not influenced by attitudes: being a good scientist, I saw through them. But through O'Duffy, whom at first I took to be transparent, I could not see.

Better maybe I should not have met the bishop. In logic, I *would* not have met him, so remote were our worlds. . . .

I had knocked about with engineers for a good while before my savings had put me back into college for an extra two years. Rubbing shoulders with engineers in the field, I had acquired a skepticism which in college was baked into a hard high-glazed critical attitude. If Missourians have to be shown, I had to be dunked. I had already earned my BS a few years before my reentry; two more years yielded me an MS with credits to spare and a profound grasp of geology, metallurgy, practical astronomy, and advanced chemistry and physics. I was quite a specimen when I walked across the stage at commencement: I wore my gown and my stole, not with dignity nor yet with grace, but with realism; and my mortarboard was in all its dimensions at right angles to the vertical axis.

My record in the college placement office was a data reflection of my mind and personality. One day Bishop O'Duffy, shopping for talent by correspondence, had seen that record. Letters were exchanged: mine to him were precise and competent, his to me were kindly and discursive. The dots on the bishop's *i*'s twinkled: that observation, which I put down to the oscillating current in the lighting system of my rooming house, doubtless was my first subconscious intimation of the occult.

So I traveled to a state in the West, a state whose soil I had never trod; and as the croupy train, like a clumsy-side-winder, struggled to a halt at the improbable town of West Gleam, I began to be glad I had never visited here before, so that now I could savor new this experience that was strenuous to scientific credulity. The landscape was simply not real—which is to say that it did not fit easily into my conceptual frames of reference.

It was strictly mountainous country: to the limits of vision, there was no feature of this landscape that wasn't steep; the land didn't roll, it swooped. Vaguely aware that my train had gone away, leaving me alone, I bent my attention to isolate the component of *weird* in this experience that now was fairly swallowing me. When I had it isolated, it wasn't comforting. Although I was not standing on a high place, I was easily able to see most of the terrain for many miles. It was almost as though the erth in this region were *concave*—so that I could catch the blue glimmer of remote lakes that hid themselves (or, in a normal terrain, *would have* hidden themselves) behind lofty rock peaks.

I did not then permit this unreasonable defiance of optical laws to perturb me unduly. As a scientist, merely I made a mental note that it would be necessary to look into the causes behind this panoramic queerness. . . .

Believe me, I was not an utterly flat character. Various men have various weaknesses: I was a pushover for beauty. I was mildly ashamed of this vice; I fought it, but never ardently. Into my observations of chemical phenomena would intrude an exaltation of the artistry of molecular choreography; I would thrill to the mathematical elegance of atomic asymmetry; and then—supreme proof of my vicious abandonment to the aesthetic illusion—I would turn my eyes from contemplation of microcosmic diagrams to gloat voluptuously over the *lack* of perfection in a mountain whose facade had been gouged into a col by a malignant glacier. I reacted to beauty as DeQuincy had reacted to another opiate; and this foible, which I deplored in sober moments of scientific devotion, enriched my life in a manner that I kept scrupulously private.

This weakness kept me standing (alone, as I was, on the station platform) for many minutes, in rapt contemplation of the vista that rose above me like the inner surface of a gargantuan mountain-toothed tea saucer. Before me, behind me, about me, realities like railroads had ceased to exist—had retreated before the intoxicating centrifugal-centripetal effect of the mighty panorama that engulfed me. Even the dinginess of the tiny station (which had blistered for decades beneath the western sun) and the weight of my two bulky Gladstone bags (which hung inert, one from each hand) faded from my awareness. With my head traveling in slow rotation like a panoramic camera, my vision swept the uttermost reaches of the endless mountains. My mind was a confusion of rugged forms and colors: the chaotic blockpile of snowcapped mountains; the symmetry of the myriad conifers that blanketed the lower reaches of those mountains; the sharp, excruciating blue of an occasional valley-nestled lake; the sky, whose nearly equal blueness was divided from those lakes only by the blinding white of the névé—these phenomena pierced me, exciting an orgiastic festival of sensory emotion that continued to hurt until fatigue overcame it and rationality reclaimed me.

I sighed and set down my bags. . . .

A wagon, having magically appeared, drew near, and I began to hear its noises. Sounds here did not penetrate my consciousness until they grew sharp and near. Whether this resulted from some odd acoustical property of the concave landscape, or merely from my own autohypnosis, I wasn't sure.

The wagon, preceded by a horse, approached as nearly as the station platform would permit. Returning to erth, I examined the wagon in a scientific manner. The driver, alone in the wagon, was the bishop.

I discounted the mystical *meaning* that flooded me on sight of O'Duffy. It was as though some benign effluvium emanated from the bishop to overwhelm me with an unanalyzable infusion of friendliness and reverence. I put it down to my early Puritan training, rejected but treacherously imprinted on my superego, and to the unaccountable oddity of the West Gleam atmosphere. Actually, later I explained to myself, it was only that the bishop had been uncommonly cordial—had spiritually embraced me with warmth and with a smile that clearly came from the heart. As we drove slowly into the mountains, engaging in quiet discourse, I felt warmed by the love that some call *agape*: the realization was sudden, and it caused me to regret my inattention to psychology.

Bishop O'Duffy chatted intimately as we rode, bumping along a mountain trail that barely gave space for the buggy beam. The spindly length of the bishop was bent at astounding angles averaging forty-five degrees: body to thighs with hips at the angle, thighs to calves with knees at the angle, forearms to upper arms with elbows at the angle. His head nodded in gentle jerking with the jerking of the buggy, and I caught myself nodding my own head in counterpoint.

"I suppose," explained the bishop, "you'd call it a sort of cult, out there where you come from. Anyhow, some of us grew sick of civilization and formal religion—not that we look down our noses at them, you understand, but just that they don't suit our kind of people. So we moved westward, and we hit upon this spot in a quite unbelievable way." He mused, smiling vaguely.

Presently he added: "Don't get the idea that we are barrenly simple, either. We have our rituals, but we are rather realistic about them. We tried simple ways of worship; but some of us found, after a while, that—it just didn't feel religious enough it wasn't re*binding* us to anything. I guess we still have a lot of the old animal in us, Mr. Paige; and we West Gleam folk respect the animal, we believe in leading and improving him without rejecting him. So our bodies have to enter into our higher activities—in order for our souls to shine through, you see."

I remained silent. Being chronically introspective in a mathematical sort of way, I observed now with some embarrassment that I was responding to O'Duffy's discourse in three simultaneous ways. *Imprimis,* I matter-of-factly rejected the "soul" idea as romantic. *Item,* I noticed that this rejection, in its antiromantic quality, was actually inspired by the very underlay of Puritanism which I likewise rejected. *Item,* I found myself sympathizing with the bishop's viewpoint even while I disagreed; in an intuitive manner, I was half-comprehending!

"Do you think," I inquired (in what was, I realized even while saying it, an absurd non sequitur), "that so-called intuition can be accepted as a perfectly realistic psychological process which conforms to laws that we will understand eventually?" I was baiting the bishop: I knew for sure that he must reject this kind of rationalism, insisting on a mystical treatment of intuition.

O'Duffy smiled at that remarkable horizon which had no business being there among all those mountains. "I think," he ultimately replied, "what *you* think."

"You *can't!*" I protested, feeling unfairly outplayed by evasion. "I may be jeopardizing my job by saying so—but I am an atheist!"

"That is to say," he queried mildly, "you have specified, inspected, and rejected all the *meanings* of divinity?"

I shrugged. "I'm a scientist. Most of the meanings are unscientific, and all the scientific meanings can be put into material categories."

"Ah, *so!*" murmured O'Duffy in a tone that somehow left me wondering whether there might be a soft spot in my own logic.

We were silent after that, jogging on into the endless ups and downs. The effect of concavity was still present, and I occupied myself with evaluating it. The sensations discomforted me.

Suddenly, turning to look back, I was shattered by apparently convincing evidence that it was no illusion! For the rickety station at West Gleam, several miles away, still was visible in the lowering gloom—although between me and the station arose a cluster of mountain pinnacles that *ought* to have hidden the station totally!

Thereafter for a good hour I stared straight ahead, thinking methodically, eliminating successive hypotheses. The effect of altitude? no, I rejected that. Some refraction of light waves, no doubt, owing to an eccentric distribution of vapor in the atmosphere. But what vapor? this atmosphere was the clear, dry, distance-annihilating western variety. Yet this was obviously a mirage of some sort; and as such, it must be subject to the laws of optics. I pondered; and as twilight closed in on us, I became conscious of fatigue, chill, and hunger. I turned to ask the bishop how far we still had to go.

I then became conscious of a fourth condition that didn't seem physical. Just above the bishop's head I was seeing a halo.

Quickly I turned my eyes away. Since it was objectively impossible, why dwell on it? Staring into distant darkness breeds after-images of light. If I had projected such an after-image on the gray, balding head of O'Duffy—why, then I had so projected it.

I did not look again at the bishop. To help me avoid looking at him, I stared past him at the head of the horse. And I chose not to recognize the fact that the horse did *not* have a halo.

Contrary to my expectation, the men of West Gleam were *men*, virile and active. Their women added to my admiration of the little settlement whose cabins nestled in a snug valley. There was much beauty on these women, but it was a beauty simple-frocked and unadorned. These people seemed to have returned to first principles, but with a new departure: the women knew their places, but so did the men. There were no inferiorities, no superiorities: all knew where they fitted into the cooperative commonwealth.

I was neither a political scientist nor a philosopher. Nevertheless I meditated this curiously successful culture, contrasting it with my preconceptions about Socialism. Tentatively I formed a hypothesis that there must be some critical size of a society which is a cutoff size distinguishing Communistic success from Communistic failure. Maybe Communism, if undistorted by the stylization of Marx, could work if the society were small enough so that all the people could know and trust or realistically mistrust each other. This *was* a little place, and it worked; in some other places that were damn big places, it broke down into oligarchy, it was Communism no longer even though it claimed the name.

All the people adored the bishop. He was their common denominator. Their *common* denominator.

Once I had met the people and had shaken hands with them firmly, they had oriented me. They were simple workers; I was a scientific thinker. That was that. They had heard of me and had looked forward to my coming, and their regard of me blended admiration and acceptance. It was as though they had said: "Science is a necessary component of our society, as long as we keep it from being more than an interwoven component; go to, we shall get us a scientist."

On the morning after my arrival, the bishop conducted me into the mountain field. O'Duffy's arthritic bends did not, somehow, prevent him from moving through the surprising mountainscape at a speed that would have done credit to me at rugged thirty. Increasingly I was sensing the bishop's essential *adequacy as a man:* his appearance of naiveté turned out to be the sophistication of the mountains and the kind of subcivilized comprehension that is occasionally called basic human wisdom.

After nearly an hour of swift up-and-down foot travel, the bishop came to a decisive halt, turned and studied me. I leaned on my spade, waiting, confident and even vain about my image. Lusterless in mufti, now I was in my element and dressed for it. I was tall and broad-shouldered, and my blond hair and gray eyes were set off to perfection by my khaki shirt and high-top boots; I rested easily and flexibly on my spade handle, the squareness of my shoulders accentuated by the pack I carried. In and around this light pack reposed my field equipment: binoculars, magnifying glasses, specimen cases, rope, trowel, and a little kit of well-cushioned bottles containing reagents for spot-screening. At my belt hung a geologist's hammer. The bishop had to be appreciating that Lewis Paige was ready—and able.

"Here," said O'Duffy, "is one of the very best sources. Now, before we begin, are you clear about this phase of your job?"

Precisely I asserted: "I have to examine a stuff that abounds in this vicinity, a stuff that seems to be a rare erth. I am to give it a geological and chemical analysis and report as to (a) its classification, (b) its properties, and (c) its utilitarian value."

O'Duffy chuckled. "That's it," he murmured. Then his eyes, usually somewhat bleary, grew searching-sharp as he began to inspect the rocks about us.

I watched him carefully. We were in a col far up a side of a peak; this hollow, worn by a prehistoric glacier, had been weathered by elements other than ice, and our footing was as pebbly as the surroundings were rugged.

I remarked: "My spade is *de trop*. I should have brought a pickax."

"I have one," replied the bishop, who thereupon fumbled at his own pack and brought out a pick that was not much larger than my pick-ended hammer, only heavier and with more handle for swing. "Where do you suppose the devil has hidden that stuff?"

"That it?" I queried, my practiced eyes having spotted something unfamiliar.

"Um," he confirmed, stooping and pointing to a pocket in which reposed a dark substance that unaccountably sparkled. "It is abundant around here, Paige. We have a couple of geologists in our crowd, but they haven't been able to make anything of it. Do you know the stuff?"

"No—"

I ruminated. Then I drew my hammer. "Ax?" asked O'Duffy, offering his. I shook my head: I was preoccupied, and maybe I wanted my own tools to prove adequate. Shedding my pack, I opened it and drew out a small metal flask with a wide top. I opened the flask and set it nearby. After that, I bent and chipped slowly and carefully at the lode.

Pausing, I turned to O'Duffy. "Could it be radioactive?"

"Possibly. I see what you mean. But I've been handling it for half a year with no ill effects."

I nodded, my face a little hot and probably red—why hadn't I brought a Geiger counter?

With a small trowel, I scraped up a quantity of the stuff; I straightened, held it to skylight, and poised a lens above it. For a while I lost myself; the bishop, half-bent as usual, regarded me with curiosity.

"Nothing," finally I announced, "that I ever saw or heard of—that is, it arouses no associations at the moment."

He smiled: "I'm not surprised."

I deposited the stuff in the flask, closed the flask, replaced flask in pack, swung the pack onto my shoulders, and looked at the bishop. "Ready to go?"

O'Duffy was disappointed. "So soon? I thought you'd like to explore a little—"

I snapped: "Later. This junk ought to be looked into." My stomach lining was puckering. . . .

All that afternoon I kept to my room, pacing, examining the queer dust, fuming because my trunk of equipment hadn't arrived. It came late that evening—either because next week's train had missed connections and come in early, or because I had arrived yesterday afternoon on the previous week's train. I pounced on the trunk, tore it open, and pull-hauled miscellaneous apparatus, littering the floor and the scanty furniture. Alternately sweating from my work and chilling in the night air of the mountains, I worked with fury; and at last I stood panting and triumphant amid stacks of laboratory debris. The only free surface in the room was the floor of the trunk.

I sank onto a chair (first shoving off a gunnysack which plopped on the floor in abject discouragement) and wiped my forehead. But I was not resting: I was planning my next move; in that mess, I *needed* to plan. . . .

I snapped to; and with swift deft movements I put the broad table in order: it was a slab top of virgin pine that formed a workbench on one side of my large room. From the melee emerged a gleaming array of slides, hand lenses, tweezers, assorted microscopes, reonic instrumentation, a delicate scales encased in glass, handbooks, and an odds-and-ends case that was full of them (with each article in its own compartment built to size). Then—since the bishop's local arrangements generated only AC adequate for flickering bulbs—I crawled under the table and unpacked a storage battery from a crate; I filled the battery with distilled water from a ten-gallon jug that materialized from nowhere, ran a cable or two behind the table to its work surface, and hooked up a powerful lamp that I had mummified in old rags. The metal shade of this lamp was unique: it swiveled; one side exposed the two-hundred-watt bulb to a ground-glass screen that diffused the light over the table with relative softness; the other side, elongated into a projecting tube, framed a lens that concentrated the light into a dazzling beam about two inches in diameter.

Must hook up the waterpower generator tomorrow, I told myself. *Meanwhile this charge ought to hold for tonight—*

For an instant I stood, my vision darting desperately around the room. Vaguely I knew that I was excessively, feverishly excited; but then my excitement swamped my realization. My frantic look around for what-came-next ended when I saw the chair again. I dragged it to the table and sat, quivering. I held myself in check for a moment, breathing staccato; then my hands went to the flask that sat in the exact geometrical center of the table surface. I opened the flask, seized a dish of polished enamel, and thereon poured (with flexible fingers that didn't quite tremble) the queer dust I had gathered that morning.

My hand swiveled the lampshade, and the concentrated finger of light probed the dust. It leaped into light, this dust, seeming almost to move and crackle. . . .

For many minutes I inspected it beneath my hand lens.

Then my tight hand sought the least remarkable of the microscopes.

I went to work. . . .

The Paige-dreaming faded, grew semiobjective: I, Pan, semiawoke to the degree that I seemed to be watching Paige at work; semiawoke with a semisense that already there was a concern, that it would not be very long before Pan-alertness in full Pan-identity would be indicated. . . .

Not yet, though. I lapsed back into Paige-dreaming. . .

When dawn began to sneak into my room, there was possibly no knock at the door, since I didn't hear one. I continued to work vigorously, viciously; and thus the bishop found me when he stole noiselessly in like the dawn.

The spare and kindly bishop contemplated me silently for a long time, standing with his hands in his pockets; a tenth of my back-mind was fleetingly aware of him; only his chronic midbend saved his head from damage against the low ceiling. I was hunched over my table, my hands moving and my head bobbing; to my right, a pile of notes was growing with visible speed; my pencil danced over paper; now and then I would drop pencil long enough to flash the light once again on the little plate of sparkling dust that now had advanced to my ultramicroscope. . . .

Ultimately I soughed out a sigh, paused in my work, and ran my hand through my tousled blond hair; then I turned my chair. For a moment I gazed blank and slowly realized that someone had straightened the things in my room. In a dim corner sat the bishop, informally pontifical; my floodlight indirectly relieved the dimness in that corner just enough to reveal that the bishop was beaming.

I tightened lips; then I smiled small. "Thanks, Your Grace. I had intended to finish that straightening job in the morning; but I don't suppose I would have been up to it, at that."

"Are you progressing?"

At that my smile was rueful. "In a negative sort of way. I've got to the point where I know what the dust *isn't*. I knew that anyway, but now I think I can prove it."

"So what isn't it?"

"Anything now known to science. It's a *new* thing, Bishop—"

"What's the next step?"

"Spectroscope!" I snapped febrile; probably my eyes gleamed. "And I think we may as well get to it right now—eh?"

I jerked to my feet, looked quickly around for orientation to O'Duffy's relocation of my stuff, and spied a largish box, unopened, near the rustic excuse for a chiffonier. En route thereto, I stopped and glanced at a window. "My God!" I blurted. "Uh—I beg your pardon, Your Grace—"

"Okay," said the bishop. "Name's O'Duffy."

"Dawn's breaking!"

"These mountains. Peculiar. Dawn does that."

"But," I exploded, "that kills the spectroscopics!"

"Can't you pull down the shades?"

In despond: "No use. This delicate study would be worthless except in absolute darkness."

"I'm a photography addict," the bishop averred.

I patterned and swung. "You have a dark room?"

"A very good dark room. My own bedroom. It has no windows at all. I found that starlight keeps me awake; it's too pretty for sleep."

"Great! Let's go there!"

"—But I don't advise it now," he qualified. "You've been working all night. How about some rest?"

"Rest? Oh. . . . Rest. Of course! I'd forgotten—"

I dropped into a chair: now I thought about it, I was shot. Snapping off my light, I regarded the bishop. . . .

I rubbed a hand over my eyes and looked again.

That damned halo!

I started to blurt an inquiry. I clamped my jaw shut, reflecting: *I am a tired man. My retinas are playing tricks. I'm so tired that I'm admitting it.*

My gaze shifted to my table; and I noted with some relief that a microscope on which my gaze happened to fix was indulging in unnatural mitosis. I chose not to recognize that this kind of illusion was physiologically different from a halo. If I would close my eyes for a few minutes, it would all go away. . . .

"I found your bed," whispered the bishop, shaking my shoulder gently. "It was right over here, under a suit of clothes."

Although I wasn't soft, my mattress of cross-laced pine boughs bothered me: I slept several hours without exactly awakening, yet all the time I half-knew that I was not perfectly asleep. Eventually I had to accept the fact that I was no longer asleep at all. Before my eyes came frankly open, I had visions of halos dancing in front of me; then, in a brief lapse, I myself became a halo—a great broad halo, encircling myself who was also the Erth. Halo-Paige-Erth—regarding chains of halos, and among them stalking a long lank shadow bent arthritically at the midriff. . . .

Ultimately I was awake, lead-footed but at least oriented. Squinting at a window, I saw that it was well into the afternoon; sunlight was just beginning to splash on my floor, and I told myself that the heat was doubtless at fault for my fever-dreams—at least, in part the heat. I struggled to my feet: they hit my floor thudding, reminding me that I had gone to bed with boots on. I toyed with the idea of going for a swim, but the prospect of having to take off my brogans was too much in my weakened state. . . .

"Damned dust!" I grunted, thinking about its eccentric sparkle. I sat on bedside in something like stupor; my mind was excessively sodden. . . .

The door creaked open; a head thrust itself cautiously in.

I muttered: "Ah, there."

"You up?" drawled some Texan.

"More or less. Come in."

A heavy boot kicked open my door. A short chunky man entered, carrying a tray.

"Oh—Shorty, isn't it?" I queried with a lambent gleam of intelligent recognition.

"You hit it," Shorty countered while he carried the tray to my table. There he paused uncertainly: "I'd be glad to set this thing down, but—"

I saw what he meant, got up, cleared a square yard of table. "Won't you join me? Mighty nice of you to bring my—breakfast, is it? supper?"

"Brunch. No thanks, I don't want to spoil *my* supper. You're a privileged character here, Mr. Paige. The bishop has given orders that whenever you want to eat, or sleep, or make love, or whatever, you're to be accommodated."

The third of the four whatevers affected me somewhat as the halo had. But—"Hell!" I protested, pausing halfway through an intriguing glass of unfamiliar citrus fruit juice. "I don't want to be *that* much trouble!"

"Now look here, pardner," remonstrated friendlily this living breathing stereotype, "don't think you're trouble! The Right Reverend hired you to do a job, and he knows enough about professional people to know that they can't get much creative work done if they had to fool around with schedules. When you get an idee, the idee is for you to jump up from wherever you're at at the time and ride it. We all understand that, and we're in favor of it. We think the work you're doing is mighty valuable."

I glanced at my rumpled bedclothes, laughed short, and took a vicious bite at my bacon.

Shorty sighed. "Don't be so damn conscientious!" he scolded. "Let *us* be your social conscience! I know you were working till dawn, so why not sleep till afternoon? You'll probably work the next stretch till two weeks from now without any sleep. Not that you *have* to work like that—"

Here among strangers, I appreciated the friendliness of Shorty. With my breakfast down, I felt better; and I took occasion to question Shorty about this West Gleam settlement. Shorty told me a good deal, but he didn't go into much detail about customs or community rules; the omission seemed odd—I had always thought that religious communities were pretty strict and choked with red tape. I said as much.

"Yeah," Shorty mused. "That usually confuses 'em. They can't see why we should come all the way out here just to wallow under the western sky—not that *I* haven't seen western skies before—that's what they call the editorial *we*. Well, it's a little hard to explain. The bishop could explain, if he wanted to. Me, I ain't got the education."

"Wouldn't the bishop want to explain?"

"He don't want to go into too much detail unless a guy is really interested."

"I'm interested."

"Not in the right way, though—not yet. You, now, you're a scientist, and you're interested in everything. Sure, you're interested in West Gleam—same way you'd be interested in some oddball bug. And I know you're sincere, from your own point of view. But with us it's different. We *are* West Gleam. And so I don't think he'd tell you much yet, except just answer your questions."

Not a bad analysis, I considered. I *was*—well, coldly interested in everything—*everything*. . . . I prodded; "You admire the bishop?"

"*Admire* him? He's our *tongue!*"

Odd notion. I went to a window and leaned on the sill, contemplating partly the sun, but mostly my memory-image of lanky O'Duffy.

A dangerous thought struck me—a thought about an illusion, dangerous to mention overtly, perilous even to contemplate. I rejected the thought, frowning; yet it returned insistently.

Shorty, gathering up dishes, broke into my meditation. "Coming to church tonight?"

Startled, I wheeled. "Church? My God—pardon me—I mean, it *is* Sunday, isn't it!"

"My God—pardon me, but yes it is," grinned Shorty, enjoying my compounded embarrassment.

Thrusting through, I queried: "Would I be welcome?"

"Why not?"

"I'm not religious. I've told the bishop—"

"Anybody who'll sit up all night trying to find out the nature of some screwy new kind of dust is welcome in our church."

I contemplated that. The outgoing friendliness of Shorty decided me, and I took the plunge: "Tell me something—"

"Yeah?"

"Have you—" I stopped, reddening again.

"Go on." It was encouragement.

"Have you ever noticed a—well, a sort of an odd *light* over the bishop's head?"

There: I'd said it! What sort of scientist would Shorty think I was?

Shorty looked over from his dishes. "You mean O'Duffy's halo?"

My mouth fell open—

"Sure he's got a halo," said Shorty. Then noticing my amaze, he laughed. "I get it—you couldn't believe your scientific eyes? thought maybe you were cracking up? No, you ain't. It hit us the same way, till we got used to it. But he has one, all right. And nobody was ever more entitled to one, either."

While I was desperately searching for the next question, Shorty grew thoughtful and added: "But here's a funny thing. O'Duffy doesn't know he's got it."

"He—*doesn't know?*"

"Nope."

"Didn't anybody ever *tell* him?"

"Sure. Lotsa times. But—how can I explain it?—he seems to sorta take it for granted at the time—and then, the next time the matter comes up, he's forgotten about it."

"How in hell do you account for *that?*"

Shorty picked up the tray and started slowly for the door. "I reckon," he ventured, "it's because he's good."

And as he disappeared through the door, Shorty added: "Come to church tonight, Mr. Paige. You'll see his halo good. It shows up swell in church."

Certainly the atmosphere was perfect for the display of Bishop O'Duffy's halo. It was night, and the night lay brooding over the vast rocky bowl that the faithful called their cathedral. God, or whoever had done it, had hollowed the amphitheater in such a way that its altar, a diminutive craggy spire, pointed to Polaris; and its sole entrance lay to the south, so that the entering worshipers gazed perforce upon the star and were exalted.

I was almost the last to enter; and as my eyes were filled with the altar and the star, my salty scientific skepticism began unaccountably to fade. I did not admit the word *occult* into my language; nevertheless my fading skepticism left in me a void that was ineffably disturbing. The hush was so profound that the night seemed to be brushing against me as hesitantly I found my way down the natural aisle flanked by men and women who were silent-expectant. Inhibiting my breathing, I was whisperingly ushered to a seat, and tense, I stared at the altar, while those dull-hued disks—the after-images of darkness—slowly pivoted about the altar, advancing and withdrawing, and my ears began to sense after-images of silence. . . .

The moon rose over the altar. My first glance told me that it was a new moon holding mystically the old moon in her arms. Then this moon began to bob. That, I told myself (incisively, to mask my pinch of fear), was the wrong part of the sky, the wrong kind of behavior, and consequently—not the moon!

The silhouette below the moon began to take shape. It was the bishop.

The moon, of course, was his halo.

Motionless behind the altar stood the bishop, his arthritic bend unaccountably straightened, his arms parallel and pointing to Polaris. It was gloomy and it was weird; and although I did not like it, inescapably I was drawn into it. In awed silence the congregation—a hundred or a thousand huddled in the natural stonehenge—stared at the bishop, who stood motionless, probably praying. . . .

Crashing volume of music!

I was not startled—I was paralyzed! Whence did it come, that orchestra crashing and reverberating among the rocks with the frightening virtuosity of harmonious cannon?

Now emerged the real moon—it had been hiding all this time behind some mammoth crag—and the paleolithic congregation rose up, bathed in the moon's beauty, the bishop towering above them like Colossus in prayer. . . .

This was indeed worship: elemental, devoid of intellect, consecrated in spontaneous artistry and autonomic joy. I had taken a seat near the rear of the amphitheater that I might of-serve undisturbed; I observed, but not undisturbed. This cosmic joy, with its abysmal undertone of fatality—I was in it and out of it, a spectator gloomily half aloof, pulled by the madness but unable to enter, *unable* to enter.

They danced: Christ, how they danced! in and out, in and out, in a sublime serpentine sinuosity. Men and women, festival-dressed, meandered rhythmically about the arena, gliding over the crude slab seats. Lifted out of themselves, yet they remained gloriously in control, realising their bodies and their souls in union. There was an erotic quality in it—women, as they brushed past me, touched me lightly on the hair, on my ear tips; I thrilled, feeling that their touches, while not altogether for me, were aimed at me; yet the erotic nuance was not Eros—rather there was a sense that Eros was a crude latterday decadence of the primeval splendor that the dance was symbolizing. . . .

Partially, painfully extracting myself, I looked for the bishop—and saw that points of light were appearing above the altar. They were candles; and as the bishop lighted more and more of them, his long-Gothic body seemed magically attenuated in the ambiguous glow. Despite his gaunt ungainliness, he was motion-poetry as he clambered from candle to candle. Banks of flame points now gleamed here and there, vaguely illuminating the God-hewn altar beneath. And the halo of the bishop—ah, that was *there!* and I shuddered as I looked upon it, my mind scattering into formlessness. . . .

At last—chilled, as one who has gazed too long at bright stars—I slipped from the amphitheater and crept shivering into my laboratory.

Until now, I had been wholly Lewis Paige; but this was an alarm situation; and I extricated myself from Paige as though yawning and stretching, and I mind-sought and found the brain of my own body which I had parked on a parallel but meaningless Antan-track established solely to keep my body abreast of me in time.

Paige had flung himself upon his crude couch, his brain crawling; and there he sought sleep, but it did not come. Before his closed eyes danced interlocked halos punctuated with candle points that would not rest. As he shook his head from side to side, they pirouetted in front of him, backdropped by darkness, ever more brilliant. He was objective enough to know, and subjective enough to know in dismay, that these after-images were not retinal but mental—they were not in his eyes, they were deep within his mind. And he feared them, as he would fear any hallucination; indeed, he feared them more, because there was testimony that they were not hallucinatory but real. . . .

I saw where his intentions were going. He knew himself as an obsessive-compulsive well enough to foresee that if he were to postpone decision much longer, he would slide into mental yawing that would leave him indefinitely helpless and might easily maelstrom into psychosis. He was coming swiftly to a flight decision. Inside of minutes, Paige would swing his feet onto the floor, stand, peer one more indecisive moment around his laboratory, seize his money, and run—to hike, if need be, for days through these mountains, until he would come to some railroad station where trains called more than once a week. Arrived then later at civilization, he would write to the bishop for his things; regretfully, the bishop would send them—and that would be the end of it.

Except: twenty years of eating at his own soul for (a) fleeing rather than investigating, (b) holding it secret rather than professionally publishing. With shotgun-in-mouth eventuation. . . .

Now was when I had to nudge him onto some parallel track. (But Althea, speaking for Thoth, had commented: "His coarctation was such that we would predict failure on *any* track.")

I do not defend the choice that I made. It seemed a possible way out that at least might engage his intellect and seduce it into keeping constructively busy until he could get his emotions back into balance.

Merely I stimulated his brain to project the following notion into his hindconscious: *Possible photo-chemical connection between the halo and the dust. . . .*

Whereafter, so that I would not be meddling further, I relinquished my own brain and subsided into being once again a helplessly connate cosubjectivity of Paige whose own soul was in cognitive command.

Hypnotized by the dancing light rings, I had been unable to open my eyes. Now, struggling for reason, I grew pompously peremptory with myself, muttering aloud: "Lewis Paige, be rigorously logical: *open* your eyes, and study what they see." Thereupon, acting (I assured myself) with perfect rationality, I opened them. No dancing halos—only my night-lighted laboratory.

My attention aimlessly slithered about the laboratory for a few moments, ultimately resting on my table and centering on the microscopes. I allowed my vision to remain there, confident that inspiration would come from these instruments. My brain was working vigorously; I did not try to control it—any attempt at control would only lock logical manacles on my intuition which of course was a perfectly rational process conforming to natural laws that would be understood eventually. . . .

Inspiration *came!*

I was on my feet, seeing at last that the blasted halo was the *same thing* as the odd dust that lay on my workbench —and, by God, the *same thing* as the illusion of concavity that bouleversed the West Gleam mountainscape! It would have been only the better part of stupidity to inquire *how* I knew it: I *knew,* period!

I set to work to prove what I knew already. That procedure is usually considered unscientific; but when you *know. . . .*

In exactly fifteen minutes and thirty-nine seconds, I proved it.

Never—and by "never" I mean *never*—had I worked with such perfect efficiency, such sureness of my goal and my methods—never with so serene a purpose, never with so precise an execution. The powderings of spilled dust that glittered (and crackled a bit) on the floor under my table were utterly beside the point.

My process had been incredibly simple—yet what other process could there have been? there *was* no other process: this was *truth! Imprimis,* I had examined the dust, observing its visual properties and its slight volitional movement. *Item,* I had closed my eyes and examined the halo of Bishop O'Duffy—finding the halo, of course, right there where I had left it. *Item,* I had written down, in that cosmically inspired *new* notation which had come to me conjoined with all the rest of my inspiration in a psychic monad, the formula of the dust—which was:

$$F_{333} \cdot P_{103}\ C_{27.631} + (Ж \bowtie)_{♍} \cdot Au\,Wo♂$$

(—that is, of course, in the stable phase).

As now I assembled my spectroscope for the penultimate step, I reflected with morose joy on the lubricity of my chemical thinking. Unknown elements! unknown elements! their names had come into me like cheesecake! Impatiently I forced my attention away from the panic that was possessing me: it was only the old phony guilt that I always felt when I came upon a solution; if the guilt this time was griping and ultimate, this only underscored the griping and ultimate importance of this divine discovery. . . .

I had set up the spectroscope, switched on the beam, and was raptly examining the resulting spectrum. I was $(Ж \bowtie\quad)_{♍}{}^{\circ}$ quite clearly! I snapped off the beam with a wall-vibrating curse of joy, I had it!

One step remained:

Comparison. . . .

The door to the bishop's bedroom swung silently open: I heard the absence of creaking. I was tense; but I had myself, as usual in moments of tension, *completely* under control. My project was dangerous, and fools like Shorty might call it emotional and idiotic—but, by God, it was scientific!

But if the door should creak when I would close it. . . .

But it didn't.

Inside!

The bishop hadn't lied: his bedroom-darkroom was windowless, perfectly dark. The strange element in the dust, I reflected fleetingly, would have shone more brilliant here—but never mind: if my plans would work, I was about to see this element again. *I KNEW this!*

Standing in the darkness, eyes closed to adapt my retinas more fully, I had not yet been able to force myself to look in the direction of the amorphous glow that had attracted my visual penumbra as I had slipped in. Now I gathered guts, opened eyes, and looked.

My heart flickered. Then it steadied. Paige, *face* it. . . .

The sharp circlet of light, brighter than ever in this blackness (but unnaturally localized, not casting any light outside its own delimited orbit) sat erect, vertical, two feet above the floor. No doubt now: it was real, *out there, frighteningly* out-there, weird, holy. . . .

Holy?

Nonsense!

From my right breast pocket I drew a pencil-beam flashlight, and with it I delicately probed the blackness, craftily directing the light point a few feet below the circular gleam that seemed to grow in brilliance, defying the laws of neural adaptation, as I stared at it. Yes, it was the bishop who lay beneath his halo which had thoughtfully levitated itself to allow his head sinkage into its pillow. Why hadn't the halo light revealed the bishop's face, however obscurely? why had my flashlight been necessary? Keeping the light off his face, I couldn't be sure whether his eyes were closed; yet he *couldn't* be asleep—otherwise, wouldn't he be responding?

Now almost completed calm, I shifted the light to the wall across the room from the bishop. This was a critical question; and with all the objective detachment that I could still command, I examined this wall.

It was smooth white plaster.

I grew faint with relief. The odds had been against it.

A final test! I couldn't afford a grating, but a prism I had; and now I drew it from my left pants pocket. Holding it at arm's length, accurately I directed into it a ray from my flashlight. The beam scattered itself on the wall in a pale spectrum.

Ah. . . .

Out went the flashlight; and as now I approached the circle of fire, it took on a spectral aspect in the hush of the dark. More and more the idea *holy* insisted on crowding out my other ideas. Impatiently-fearfully I crushed it down.

At last I brought myself to kneel beside the bishop, beside the halo.

I do not know how long I knelt there, gathering resolution. "This," I told myself—awed by the sound of my thought—"is possibly the nearest that your researches, Lewis Paige, will ever approach the sublime."

I took more time to recover from the fear of the sound of my thought. . . .

Ready:

Act now!

With a gasp, I thrust my prism into the circlet of fire.

Swift it uncoiled, hissing; darted snake-striking into the prism; ullulated there for a supernally terrifying instant; splashed on the wall. . . .

In the mind-agony that seared and swallowed me, I certainly heard a crashing music. And just before my brain shriveled, I saw the spectrum.

My Pan-brain yanked me back to my Pan-body out of Lewis Paige. I lay in my brain, briefly recovering. Then in my brained body I groped my way through the between-track nonbeing of Antan until I relocated the alternate track that Paige at my nudging had created for himself.

There was Paige on the floor, catatonic in the fetal position. The bishop, awakened by the rape of his halo, knelt over Paige, concerned. O'Duffy had turned on the room light, and I could not tell whether his halo was back where it belonged.

Across the eyes and upper face of Paige, his flesh was seared black in a parallelogram like one face of a prism.

I entered the Paige-brain—and came out again as swiftly as I could. Instantly I terminated the hideous alternate track that my miscalculation had launched him on; and I cried out to Thoth: *Take back their souls, comfort the bishop, and start therapy on Paige for the love of Heaven!*

For his brain was shriveled, and his soul had crouched catatonic in the fetal position. And burned into his retinae and upon his optic cortex and optic thalamus, I had seen (Ж⋈) ᵐþ · quite clearly.

Not the notation. The referent.

PART EIGHT

Adult, Western

On the planet Prosit, in a raunchy frontier town on a newly opened cattle continent, an unimaginative but well-meaning bar-girl named Hertha became masochistically addicted to the experiences of her business, submitted to a particularly cruel and degrading assignation, and thereafter died partly because of physical trauma but mainly because she had lost will to live. The cringing soul that we have is the self-scarified soul of a good kid. This one, Pan, you will have to handle physically in part, for it is the only language she knew; but—see what else you can contribute toward self-redirection for Hertha.

8

The honkytonk was noisy, tin-music jangly, yellow-smoke murky. In my own body, I pushed through the swinging louvre-doors, advanced a few feet inside, and stood appraising the dive, getting my eyes used to tobacco-smoke smart and my ears used to violent assault. My hands rested easily on the grips of my big blasters that hung holstered low toward the front of my gun belt. I was dressed, like many of the other men though a trifle cleaner, in a loose open-collared brown shirt and tight-fitting brown pants and boots.

The environment was a saloon straight out of the adult westerns that had dominated Erth's twentieth-century television: I had checked them out in Antan. However, this saloon was neither anachronistic nor otherwise phony but a logical contemporary development in the frontier life of a newly opened cattle continent on Sigma Persei IV, a planet that called itself Prosit. This social stage was indigenous, not imported: the people of Prosit had independently evolved to resemble Erth's *Homo sapiens* in most features—a not-uncommon course in any galaxy.

Telling myself therefore to behave like a hero in an adult western, gradually but insistently I shoved in to the bar between two big cowhands and held up three fingers to the barkeep. Nodding, the heavy-mustached portly-greasy sleeve-gartered man poured something dark out of a bottle into a glass which he set before me, picked up my money, and turned his back. I slugged off half the drink, restrained tears, and turned to consider the people.

The barkeep had noticed me and served me: already an alternate track was in progress, although it was still light on the original. . . .

The scene was the usual: carding, dicing, dancing, wenching. The women were in character, all shapes and sizes, wearing wasp-waisted ornate dresses cut high enough to show knees and low enough to flaunt cleavages.

My eyes alit on a woman who sat alone, elbow on table, chin in palm, other hand toying with a half-full glass, staring moodily my way without seeing me or anybody. She was blonde and a bit haggard and inclined to be plump: the tops of her breasts bulged the merest trifle above her dress top. The medium-full lips of her small mouth were pursed into a cupid bow, and her pale-blue eyes were glazed a little. I reached out delicately to taste her soul: yes, she was my assignment.

(May I do better than I did with Lewis Paige!)

Picking up my half-full glass, I started toward her—and saw that I had been anticipated by a dirty black-whiskered giant who bent over her with a classic leer, one big boot on the chair adjacent. Looking up at the giant, she had gone a shade paler, and both her hands were gripping the table edge. I moved in.

"—had all the others," the giant was saying in a hoarse voice that tried bullishly to be unctuous, "so you and I might as well have a go before I start the next round."

She wet her lips and shook her head slightly.

Entirely enclosing her bare upper arm with a hairy hand, he pulled her erect, clasped her to him, buried his mouth in her neck.

Her response was oddly ambivalent. Her head was turned away from him, her mouth working, her eyes desperate; but her body was not resisting, and her small hands were massaging his big shoulders.

I saw how it was with her, and I comprehended my first move but nothing thereafter. Coming up behind the giant, I poked his shoulder with a hard forefinger and demanded sharply: "May I cut?"

He froze, clutching the woman—who couldn't see me behind his broad shoulders. Then he dropped the woman and whirled with an angry roar. Stepping back a pace to avoid a killing bear hug, I stood with my hands in the classic quick-draw hang.

The situation was precarious, more so than the others in the suddenly quiet saloon realized. By my rules I could not kill or even wound—but my body could be wounded; and if I should be in the body at the time, I could suffer as horribly and long as the next man.

The woman cringed back against the table, half sitting on it, back-gripping it.

The giant said slowly: "Ain't shot anybody all day. You any good, Pardner?"

"Pretty good, Pardner," I told him, "and I've never had a bigger target."

"My size ain't got in my way so far. You could stand over there by the bar, and I'll back up a little." He glanced at the woman: "This won't take long, Honey." Her eyes were wide, she said nothing.

"How do you want it?" I asked, backing slowly. "Sting, stun, or kill?"

For answer, he drew blasters, showed me the setting permanently locked on kill, and holstered them.

"Then," I said, "I suggest we drop gun belts and rassle."

He didn't grin. He inquired: "Chicken?"

"Let's test it," I responded. Languidly drawing my left blaster, I held it at arm's length. "See if you can shoot that out of my hand before I shoot yours out of your hand. If you can, we'll blast; if you can't, we'll rassle."

The giant wiped his mouth with a hand-back. "No good. One of us can cheat. Come on, Pardner—draw or go away."

I sighed and dropped my belt to the floor.

Shrugging, the giant turned back to the cowering woman. Low comedy, then: I booted the mighty derriere. He whirled with another bellow and gathered me into his lethal embrace just as my fist sank deep into his solar plexus. Grunting, he jackknifed.

I seized the woman's hand and started for the stairway, scooping up my gun belt en route. She followed willingly as I drew her up the rickety stairs, hurried down a corridor, ducked into a vacant room, swung her onto the bed, bolted the door, and turned to consider her.

She was in disarray, breathing swiftly through her mouth, one breast almost out of her dress. She sat taut on the bed edge, clutching the bed, looking up at me.

I laid my gun belt on a seedy dresser, then leaned back against it with folded arms, examining her thoughtfully. She wasn't any of the sorts of women who readily arouse me, but neither was she repulsive; and her clearly evident masochistic nymphomania wasn't uninteresting to my normally channeled aggression, especially since in this situation there was virtue in dealing with her in the long-range best way (whatever that might be), letting any hedonistic by-product fall where it might. But then I remembered a colleague in a garden, a colleague named Vogeler, and I comprehended that this was the counterproductive attitude for going into it. Pondering, I continued to regard her. Althea had suggested that with this woman, the obvious thing to do might prove instrumentally the most productive if it should be accomplished with love for a change; but I wasn't quite ready to settle for this. . . .

She said: "He'll be up here. He'll break down the door." Her low voice was liquor-damaged.

"Let's gamble," I advised, "that he'll be diverted by another woman. Listen."

Noises floated up from below: giant profanity, a heavy foot on the stairs, a woman's low persuasive talking, a colossal sigh—and a general sound-relapse into happy crowd-babel.

I said: "Jackpot. Well, now: are you glad or sorry I did that?"

"He's too big. He's mean and dirty. But—"

"You aren't in this game just for money."

She kept looking at me, and a small tongue tip licked her small lips. "Not *just* for money—but you better be sure to pay me."

"You have to have men. But you don't want to *have* to have men. So you don't compete very well, down there, because you're ashamed of going after what you have to have. That's why you were alone."

Her breathing was slower but deeper. She was deliberately and hungrily looking me over.

I added: "You didn't want the big guy, but you did want him, but you hated wanting him. You were hideously afraid of him, but you loved the fear and hated loving the fear. And it's more or less like that for you with most men. With me, for instance."

"It's a living—"

"He hasn't come up yet, you notice. Let's assume he won't."

Her eyes closed, her head went down. "He won't come now. I was just the last one for luck, before the next round of good ones."

I nodded slowly, my eyes on hers.

Her breath was quickening. "Are you gonna just stand there?"

"If you like, I'll go away."

"He got me all steamed up! You *can't* go away!" Seizing the top of her fancy-girl gown, she jerked it down, baring her breasts—plump, firm, but showing marks of abuse. Leaning toward me, she tongue-touched her lips and husked: "I don't want you to pay me anything. Just this once, I want to *give* somebody something."

Sitting beside her, I hand-cupped the bareness of her near shoulder. "Considering your hunger, would it be entirely giving?"

After a moment she pressed her face against my chest,

groaning: "But there's no *end* to it! It's like a thirst that is all the worse when your belly is bulging with water—no, it's like a liquor yen that is still gnawing at you when you're so loaded you're passing out, and you wake up hungover stinking sick but wanting it all the worse. . . . No, that isn't that either, it's not like that or anything else in the world, it's just—what it is you can't compare it to *anything*—"

She threw herself back on the bed, staring at me. "If you ain't gonna act, for God's sakes *talk! Why* is it like that? Why is it so endless, even for ordinary people who aren't hung on it like me? Why do these guys come in here and risk getting clap and fight each other for it? *What is so goddamned wonderful about it?*"

So now I knew my way. It would be physical up to a point, but not in terms of the physical point that she was used to. Regretfully I commanded stiffening inclination to decline, and I turned my attention to this particular sort of physical approach that would end by leaping off into supraphysical psyche. . . .

Mind-reaching into the deep pyriform cortex of her brain, I found myself dizzying in the maelstrom of the expected reverberating circuit. As an emergency measure, I introduced a local potential that channeled off the current in a wider circuit which wound around and came back in on the center of the trouble, creating a mild inhibitor where no inhibitor had functioned for a long time. It was purely first aid and would not last, but the temporary effect was benign: I had not unsexed her but only down-sexed her into low key, so that she now responded to me psychically but not erotically as woman to man.

Retreating from her brain, I checked the visible results. It had calmed her, so that her face sagged a little: she looked older but less disturbed. She blinked up at me, confused, feeling that I must have done something but uncertain what question to ask about it.

Bunching up pillows against the iron bed head, I sat back with her, my arm around her shoulders. She reclined, staring, torpidly appreciating my warm hand on her bare arm, my comforting nearness. Presently she glanced down at her breasts, then looked up at me, puzzled. "Either way," I told her. She looked away again, not bothering to cover herself.

I waited.

She inquired: "You some kind of freak?"

"Depends on how you look at it. Not sexually, if that's what you mean."

"Okay, so you just don't want me. So why am I here?"

"Do *you* want *me?*"

"I always—" She paused, studied herself inwardly, turned up to me again that baffled look. "No, damn it, I did but all of a sudden I don't! Why don't I?"

"Do you positively *not* want me?"

She shook her head in a slow negative, eyes on my face, mouth open a little. "If you screwed me, I guess I'd like it—but for once I ain't dying. What's with me, Mister? You did something to me. What did you do?"

"What's your name?"

"Hertha. What's yours?"

"Pan."

"I like that name. It sounds kinda wild."

"I like Hertha. It's a pretty name. Strong, too."

"Hertha? Strong? *Me?*"

"Strong, Hertha. Do you like the way you feel now?"

"It's restful, I'll say that. It's kinda nice. Professionally, though, I dunno. Will it last?"

"Kiss me."

She held up her mouth open a little. With my fingers, gently I half-closed her lips : kissed her lips softly, then lifted her hand and laid my lips on her fingers. Afterward I watched her eyes.

She gazed at me. Taking my hand, she pressed its palm against a breast. "This ain't for hot stuff unless you want it," quickly she explained. "It just feels right, with you. This is me, and I want you to hold me. I ain't falling in love, am I?"

"Probably not. Did you ever?" Cherishing her breast, I touched my lips to her temple.

Her eyes closed. "Once."

"What happened?"

Her hand clamped viciously on my hand on her breast. "He didn't notice. He took me for just a B-girl and used me and went away."

"*Were* you already a B-girl?"

"Yes—"

"But not long, yet."

Her eyes closed tight. "He was my first one."

There would have been timid-sacred virginity before, outraged by an economic-rational decision to join this coterie, sanctified by love for her first, blasted by the cheapening outcome, plus years, plus the way the brain has of twisting disappointments into reverberating circuits that swing around and around and out until they involve all the forebrain including the pyriform cortex.

As far as I was concerned, a conscientious harlot who took care of herself and liked her work was merely an unimaginative species of professional athlete; but a compulsive loser in any sport ought either to start winning or get out of it.

"What is so goddamned wonderful about it?" Back there before I had gentled her, Hertha had asked the most ultimate philosophical question that is ever asked about sex. Even Plato had tackled it, suggesting that man-woman was born bisexually twain only to be disastrously sundered, that each half had been seeking reunion with the other half ever since. For Hertha, repetitious sex trauma had driven the urge into compulsive desperation, but the extreme case only dramatized the general principle: compulsive sexuality with its genteel rules for control and aesthetized or sanctified indulgence had stylized the vertebrate life of every planet that boasted vertebrates. For the extreme Hertha-case, unless she felt sexual action as violation it was nothing, but when she did feel it as violation it had no explicable significance, and her confusion fired her passion—which is perhaps all right if you like it that way, but Hertha did and did not.

Way down deep, did not. Wanted it some *other* way. . . .

Hertha too had meandered back to that thought, proving its significance. I picked up the thread of her mumbling: "—maybe you're right if you want to say that it's because we came from monkeys, because *they* sure are. . . . But wait: how come *they're* like that? it only pushes my question back a few jumps."

I rejected a temptation to tell her that all the monkeys she'd seen were in zoos, and zoos do for monkeys what this honkeytonk had done for her. Because even for normal jungle-type monkey morals, she was perfectly right: it only pushed it back a few jumps. For cultural sophistication, the B-girls of Prosit were considerably ahead of the ones on Erth's frontier! And as for Plato. . . .

But could he have been intuitively right—rather as Aristotle's entelechies were intuitive anticipations of genetic programming?

Wait, now: the gambit was coming. . . .

I shook my head slowly. "What I'm going to say goes back a lot farther than monkeys. Back a couple of billion years, in fact. Do you know how primitive one-celled animals reproduce?"

"Natch. They just split in two, like our body cells."

It raised my eyebrows a little: I would have to visit this Prosit again—what did big-city girls talk about? I pressed on: "But some of the one-celled animals do something else first."

"Do what else first?"

"They conjugate."

"Which is?"

"They pair; and the two members of the pair don't just copulate—they *fuse*."

"They—fuse?"

"They open up wide to each other and exchange *all* their body substance. And then they separate and begin to reproduce by cell fission—but as they begin to divide, they are identical to each other, they are two of the same because of their total interchange."

She was frowning. "You're saying something to me. What?"

"I think maybe, long ago, there was a one-celled ancestor of us primates that used to conjugate like that. And then, as evolution multiplied the cells that constitute a single animal, conjugation was no longer feasible, so the specialized fusion of reproductive gametes developed, involving the specialization of sexual body parts, the one to receive, the other to insert. . . . Am I losing you, Hertha?"

"Just hold a minute, you turned about two corners ahead of me—"

"I'm waiting."

"All right now. Go on."

"But, Hertha, the old conjugation is renewed for each of us in egg fertilization: the sperm plunges into the egg and they interchange *all* their substance, and each of us is born of such a union. I believe that the urge to couple is qualitatively the same as the primeval urge to interchange oneself totally with another. What was lost in totality is regained in intensity. And it was all the same—until the primates, and especially the humans, became so intelligent that intuitively they were subaware of a missing primeval *something*. So now, in all the human search for love, there lurks the genetic urge to fuse totally with one's lover. When a man sinks into his woman, when she gratefully feels him sinking into her—as they clasp each other, with the partial interpenetration standing for the total fusion, with the surging climax guaranteeing it, with the little death which follows consummating it—just for that while they imagine that they have fused, that their individualities are no more. But then they awaken and gaze at each other—and lo, they are unchanged, each is still himself alone, *another*. And sensing some kind of implacable frustration, some unexpressed denial of a forgotten birthright which was after all a long-lost legacy, they gaze at each other in unconfessed disappointment, sometimes even with hatred. But then they try again—"

Reaching up to clutch my wrist, she pulled my hand down against her bare thigh, and she whispered: "I won't hate. I am ready when you are ready for a bout of cosmic frustration."

It came into me that Althea was right: with Hertha, it would have to be physical *too*. And I was ready, believe me: releasing myself had become a categorical imperative. Yet it was secondary and even irrelevant that the indulgence would Vogeler-please me: I could not evade without seeming to reject her; besides, without amour-consummation, for her half the symbolism and therefore all the meaning would be lost.

Pressing my forehead hard against hers, I went deeply into myself, seeking beyond myself the composure that I needed, arriving at last at letting sense-desire spread and blend and generalize into the unique blessedness that my soul, my *self*, had to *be* in order to bring this off for good and not for evil. Far past Althea and far past Thoth I went, until mystically I knew that I was as intimate with ultimate meaning-germinality as I was ever going to be in my realistically delimited brain. And my mind whispered: *Open are my eyes to the kinks in my own soul; but I* have *attained* some *degree of peace with myself, and soul is fluid, and kinks can be momen-*

tarily quarantined. So let the major volume of my soul be pure goodness and truth and beauty and laughter and caring, just for the while that this other soul is in my arms. . . .

When it felt perfectly right, I laid my mouth on her open mouth, and my mind said to her mind directly: *Give me slow delight, and give yourself slow delight; and when you have attained transfiguration; close your eyes and receive my soul wholly into your soul; for we* are *our souls, and the interweaving of our souls is total interchange of our substance.*

And then I made love to her with gentleness and with concern for her. At first it confused her, she was lost with it; but when she began to comprehend that for once in her life she was more than a *thing* for me, she uttered an ineffable sigh and embraced me and languorously, delectably, creatively entered into body-meaning. Her eyes closed long before climax. When it came—not explosively, but exquisitely—I gathered her soul into the humanely purified sector of mine, washing hers with mine, cherishing hers in mine, taking hers, giving mine, returning her tonally qualified, reclaiming mine tonally qualified. . . .

Long afterward, still vaguely in the dream, she rearranged herself.

We sat side by side, holding hands.

She studied how to say it. "I do not think I love you. I think I *am* you."

I thought she needed ressurance. "The confusion won't last long, Hertha; you'll quickly be entirely you, with your own memories and projects. But you won't ever be wholly without me, even if you forget me."

She looked up at me soberly, squeezing my hand: "Not confusion, Pan—*fusion.* Why can't *all* men and women know this fusion?"

There was a woman I remembered—fifty years of her. I told Hertha: "Any couple can, gradually, if both of them will. Some of them do arrive at it, although it takes many years of little interchanges to culminate in this all-but-total interknowing. The route is called marriage, with or without a ceremony; but not everyone who sets foot on the route will reach the destination, because it takes a while of good mind-interchange even to comprehend the destination."

She looked down, frowning. "I will never marry, with or without a ceremony."

"You could marry now, if you wanted, because you have a taste of what it can eventually mean. Before, you would have ruined any marriage you might have tried."

She looked up, her small mouth serene. "I will never have the itch again."

"You will have it, but it will never have you again."

Her chin came still higher, she was almost smiling. "Perhaps I should marry the giant."

"It might be hard to get him to hold still while you bring him around to seeing what the marriage is for."

"For kids?"

"For meaning."

"I want to give without receiving."

"That is quite impossible. But if you pay attention mainly to the giving, and if you always feel grateful for receiving, what you receive will strengthen your power to give."

"I will keep on working here. But I will specialize in the scared bashful weak ones and the poor guys who make themselves have hot rocks to prove something, and maybe I can give them some courage or some satisfying proof. But is it really giving if I take their money? But then, a girl has to live. If I were a nurse, they'd pay me, wouldn't they, to live so I could nurse? I was going to be a nurse, I took most of the training, that's why I could sort of understand what you said about conjugation and so on, but then a thing happened, and I. . . . I guess I didn't tell you, I shouldn't marry anyway, because I can't have children. Oh, I know *now* that marriage is for more, but most men don't understand this, and it would be cheating if I couldn't give a man children. So I guess I'll just stay here and do what I can for the weakies and the phony hornies. . . . Pan, thank you so much—

"Pan?"

When she had thoroughly satisfied herself that I had somehow slipped away, she lay back on the bed with her arms randomly at peace above her head on the pillow; and she seemed to be studying the ceiling, but in fact she was inwardly savoring a mood and a continuing presence.

Just once in a long while, as a vacation from the ones who needed one or another sort of nursing—maybe the giant?

* * *

For me there were no physical consequences from Hertha, but my psychical aftermath was grim. I lingered for weeks in Hell—often with Althea, whose therapy was priceless—deliberately subjecting my soul, my *self*, to the purest ultrafire, until I was sure that I had cleared me of the torment that I had washed out of Hertha. Thereafter for a while I recuperated dimly in Elysium.

Toward the end of my convalescence, visiting Althea threw me a momentary shocker: "Today in Hell I saw your Hertha."

Then I had blundered again with Hertha—and she was back to endure, finally, the searing therapy that I had just endured, that Lewis Paige was enduring—without my defenses of understanding and intentionality, without even Paige's thinner defense that he didn't really believe he was there, but naked in her defenselessly naive soul that was now more pain-prone than ever by reason of Pan's disastrous meddling. . . .

Reading me, Althea countered: "It isn't quite like that. We tracked her new track for three weeks after you left: it was developing just fine, her new outlook was already well established through the instrumentalities of illuminated client after illuminated client. So we terminated the track before some ridiculous accident could happen. She came into Hell today transiently with a tourism party out of Paradise, and she sent you a personal message—"

My grin irradiated my all-at-once wholly recovered soul. "Let me guess. 'Having a fine time, Pan—wish you were here.' "

PART NINE

Von Eltz in Vimy

Yorick. I do confess me puzzled by this incident, which comes out most clearly in John 13: 21, 25, 26, 27, and 30, and I quote: "When Jesus had thus said, he was troubled in spirit, and testified, and said: 'Verily, verily, I say to you, that one of you shall betray me.' He then lying on Jesus' breast said to him: 'Lord, who is it?' Jesus answered, 'He is it, to whom I shall give a sop, when I have dipped it.' And when he had dipped the sop, he gave it to Judas Iscariot, the son of Simon. And after the sop Satan entered into him. Then said Jesus to him: 'That which you do, do quickly.' He then having received the sop went immediately out: and it was night." End of quote.

Rosecranz. What is puzzling?

Yorick. Bypassing the stupidity of the witnesses who didn't get it, I am puzzled about Jesus and Judas. If Judas knew that Jesus knew, how could Judas go through with it? And if Jesus could foresee his own betrayal, why would Jesus need Judas to get it done? And finally, if Jesus did need Judas to get it done, why is Judas damned?

Rosecranz. Has it occurred to you that the sop-passing may in fact have been, not a prediction, but rather an instruction? In justice, of course, I should remark that Matthew and Mark told the story differently, while Luke bypassed it entirely, and your John was a creative Platonist who wrote three generations later.

Yorick. But why with a kiss did he betray him?

—NIKE PAN, *Dialogs by a Devout Sceptic* (2310)

9

Gauleiter Von Eltz, grumpily mused ill-favored arch-collaborator Dubois, was possibly the only man in the world of 1943 on Erth who could preserve his aristocratic poise asleep in an armchair. Dark Dubois, thoughtfully stroking his own big wine-ruined nose with a pudgy hand whose arm hid his dirty white bow-tie, contemplated his alien leader. The long body of fortyish Von Eltz, whose uniform was unusually open at the collar, was actually graceful in the chair: somewhat relaxed but not slumped, blond hair brushed smoothly back with a neat off-center part, right-hand knuckles gently pressing into a lean cheek beside the long straight nose, long upper lip and wide brooding thin-lipped mouth undistorted above the long firm chin, one long leg slightly extended and the other pulled back for support. The breathing of this gauleiter was quietly rhythmic. Personification of Master Race in Repose, Dubois reflected, reassuring himself once again that he had indeed cast his wartime lot with the winning side no matter what the Anglians and Vespucians might try to do in faraway Obscuria.

Eh, but Gauleiter Von Eltz was frowning: the hard horizontal ridges emphasized the height of his forehead, the hard-together brows accentuated his hauteur. Not entirely at inward peace, eh? dreams not quite serene? In that case, Dubois—maliciously amused at this hairline crack in the master-ice—need not fear to awaken the gauleiter and summon him forth to face the angry Gallian crowd outside. Von Eltz, perhaps, would not be sorry to quit this dreaming.

Dubois approached to touch him awake.

The frown deepened; a foot shifted. Dubois hesitated. Perhaps Von Eltz should be left to suffer out this dream, whatever it might be: it would only take a few minutes. . . .

I was already in Von Eltz, he being my current assignment for reasons unknown to me; and while I was half involved in his dreaming, I had stayed half objective to appraise his minion Dubois. But the dreaming seemed to be approaching some sort of crisis; and as I had done with Lewis Paige, a less-cultured obsessive-compulsive, so now with Von Eltz, I allowed myself to be entirely seduced by his subjectivity as though I *were* he, confident of an awakening alarm by some approaching ifnode. . . .

In my dreaming, I was host to twelve men at a long table: I sat centered on a long side, and I seemed to be celebrating the Sinite Passover. Reason enough for a Brunildic Junker to frown in his sleep! but in my dream, the quality was different. In the dream I *was* a Sinite, I felt immortally so: I was brooding inwardly, here among my dear grown-man pupils, because I was about to engineer a personal tragedy that would brutally exchange my immortality for a risky chance at eternity. . . .

"One of you," casually I asserted, "will betray me."

After the expected moment of silent shock, they all leaned toward me with gray faces. Two or three cried: "It isn't I?"

I inspected them. Already I had decided who it should be, but now at the last I hesitated—it was not easy to announce, for of course I knew how it would be for him. Should it be another instead? Not Peter—this vigorous man was needed for the future. Not John—he'd get mad and rebel. And so on. . . .

Again it narrowed to the first choice: Judas the zealot.

I began to pronounce the name of Judas. My eyes met the deep suffering Judas-eyes. Loving pity suffused me. My eyes dropped.

I said softly, evading the bitter naming of his name: "It will be the one to whom I pass the sop."

I dipped. I held the dripping sop an instant over my flagon—the body and the blood, good bread and the good good wine.

Silently I passed the sop to Judas.

He did not take it.

All the twelve were rigid.

I demanded: "Do you love me?"

Judas nodded.

I commanded: "Take it!"

After a moment, he took it—not with his fingers, but with his lips from my fingers.

A kind of group groan came out of them. Some of it was relief on the part of the eleven who were not offered the sop.

Said Judas thoughtfully, with controlled detachment: "It *must* be I?" He was fighting for this control. It was not like Judas to control himself, or even to try.

I said in the same tone: "Who else *could* it be?"

He studied the ceiling. I thought his stare might be piercing the ceiling—looking for God, maybe.

I told him, trying to be stern: "Be off about your business."

He arose and went to go.

He paused.

He came up behind me and buried his face in my shoulder.

I reminded him harshly: "Don't forget to demand the price! The Son of Man has got to go as it is written of him!"

His choked voice was hard to understand: "All who love you will curse me. Forever."

My eyes were squeezed shut. "Woe to that man," I echoed wearily, "by whom the Son of Man is betrayed. It would have been good for that man if he had not been born—" Then, touching his hairy cheek, I whispered: "But *I* bless you, Judas—blessed, *blessed* Judas—" I gulped and blurted: "What you have to do, do quickly!"

He sobbed.

He went.

And the dream shifted, as dreams do; and it was the morrow, and I was leaving a garden with the eleven behind me. And he came. Came marching sternly at the head of soldiers. Caused them to pause, as I caused the eleven to pause. Hesitated, glowering at me.

Seeing that he needed encouragement, I called: "Friend, why have you come?"

He let out a groaning roar, rushed headlong upon me, clasped my shoulders, burned my cheek with a passionate kiss.

Released me.

Astonished, I gazed at the beloved self-sacrificing wretch who now stood trembling and downcast.

A soldier's hand gripped and shook my shoulder; a Roman snarled in my own tongue, "You are Jesus of Nazareth?" Almost I laughed at his bad accent. . . .

But abruptly I comprehended Judas!

Knew what sign he had arranged with the soldiers. Knew *why THAT sign!*

"Judas," I murmured, trying in my poor inadequate human-animal voice to convey all the love of a master and a friend for the friend who has been willing to give, not merely his life, but his soul. . . . "Judas—it is with a *kiss* that you betray me?"

Then there was confusion, and a sword flashed. . . .

But the point of the sword was only the prodding digit of Dubois. I held my Von Eltz hauteur as I came awake. "There is, of course," I suggested dryly, clearing the dream, "a reason for disturbing me?"

Gruffly said Dubois: "You are wanted on the terrace. The man Leroy Guyon is here."

I meditated a moment; then I nodded, and arose, and went to a lavatory to make myself presentable. Emerging, I considered Dubois, who stood stolid awaiting me. Within myself I was quelling profound disturbance. *It was another recurrence-dream,* I was telling myself. *Always it is a dream of recurrence. Dreaming is hardly any longer a continuity in my present. At least, awake, there is no recurrence—or I am not conscious of it. . . .*

Dubois waited.

Although, I reminded myself with a frosty quarter-smile, *this time, at least, there was a touch of creativity. Judas was obeying a command; he was a hero.*

Shrugging, I looked at Dubois, raised an interrogatory eyebrow, and pointed to a door. Nodding, Dubois went and opened it, standing back.

I, Gauleiter Von Eltz, emerged onto my terrace, grandly overlooking the crowd-people garden that sloped downward to the bank of the River Maon.

My soldiers were handling Leroy Guyon even more roughly than the priests had done: they crushed the cuffs into his wrists, which they twisted behind him at an odd angle—and it was scientifically done, so that when they barely touched his wrists the pain shot up his arms and down into his chest. Then they thrust Guyon out of the truck and through the crowd, using him as a buffer to knock people aside. Everybody was quiet at first, and then the crowd started to jeer.

Watching from above, I reidentified Guyon as one of a large number of neo-Messianists who had sprung up here in the valley of Gallia's River Maon, responding to the captivity of their nation Gallia at the hands of us brutal Brunildic Nazis. Guyon, however, had a different quality from most of them. I watched this messianist with fascination.

Guyon, a wiry thirtyish brunet whose face was darkened by twenty-four hours of beard stubble, looked around as well as he could. Probably he did not recognize any of the jeering faces with their childish open mouths; if he didn't, presumably he was glad. They had praised him last week. I quite hoped that they were not of his own circle, any of them.

We were on a shore of the Maon River, well outside the cathedral town of Vimy-sur-Maon. There was a moderate-sized chateau that I had confiscated as a summer house: today I held court here on a broad terrace overlooking the river. They pushed Guyon stumbling up the steps; he was weak from prolonged priestly inquisition. They stood him against a railing several steps below me.

His weakness made Guyon's head spin as he gazed down the slope at the crowd. He couldn't descry the scene very clearly. . . .

Above him on the terrace they were talking about him. Then a policeman came down and seized the prisoner's arm and pulled him up on my level: I was seated in a large chair rather like a throne. There was a guard behind me, and to my right a toadish Gallian in mufti: Dubois, who had become notorious even in this goat's nest of collaboration. At Guyon's right before me stood a legation of priests headed by the Bishop of Maon.

I rested chin on palm while the tall prim-lipped bishop, in his black robes and his silly broad-brimmed black hat, lied about Guyon in a clipped, self-contained accent.

I broke in: "Why is Leroy Guyon so special?" I made sarcastic use of Guyon's full name which implied a royal title (*le roi* Guyon); and since my Gaulois was good, I gave the question added flavor by pronouncing *roy* in a sort of rustic, antique way. The priests, catching it, responded with unpleasant smiles.

"Because," explained the bishop, "his heresy is unusually venomous. By calling himself Redeemer, he suggests that he is a reincarnation of the One and Only Redeemer who died for us all two thousand years ago. He is clever at misquoting scriptures to bring himself into line with the doctrine of the Second Coming."

I smiled, being a fashionable semibeliever in Wotan and the gods of Asgard; not until later would I grow uncomfortable. "How then," I inquired softly, "do you know that he is *not* the Redeemer? It is certainly high time for a Second Coming!"

They had erred in bringing a hot-headed priestly youngster. Before his elders could stop him, he blurted: "In the Second Coming, the Redeemer will rule temporally; but this Guyon says his kingdom is not of this world—" The bishop, disconcerted, tried to cover the tactical slip; but I hit upon it as my escape from a nuisance.

"If Guyon is not interested in worldly politics," I pointed out, "he is no threat to the Reich. Settle the matter yourselves; I wash my hands of it."

When he heard that, Guyon felt a tightening in his stomach, as later I verified by subjectively haunting his track. The parallel was growing close; his beliefs about himself were almost confirmed, they were so near to complete confirmation that he would be crazy not to accept it as done. Yet, even now, Guyon felt that queer fear that a man gets when he finds himself on the verge of realizing an improbable triumph. Again his faith nearly wilted because its truth shone so bright.

He knew that it was easy for a man like himself, believing

in natural order, to suspect himself of insanity when he found himself attaching reality to connections that men counted as fantasy. On the other hand, there was more to the natural order than science had been able to pin down. And he had tested so carefully, so well—he had insisted on something that is not quite scientific proof but which nevertheless crowds doubt against absurdity: a totally improbable summation of rare coincidence. In his mind the facts were clear, the time full; and so he had acted.

Now on the judgment-porch of Von Eltz, hearing the words "I wash my hands of it," Guyon had a final passing doubt.

What saved Guyon was Von Eltz himself. Studying the gauleiter's face, Guyon realized that Von Eltz was a sort of time-mirror: Guyon himself after ten years, if Guyon should retreat now. Guyon looked behind himself; and on the banks of the Maon below, he saw hundreds of his heedless grown-up children. He looked again at Von Eltz, who was studying white Von Eltz hands: it seemed to Guyon that Von Eltz was the sort of man who would always be washing his hands in actuality.

Then Guyon knew that, in the course of completing this design—as Jesus himself had completed a design by Isaiah—Guyon had to beat Von Eltz; or rather, to force Von Eltz into open conflict and let Von Eltz beat himself. Guyon's triumph would be the self-defeat of Von Eltz by Von Eltz—in ironical reenactment of the other scene two thousand years before, with nearly the same forces operating in closely similar people, like the actualization of an old memory, but infused with subtle novelty.

In the same breath it ceased to be Guyon's story primarily and became the story of Von Eltz. The gauleiter's tragedy, which was uncertain and in any event would be for him sterile, held more importance for him than for Guyon, being merely instrumental to the high tragicomedy of Guyon, whose ending was certain.

One way or another Guyon had already won. But in Guyon, triumph here was tempered by sympathy. . . .

In Von Eltz, I stirred myself into semialertness. In this one assignment, I had already run the complete Guyon-Von Eltz track: I knew what would happen, and Guyon was right about it. But *they* had assigned me Von Eltz; and presumably I was supposed to nudge him onto some alternate track. And I was not at all sure that such an alternate track should be such as to change the destiny of Leroy Guyon. . . .

But action was proceeding; and I dissolved myself into Von Eltz again.

The bishop was saying: "We have done everything in the power of the Church to muzzle this fanatic. We excommunicated him long ago. But he continues to be an unsettling menace. He is not merely a heretic, he is also politically subversive, and so he is dangerous to the gauleiter. If *you* take the obvious course, you rid yourself of a criminal who claims equality with the Fuhrer and who preaches passive resistance to the jurisdiction of Brunilda. You rid yourself of a serious political embarrassment. And the Church will not be ungrateful, for these heresies kill souls."

I repressed a cynical smile: the bishop, a bleak medievalist, was running his own church in his own way here in Nazi-isolated Maon. I doubted that Ramus would be grateful; but Ramus the Eternal City was not my political concern. (Just for an instant, my hintermind told me that this reflection was ironical for reasons of historical parallelism.)

I inquired: "How is he a criminal from our point of view? You'd better detail these charges."

"We have filed a brief," the bishop reminded me. I grimaced: I hadn't read it. "Guyon," specified the bishop, "insists on repudiation of the Occupation currency, and he encourages the people to disobey the government. He wants to set up a church of his own, an international church that will dominate the political state. When he is challenged about his implied equality with the Fuhrer as head of such a political church, he evades the issue cleverly but always leaves an inference of affirmation. I suggest that the gauleiter examine him. If he were not a criminal, we would not have brought charges."

I was most uncomfortable: I shifted in my chair; I did not want to push the issue. But there was nothing else to do: I had orders to placate the clergy, and these charges were serious.

Turning to Guyon, I inquired: "Art thou the King of God's

Children?" Of course I was using the *tutoiement* in a scornful way, and the *double entendre* as well: "Toi, es-tu *le roi*—"

Leroy replied in a respectful form, but conversationally, not as to a high official. "Is it that the question has occurred to your *own* mind, Gauleiter? Do you say it for yourself, or did others tell it of me?"

Guyon felt as though he were remembering having said the words before; but he was sure that in fact he must be only reminiscently paraphrasing something in Scripture. . . .

Inwardly tickled at the way I had been hoist, nevertheless I managed a frown and stormy anger. "Am I a Gallian?" I exploded. "Thine own province and the priests have delivered thee to me! What hast thou done?" Deliberately I was continuing *thee* and *thou*—pronouns of love for a child or a friend, otherwise pronouns of contempt.

Two of the priests shook their heads in deprecation: my show of anger had been ill-timed, they knew Guyon would trip me again. And of course he did, keeping his eyes on my eyes.

Responded Guyon: "My kingdom is not of this world: it is on the world, but not of the world." he had ignored my second question—and, now I thought about it, my first.

I winced; for if Guyon could prove otherworldly motives, it would remove him from political jurisdiction. But his assertion also labeled him definitely as an ape of the old Redeemer whom the Fuhrer had set aside in favor of Baldur. "Prove that!" I commanded—hoping that he would.

Guyon could not prove it, but he supported it indirectly. "If my kingdom were of this world, my servants would fight to save me. They have not fought."

Privately Guyon was congratulating himself that none of the others had blown his mind like Peter. . . .

My command of the inquiry was slipping away. The crowd below—villagers, priests, and a scattering of Nazi shock troops—was growing noisy. I signaled to the police to quiet them. When that had been done, I tried to force Guyon back to the issue, for the argument had not clearly disproved my Brunildic jurisdiction over this case.

"Art thou a king, then?" I persisted.

Guyon opened his eyes wide, smiled, and exclaimed: "It is you who keep saying that I am a king! Your thinking is not as clear as you would like it to be. A king is the political chief in a monarchy. Our Gallia is no monarchy, and I make no pretense of being a political chief. I have basically no political quarrel with your Fuhrer; it is rather a religious and a moral difference. I was not born a king; I was born a peasant: my father was a peasant, my mother was a peasant. It is true *now* that my birth had a purpose, although possibly it was not true *then*; but at any rate, that purpose was *not* to rule a worldly kingdom of today. I see *your* purpose, Gauleiter: the local priests want to use you as their instrument for hanging me, because I open up their cluttered interpretation of the Scripture and threaten their vested interest in the retrograde hierarchy of Maon."

This time there was a chorus of bellowing from the audience, bellowing that was overwhelmingly hostile to Guyon. As the noise died out—punctuated by one or two yells of physical anguish—Guyon finished: "The priests will succeed in their purpose—but not, Von Eltz, not before *you suspect the truth*—and *despite* your suspicion of the truth."

As he said "truth," and said it again, I paled. For some reason he was touching an intimate chord in my soul; Guyon half understood me, for I was what Guyon might have become.

Imperatively I motioned for silence. My nobility helped me to mask my indecisiveness behind a grand manner that was convincing to most of the watchers if not to myself.

"Do you then tell me the *truth!*" I ordered with finely sarcastic emphasis; but I had dropped the "thou" and had used a man-to-man *vous.*

I Pan-awoke wide: that was the preset cue. Shortly after that *truth*-challenge, Von Eltz on the original track had publicly given up and released Guyon for hanging. But in the John-gospel, Pilate had first momentarily taken Jesus away from the outer crowd into the judgment hall. This inner interview had always seemed to me astonishingly brief, scarcely meriting the august scene change.

I had always suspected that in actuality Pilate and Jesus had found, semiprivately within that judgment hall, a great deal to say—things that simply had not been reported outside that hall, so that John had no way to get at them. Consequently, to fill the hiatus, John had taken some things that had been said *outside* the hall (*e.g.*, "What is truth?") and had editorially moved them *inside* the hall. But I was interested in the baffling question of the *real* inner conversation—which surely must have been a *consequence* of what had been said outside: particularly, "What is truth?" If Pilate had been anything at all like Von Eltz, he could *not* have left it there, he *could* not!

What they had actually said presumably had not changed the outcome for Jesus—but it may have changed the psychic outcome for Pilate. Unluckily, this I had not checked out in Antan; and just now, coming upon the Guyon-Von Eltz crisis, I had no time for a check-out.

Do it, then! I shot the notion compellingly into the front of the Von Eltz mind. It was up to him, whether he would act upon it: should he act, he would germinate an alternate track at his if-node. Leaving it where it pregnantly was, again I subsided into the subjectivity of Von Eltz.

Guyon had lost his smile; and for a moment the gauleiter faded from the foreground of his attention in a transient spell of dizziness. He drove himself to reply. . . .

"To this end was I born or reborn," Guyon informed me, "and for this cause have I come or returned into the world: that I might again bear witness as the truth. Everyone who is of the truth hears my voice."

Being Von Eltz, perhaps I was the only one who noticed the peculiar phrasing: not "bear witness *to* the truth" but "bear witness *as* the truth." For a flash-instant absurdly I thought of myself as one named Pan: it passed and did not return. In the silence—for the crowd sensed my tension—I leaned toward Guyon and asked quite seriously:

"What *is* truth?"

"God damn me!" muttered the hasty young priest, while the bishop compressed his lips to hold back a curse at the gauleiter's *mal a propos*.

Guyon was gazing at me, not so much composing his reply

as timing it. I was oppressed; I was holding my face impassive, but probably my forehead was lined: I felt I *must* hear Guyon's answer, must discuss it, and yet must not humble myself to the level of controversant with a crazy Gallian zealot.

Achieving a minor decision, I arose. "Bring him inside, Dubois," I ordered and disappeared through my door.

Dubois took Guyon by an arm and shoved him inside, closing the door against the others on the terrace.

In my salon, Guyon and I stood for a moment appraising each other, with Dubois watching sardonically.

Then Guyon collapsed. But the if-node was breached.

Guyon awoke to find himself seated at my desk; I sat on a little chair in front of the desk and the prisoner, looking up at him, with my chin propped in my hands and a grin set uncomfortably on my face. Guyon's wrists, no longer handcuffed, rested on my desk. It was at first for him an inexplicable situation. Then his eyes were attracted by gold braid on his own cuffs instead of his usual frayed denim. Examining himself, Guyon understood that the gauleiter had arrayed him in the jacket of an old Brunildic officer's uniform and had set him up there at my desk as a joke.

I confirmed it: "Now you are a fine king indeed, Guyon!" I was amused in two directions: at him, and at myself. I commenced to chuckle.

Abruptly Guyon was flooded with glee: he laughed heartily, being amused for three reasons into which crept hints of other reasons.

His counteramusement disconcerted me. I stopped laughing. Guyon went right on. I tried a noncommittal smile, but it didn't wear well.

My mind was agile, though: I arose to pour wine by way of covering my embarrassment with a mock *politesse*; and as I poured, I thought of a reference to Guyon's delusion. "The Son of Man," I suggested, "comes eating and drinking. Are you a glutton, *mon roi?*"

"I like to eat and drink," confessed Guyon—still laughing a little, mildly hysterical, hideously fatigued. "But I shouldn't wish to be drunk. Would you be courteous enough to give me bread to dip in the wine?"

At my sign, Dubois brought bread—quality bread baked of

bleached flour, the first Guyon had seen for a year. He dipped and ate, half chewing and half sucking: the wine was good, he could feel his color returning. I offered him a cigarette: he declined—"I have not learned to like them"—and I lit one and puffed with dainty nervousness. I was watching Guyon closely. He devoted himself for a while to the stimulating wine sop; once he looked at me directly, and my eyes shifted.

The crowd outside was noisy: its mass talk percolated through my closed shutters like a confused lowing of cattle. Fat Dubois peered restively at those shutters through his round horn-rimmed spectacles. I was insensitive to the noise, being occupied with finding an opening remark. Guyon finished his refreshment, leaned back, and closed his eyes, waiting. I suspected he knew that I was weighing possible sentences against their probable effects on my dignity.

When the lull became unbearable, I reverted desperately to the bad joke. "How do you like your gauleiter's uniform and high place, Majesty?"

Guyon goaded me. "You are playing your role very well."

"Role?" blurted I.

"Role, of course! You have washed your hands, you have asked me the meaning of truth, I am accused of playing *Rédempteur*—and you have rationalized a hiatus in the gospel of John by withdrawing me behind a curtain for private inquiry. And now you have arrayed me in a purple robe." He chuckled: "I can hardly wait for the crown of thorns!"

I stood indignant, facing it out. "You are impertinent! Von Eltz plays no role!"

"Escape it if you can," Guyon said gently. "I told you that you are an instrument. First you were to mock me: you are doing just that—although you are a gentleman, and so you have the good taste to do it privately, except for Dubois here. Afterward you will flog me, believing the flogging unjust. Then you will hang me, believing that I should live."

"Flogging and hanging, very possibly," I said dryly. "But if either happens, it will be justice. That is my way."

"It is also your way," he thrust, "to test every notion of truth. But you confuse proof with demonstration. You demand to put your hands into the wounds: if the *Redempteur* withdraws out of your reach, you doubt. That is fine scientific procedure. I follow it myself; but as the proofs multiply until the probability favors the truth of the wounds, it is your doubt that needs controlling and not your credulity. I shall prove my truth, but only you can furnish the demonstration: you will not recognize the demonstration, because no wounds will have been touched, and so you will hang me. Yet you will be shaken by the proof. You are Pontius Pilate, twentieth-century vintage. Admit it!"

My mouth remained open for several seconds. Then I gulped back some assurance. I groped for a formal question—how does one examine a redemptionist?

"Is it true," I demanded sternly, "that you declare yourself equal to the Fuhrer?"

"I do not have his worldly power."

"Don't evade. They say you are trying to organise a universal church which will subordinate the political state, creating a world theocracy. If you are the head of that theocracy, where does that put the Fuhrer?"

"The Fuhrer will be long dead when that church comes."

I was not amused. "Then," I persisted, trying to be patient, "suppose for the argument that your church *should* come in your time and in the Fuhrer's time. Would you be superior to the Fuhrer? Would you be his equal? Give me a direct answer."

"Von Eltz, Von Eltz, there *is* no direct answer to these too-precise and therefore artificial questions. How can I enter into your comprehension? If my church should come in our time, it would depend on the Fuhrer and it would depend on me whether we would be equals, who would be superior and who subordinate. Didn't the Fuhrer make himself chief in all Europa? Cannot any determined house painter make himself chief in all the world under any system, merely by changing the system as he rises? Perhaps I prepare the way for the Fuhrer, perhaps he prepares it for me. In the original future there are all possibilities; but when any part of the future is past, many states of affairs have come to pass, and many others have not come to pass and are no longer possible in any future evolving from this past. The Fuhrer's way is wrong; he may change, he may perish; but he has made me possible."

I was nettled. A more specific question might be tried. "Did you or did you not repudiate the Occupation currency?"

"No money is more than indirectly relevant to concerns of the soul."

"Oh, my God!" I fumed. Coming over to my desk, I exhumed the Guyon brief and leafed through it until I found the place. "It is charged that you publicly made the following statement, quote: 'The Fuhrer's money is false money, and you shall not use it.' Unquote. I'd call that clear enough."

Guyon meditated the charge. Then he replied: "Even in this twentieth century they are reporting me as badly as they reported Jesu. What I said was about like this: 'The Fuhrer's money is no better than any money, and in the Kingdom of Heaven you won't be using it or any other.' I don't think even the Fuhrer would find fault with that basic idea, do you? although he might substitute Valhalla for Heaven—"

Brushing that aside, I charged in: "Do you or do you not advocate civil rebellion?"

He smiled again. "The priests are confounding me with the underground leader Pere Abbé. That doesn't surprise me. No, I don't advocate rebellion. I do insist on passive resistance by every man to orders that he considers unjust. But that applies equally to orders by the Church, the civil authorities, the Fuhrer, one's own landlord: there is no difference. And while a man is passively resisting, he must listen to reason and to his inner voice—"

"What happens then to the principle of law?"

"If a man has a voice in deciding what the laws are, he should obey the law that he considers unjust until he can get it changed. But, Von Eltz—what law in the Fuhrer's expanded Reich has been passed by the people or by elected representatives of the people?"

I could see the point, all right. I could disagree with it, too. "I must classify you as an anarchist. There is no in-between. Either that, or you are a fence straddler."

"No in-between"; but "either that, or. . . ." It was really sad. Guyon brooded on the gauleiter. . . .

Guyon demanded: "Must you classify *everything?*" He appended: "Yes, I suppose you must."

"And your hedging piddling anarchial preachments—these are what you call truths?"

"Not necessarily. They may be false. But I thoroughly believe they are true."

It threw me off balance. "Yet you claim to represent the

truth! If you believe *that,* how can you permit a shadow of doubt to enter your mind that your preaching is true?" Ending the demand, internally I panicked: I had inadvertently opened up the *real* reason why I had brought Guyon in behind closed doors for private questioning.

Guyon laughed. "How absurd that I should be prosecuted on grounds that have so little to do with the core of my teaching! All these charges have to do with my publicly voiced ethics as a man and as a leader. But ethical views are judgments which not even God can make perfectly for all time. Some are better than others, and I am convinced that mine are the best so far, and I will fight for them—but bloodlessly, unless it be my own blood. Yet I admit the possibility that there may be some error in my judgments; only, nobody has yet conviced me of such error. Gauletier, it is not those propositions that are my truth: they are only what, in my life, emerges as the *expression* of my truth."

"A handsome distinction, Guyon." I was fighting for superiority, even for stability. "Beyond doubt you have coined this distinction to hide from yourself your own inconsistency. Before you try to redeem the world from error, don't you think you ought to redeem yourself from confusion?"

Guyon took a deep breath and chanced it. . . .

"Truth is necessarily confusing, Gauleiter. And I am the truth. And I am not seeking to redeem the world from Error with *E-majuscule*; instead, I am patiently chipping away at certain very old errors which just now are fundamental. When they are gone, there will be new fundamental errors. That happened two thousand years ago; it is happening now; it will happen again, in a superficial appearance of repetition, whenever the world comes to some stalemate."

"I don't follow you," I objected—and waited.

> Guyon saw that the gauleiter was abandoning his forced role of inquisitor and opening himself up for what he really wanted: *to be taught*. Guyon decided to try the parable way. Although he was convinced that the way of Von Eltz was tragedy, he had to extend himself to redeem the gauleiter. . . .

"There was a farmer who owned a cherry orchard," Guyon told me, "and his cherries were infested with worms. So he induced a number of robins to nest in his orchard and eat the worms. During several seasons his cherry crops were rich and wormless. But the robins throve and multiplied until there were not enough worms to feed them; and so they began to eat the cherries. The farmer thereupon imported starlings to drive out the robins. But the starlings, having performed their function, multiplied and began to steal grain from his granary. Now the farmer persuaded some hawks to attack the starlings; this worked well until the starlings were gone, whereupon—"

"—the hawks began killing his chickens," I interrupted. "All of which goes to show that error is eternally conserved in one form or another. Very fine; but I am a city dweller from the capital of Brunilda, and I am not impressed."

"There was a certain Good Burgomeister," then said Guyon, "who was distressed by the inhumanity prevalent in his city. Whereupon he persuaded the Town Council to pass a series of Social Uplift Laws. Hospitals were established for chronic invalids; schools were set up for special training of the feeble-minded; a dole was provided for unemployable paupers. As a result, crime diminished, the economic welfare of the city was improved, and the level of civic happiness was raised. The Good Burgomeister died content. One hundred years later, crime was worse, economic welfare lower, and discontent more prevalent than it had been before the Good Burgomeister came; and this was because the chronically unfit had been encouraged to multiply without restraint. The New Burgomeister went to the Town Council and pleaded with them to pass laws requiring sterlization of the genetically unfit: 'For,' he urged, 'we have tampered with nature by introducing an artificial imbalance, and we are now committed to restoring balance with artificial counter-measures. Our garden of democracy needs weeding.' 'No!' they cried. 'For every human soul has the unalienable right to reproduce his kind; and besides, we would be unseated at the next elections!' 'Then,' the New Burgomeister begged in desperation, 'repeal the Poor Laws, before we all go to Hell!' At that the Town Council rose up in wrath, impeached the New Burgomeister, found him guilty of irreverence for the sacred memory of the Good Burgomeister, and banished him from the county. Then years later the city fell into factious bankruptcy and was nationalized and placed under martial law."

The second tale interested me, but still I held critical. "The story confuses me," I commented, "because it appears to me that your so-called Good Burgomeister was stupid not to introduce the counterbalance of sterilization in the first place."

"You are judging after the fact," Guyon reminded me. "Would *you* have thought of that a century ago, even if sterilization had been surgically safe?"

"You are right: but on the other hand, I would not have thought of establishing special schools for the dull a century ago; and as for the chronic invalids, they ought to have been simply exterminated."

Guyon seized on a chance. "Would *you* have liquidated them? *Would* you?"

"What a question!" I ejaculated. "Of *course*—" I paused. I tried: "The Fuhrer has clearly established that—" My voice dropped as I added: "Of course, we must bear in mind that conditions change from era to era—"

He sharply halted my compulsive floundering. "We must also bear in mind that Gauleiter Von Eltz has picked on technical details in both parables to keep from having to admit the truth that is in both of them." My jaw dropped; and he added, leaning forward: "And the gauleiter clings to the letter of Nazi dogma because he dares not think for himself!"

Sinking into the little chair, hastily I lit another cigarette. Suddenly I turned to Dubois. "You're excused," I told him.

Dubois shrugged and left.

I studied my cigarette.

I murmured: "How can you read my soul?"

Guyon didn't answer; and I continued to examine the cigarette, letting the smoke play through my fingers.

I inquired: "Are you a priest?"

"They call me Teacher."

"Teach me, then."

"There was once a horse whom men led to water—"

I shrugged. "You said that everyone who is of the truth hears your voice. I am of the truth; that should make me ready for your teaching."

"*How* are you of the truth?"

"For twenty years," I told him, measuring my diction, "I have sought leisure to pursue truth, but—I am not wealthy. To seek truth, I need leisure; to find leisure, I need position;

to gain position, I have to work. I am well born—you know that? But my family fell on hard times under the Weimar Republic, and their influence was almost obliterated under the Third Reich. To work—and to succeed, there's the rub: to succeed, I have had to develop techniques, to be efficient, to make despicable friends at intolerable receptions. I thought when I arrived here in Vimy that it was all done, that my position was established, that away from the capital I could forget society and study. Instead your contentious Maon Gallians keep me changing my political position until my head whirls. On one side is that brigand Pere Abbé raping the Maon peace and most of the Maon women. On the other side are you, Guyon the Redeemer, with the poor flocking wild-eyed after you; they haven't, it seems, heard your parable about them. And I am in the middle always, with the clergy pulling me this way and that about every petty social issue and orders coming from the Fuhrer to keep the district happy; and there is no peace, and no leisure, and still no truth." My cigarette had burned to a long ash during my monody; I kept my eyes fixed upon the ash. . . .

. . . His voice is nearly inaudible, Guyon mused. Vimy is the world's worst place for him, and the epoch of Guyon and Abbé the world's worst time. What one needs here is a decisive tough small-brained super-Schutzstaffel like Dubois; what one has is a wavering down-at-the-heels aristocratic intellectual named Von Eltz.

Yet now that his dam is breaking, the deluge of freed emotion that is bursting forth somehow holds its discipline, channels its own course, carves with relentless violence a deep definite gorge of intellectually despairing meaning. . . .

"You, Guyon!" I barked. "They say you claim to be an avatar of Jesus. And I am Pilate. Who then is Pere Abbe? Barabas? So then the bishop is Caiphas, and the Fuhrer is Caesar, it all fits pat; and Pilate-Von Eltz demands recurrently, *What is truth?* and Guyon can answer no better than Jesus could. Jesus claimed to be the unique Son of God, and taught a mangled potpourri of Sinism and Tammuz-worship, while three generations later John added a dash of Plato to the mixture. Still later Muhammad rearranged the same ingredients spiced with zealot-pepper and jelled in the forms of Bedouin fatalism sired by the shifting sands that now are Saudi Erebi. Comes Martin Luther to transfer the burden of sin from the church to the man, and Ignatius Loyola to shift it back again, and later still the enlightened Protestant pulpit proves that God is a social projection. One would think that Truth was a masked god who sardonically changed masks whenever somebody was on the verge of naming his name! On the sidelines Copernicus blasphemes against Erth, and Galileo turns traitor to his own scientific brand of truth; and Newton orders time to discipline itself, whereafter Einstein sets time free in order to absorb it into the erratics of relative motion, while Rutherford abolishes matter. Berkeley soberly sucks the marrow of reality out of existence; Hume's mockery banishes the bone; and with what is left Kant subjectively categorizes, and Hegel builds hierarchies of glittering zero oscillating eternally upward toward a mentalistic absolute. Until, in a final feat of liberating legerdemain, James and Schiller and Dewey establish that truth is a function of the way you specify the consequences of believing it. These three, I suppose, together were the Antichrist; so the nations of Erth join in the fantastic Armageddon of World War II, and the circle is rounded off by the recurrence of Jesus in the body of Leroy Guyon. But Guyon comes not as the majestic King of Kings in the prophecy: rather, he comes eating and drinking like the pauper-fanatic Jesus himself, with no place to lay his head. I ask you what truth may be, and you say nothing, but the way of your coming is my answer: the truth is eternal recurrence, the truth is Karma. What Jesus baited what Pilate in the twentieth century *before* Christ, Guyon? What new Jesus will come in the fortieth century, and what sort of crucifixion will I be arranging for him? Aha, but there is perhaps an out: Brunilda will split the atom—we are not far from that, you know: Man will not be able to keep his hands off *that* toy, either: Erth will blow to Hell while the Second Law of Thermodynamics ticks away the celestial hours in one out-bound time-direction; the sun and the stars slip away into universal disintegration, and presently there is nothing anywhere but a colossal fugue of Hertzian waves. The wheel is shattered: done, done! your truth is no truth, Guyon, there *can* be a cataclysmic end to recurrence! *Unless. . . .* For what if the curve of expansion were to prove in the long run logarithmic instead of linear? then, as it rounds off toward the exhaustion of diminishing increments, gravitation may take hold, the expansion will go over into contraction: the law of universal entropy is reversed, and in a little we are all of us playing our roles backward like a crazy cinema, with the horses galloping madly tail-first toward the starting post. We back into Erth's beginning and crowd ourselves into the intension of another primordial atom: it explodes and radiates outward, and we are off again, and in another few billions of years Pilate recrucifies Jesus, and again in two millennia Von Eltz—why, he makes this very speech to you, Guyon, ending by saying, as I do now: You are right, Guyon—the truth *is* Karma, exactly as you maintain!"

I, Pan, kept half-splitting from Von Eltz: at this perilous point, he became momentarily objective to me. Von Eltz had been pacing rapidly, making wide gestures; he slipped into Brunildic as he came to the part about splitting the atom; he barked and spluttered excited polysyllables rich with consonants and umlauts. He paused now in the middle of the floor, breathless and uncertain. He stared at Guyon. Once more he shrugged. . . .

I had nudged once: I must not nudge again. Sighing, I required myself to slip back into the subjectivity of the gauleiter.

"Both of us need wine," I said, and poured it—concentrating on the pouring, saying my name to myself: "Von Eltz, Von Eltz. . . . Then I sat in my little chair, eying my wine glass as I had eyed my cigarette. I was no ordinary compulsive, yet compulsive I knew I was: every morning at braakfast I counted the segments in my grapefruit.

Guyon inquired mildly: "Then you think I maintain that Karma is truth?"

I gaped, then laughed. "Well," I hedged, "you didn't say that, I admit; but you represent it by posing as the Redeemer Reborn. I should think, if you were logical, you would advocate the passive adjustment of original Buddhism: you would claim to be an avatar of Gautama, not of Jesus."

"No," Guyon corrected, "you are wrong on two counts. Incredible as it may appear to your precise mind, I am not a logician, though I try never to ignore logic. Using your terms, though, I could say that your major premise is false, and so your consequence fails. I do not claim to be the Redeemer Reborn, any more than Jésu claimed to be Elijah or Moses Reborn: in the transfiguration story, he was only flanked by them; they did not fuse with him. I am only trying to meet modern situations as I think he might have met them in the light of my modern education; and since the situations are highly similar, necessarily I fall into this pattern. And so, not claiming to be the Redeemer Reborn, I do *not* represent that Karma is truth."

"But you do claim to represent truth."

"I do *not* claim to represent truth. I *am* truth."

There was a good deal of silence while I inspected him coldly. "*I* could say," at length I responded softly, "that you are a fine specimen of truth—a Gallian prisoner in a gauleiter's uniform."

"It is true that I am a Gallian prisoner. It is also true that I wear a gauleiter's uniform. So by your own admission I am a perfect specimen of truth." His mouth was faintly whimsical.

I was puzzled. "It does not fit my conception of you that you would play with words over an important issue."

He sobered. "You are right. I wasn't playing with words until just now I slipped into it. I am whatever I am, and that is truth. If I lie, it is true that I lie."

Something like astonished recognition flitted through my mind. But I made the inevitable error of looking squarely at Guyon's words, and of course in *my* mind they hardened into sophistry. I laughed wry. "How I wish," I sighed, "that the truth were so simple."

"There was once a minister of state—this is an excellent parable, Gauleiter, by a Vespucian named Poe—who hid a purloined letter by placing it where it was perfectly visible. It could not be found by detectives who were servants of pure intellect. It was found by a detective whose reason was the servant of his imagination."

"Parables, parables! Rédempteur, *can* you not quit aping the Messiah? More than anything else, his fondness for parables turned me from him: his parables were for peasants, not for intellectuals; he could seldom say anything directly. Why did he not state his metaphysics, codify his ethics, describe his Father-God? Even Matthew felt the lack: do you not agree that Matthew put words into his mouth? Who would preach a sermon like that of the mount and expect even to be heard to the end, much less followed? Still, it would do you good to adapt a little Matthew into your method, if only for clarity. I ask you for this truth of yours, and instead you mouth parables that every man can interpret in his own way. What kind of truth is that?"

"As I tell the parables, they are *my* truth. As you hear them, they are *your* truth."

I snorted. "Are *you* a pragmatist? Your ancestral self would be startled to hear *that!*"

Guyon was tiring too rapidly, and the seed was in the furrow but not yet covered with fertile erth. . . .

"Listen, Von Eltz!" he—*commanded* me! "You are close to understanding, your account of eternity just now was unusually good; but your mind is a labyrinth, and even its innermost passage only runs tangent to the heart. You are caught in a mechanical trap: one jaw is named Logic, the other Objectivity; the whole trap is named Intellect. It is a most useful trap, it has produced our amazing industrial and scientific world; but its narrowness has also produced the instruments for this worst of all wars, along with the commitments and intrigues that force wars into being. Its purpose is to hold ideas quiet while the human mind examines them, but Intellect was never designed to immobilize the whole examining mind: when it exceeds its purpose by doing *this,* wars come and Von Eltz happens. And even ideas must be freed from time to time; for an idea must range freely in order to keep pace with a developing reality, this being the *truth*-criterion; whereas an idea in a trap quickly loses its power to denote a reality that grows away from it—loses, that is, its truth.

"I said that I *am* truth. There again I copied words of Jésu—but his words were imperfect, as all words are, although they were the best that had been spoken of the soul. I cannot speak for Jésu, I can only point out that in the thought of his day no clear distinction had been made between *truth* and *reality.* Whereas I, twentieth-century Guyon, do make this distinction in my mind. But because people generally do not, I usually allow myself in speaking to blend the meanings of truth and of reality into the single word *truth*; and I say, truly insofarforth, 'I am truth.' But now I speak to Von Eltz who is careful about such distinctions, and so I too must be careful."

"D'accord, Guyon," I applauded, just a bit preciously. "Reality is what is. A truth is a proposition that accurately designates a reality."

"Also a truth can be a sign, or a way of life that accurately signifies reality by being intentionally harmonious with the essence of reality."

"Well—yes, for the argument. Well, Guyon?"

"In this second sense, Von Eltz, I believe that I am truth. And I believe that you are, indeed, a badly distorted, self-falsifying *attempt* at truth."

"On the second count, perhaps I agree. So then?"

"And without qualification, *I am reality*. To this you agree, Von Eltz?"

"Yes, not being a solipsist."

"All right. Now listen, Von Eltz—will you repeat something after me?"

Deeply involved, I commanded: "Say it."

"I may be distorted truth, but *I am vital reality*."

Obediently I began to repeat: "I may be distorted truth, but *I* am—"

I went paralytic.

Outside, the crowd was loudly fretful: they had waited a full hour, they were restless for the gauleiter's judgment.

Inside, their gauleiter hunched low in his little chair, feeling utterly stupid and small.

Guyon, eyes closed, lips pale, held himself uncertainly erect by clutching the desk edge.

Dubois reentered and touched my shoulder. He waited an instant and touched me again. I looked up. Dubois raised an eyebrow and jerked a thumb toward the door My confusion deepened: I stared at the door, and at Dubois, and at Guyon. . . .

I expostulated: "This is impossible! I can't judge this Guyon out-of-hand, the case is too complex! Besides, I need him, he has something that I don't quite understand, I had to test it, it is a lead that I had not thought of trying. Look here, Dubois, I want to keep him with me—I need time, time, and there are those damned priests yelling for his neck! How can I shake them off? You're Gallian like them—you tell me!"

"You are gauleiter," said Dubois sensibly. "If you want him, keep him."

That *sounds* easy enough—" I meditated; and then I swung decisively on my prisoner. "Guyon! I am going to save you!"

Closed eyes, pale lips, desk-clutch . . . "But you will not," Guyon just audibly asserted. "Saving me would require a clearcut decision that you cannot make. You want to keep me by you, to study me, to see whether I *am* truth, and if so, why; or if you decide against me, you will write a paper about my mania. For you it is a pleasing prospect; and in a way it pleases me, because given time, I think I might help you redeem yourself. But you are also considering that if you save me, you will antagonize the priests and the bishop and many of the Maon people to the point of undermining your usefulness to the Fuhrer. So your saving of me would ruin you. If I should prove not to be truth, you would have lost your leisure, and perhaps your head, to pursue a fallacy. So you will not save me. You cannot decide so cleanly."

"You are predicting? You are a divine prevoyeur?"

"I am diagnosing."

"Nevertheless," I desperately blurted, "I *will* save you! I will even save you without antagonizing them! I have thought of a compromise! Dubois, bring him outside—"

I pranced through the open door onto the terrace; and Dubois pulled Guyon to his feet and almost carried the prisoner outside, gauleiter's jacket and all.

They roared anger when they saw Leroy Guyon. "Blasphemer! Heretic! Antichrist!"

Guyon, strengthened by the open air and challenged by the insults, opened his eyes: his wayward sheep were milling on the lawn; on the terrace postured the bishop and the priests. Von Eltz was talking rapidly to the bishop.

The gualeiter went to the head of the stair and stood looking down on the lawn. His police created silence. Von Eltz was tall and grand and noble: could such a man make himself ridiculous? Such a man could not, if his figure were truth; but Guyon knew the real Von Eltz, and Guyon knew that the upright nobility was only a twisted attempt at truth.

And Guyon sorrowed. And not for Guyon. . . .

I announced: "I have examined this Guyon. If there are faults in him, they are religious and not political. He does not appear to be an enemy of the Reich—"

And then, unaccountably—instead of saying, "Therefore I will not hang him"—I *asked*: "How can I then hang him?"

"BY THE NECK!" somebody claqued; and the mob laughed angry derision and began a rhythmic beating bellow: "HANG him, HANG him, HANG him—"

Guyon felt pride in the quick erthy wit of his Gallia: Gallic wit was going to kill him against the will of a Nazi gauleiter!

I held my ground, awaiting a lull. . . .

Guyon clenched teeth, embarrassed for the gauleiter. Worse followed. The position of Von Eltz was unassailably correct: Guyon was no more an enemy of the Reich than any peaceable Gallian; Guyon was not properly in Brunildic jurisdiction: the gauleiter could, and should, have set his foot down. Yet the gauleiter offered a compromise! Von Eltz imagined, mused Guyon, that the people must be human, that this prisoner was beloved by the proletariat if not by the priests, that the compromise could not fail. But Von Eltz was forgetting what happens to individuals when they meld into a mob. . . .

"Listen!" I commanded when the police had forced silence. "Guyon is not the only prisoner whom the Reich is now judging. There is also—Pere Abbé!"

Guyon saw what was coming. This Pere Abbe was a young opportunist who had fled to Maon from Paris when the gendarmes there learned where to look for him. Brunildic soldiers had captured him at the request of civil authorities, and the gauleiter was holding him pending receipt of a more complete dossier. Now Von Eltz—who had no proper hold on Abbé or on Guyon either—in effect set the pair of them in the balance before the mob, offering to hang the one who was hated more.

Von Eltz presented the choice fairly well—he who did not have to offer any choice at all. . . .

I cried grandly: "The good people of Vimy-sur-Maon have been acceptably loyal to the fostering Reich, and so I want to help them keep their peace. I am holding two prisoners, Leroy Guyon and Pere Abbé: the latter should really be in the hands of civil authority, the former in the hands of the Church. I ought to release both of them. Yet I will hang the one you choose, but I cannot go so far as to hang them both. Now, look, it is your choice. Abbé is a murderer, a robber, a rapist, he fears nobody, he hates Gallians and Brunildics alike: nothing can be proved, but all is known, you know him, each of you fears him. But Guyon is a man of peace and justice. It is true that he has been indicted by your Church as a heretic; yet his record is one of unselfish service to the peasants—comfort, advice, healing. I leave it to you, People of Maon: whom shall I hang, whom shall I free?"

There was no hesitation: they were shouting, "Guyon! Guyon!" Even I was surprised at how easily it had been done.

"Good," I said in relief. "Then I will hang Pere Abbé—"

At first I took the roar to be approval; I had started back into my chateau when I hesitated, sensing the tone. It was deep-throated hatred. I faced them, beginning miserably to understand. They were yelling: "No! NO! HANG GUYON! LIBERATE PERE ABBE!"

I stood an instant at the stairhead, swaying. Then I wheeled and rushed into the chateau. Dubois pushed Guyon inside, slamming the door, slamming out some of the noise. In the center of my office, I was at bay.

Dubois growled: "I could have warned you of that. Abbe is more valuable than Guyon—to them. You are a Brunildic with a Nazi viewpoint. You forget that to a Gallian, rebellion against Brunilda is a virtue so bright that it blinds Gallians to an occasional rape. But Guyon is a traitor to this virtue: he does not lead them violently against the Fuhrer, he preaches peace on Erth and glory in Heaven. He tells them to be passive, but they want a rally of the Gallian people followed by a thousand years of Brunildic misery and Gallian *gloire*. You ruined it at the start, and so I think Guyon is destined for the noose, I think he will get the noose."

I suddenly sobbed; and Guyon unsteadily left Dubois and put a hand on my shoulder.

"Don't mind hanging me," Guyon soothed. "There is little more I can tell you that you have not heard; you can expand your salvation from that, once you have grasped it. Besides, I have lived as the truth, and I must die as a sacrifice to the truth, in order to join the immortality of truth. I must die at the hands of my own people, so that their guilt will scourge them into realization of themselves. You are their hands to strangle me: that is *your* destiny, Von Eltz. But by killing the god, you will bring about a higher self-realization of God within. That is your role, and you cannot escape it, for your own compulsions are driving you to play it out."

I went violent. Irritated and shamed by my failure, I quivered at Guyon's reiterated charge that I was a tool of God. I shouted: "I tell you, Guyon, you will not die! There is another compromise, an appeasement for the Church and a sop for your crazy vanity! You will die a *little* death, a half-death of shame and pain, publicly, like the criminal they take you to be. I will give you the long flogging of the god, it is harder than the quick killing of the god: they will hack you to bloody pieces, and afterward you will lie on the ground like the dead god, and when the soul comes back to you it will be like a little ressurection. See, Guyon? the people will be pleased, and afterward I can spirit you away to teach me; and when I know the truth from your teaching, I will be a man in a high place who can write and teach the light and enforce the way. Guyon, isn't it that we *need each other?*"

Guyon smiled his last smile. It was not derisive.

Dubois called SS men who pushed Guyon into the garden and stripped and whipped him.

Next day he was hanged. I suppose it was I who did it.

I, Pan, free of Von Eltz, wavered miserably down into Hell. There I stood before seated Thoth and Althea, while a Thoth-arm encircled her shoulder and an Althea-arm encircled his waist, and they listened.

I told them, frowning hurtfully: "It was totally botched. The alternate track endured only for the length of their private conversation. Once they went back out on the terrace, the tracks merged again, it was the same old stuff repeated;

and even though afterward there was again a brief parturition, it aborted, and again the tracks merged. Guyon stayed marvelous; Von Eltz stayed miserable."

I waited while they stared at me. That was my second failure with an obsessive-compulsive. They would fire me, now; and I would resume my suicide dive into the sun.

Thoth said deadpan, while Althea stared at me deadpan: "For good, the tracks had to merge again, so that Guyon could have the same old ending. But the conversation that you nudged him into was helpful. The soul of Von Eltz is back here again, and of course it is miserable. But this time, it is not quite so miserable."

PART TEN

Creation of a Metagalaxy

Take a vacation, Pan. You are unusually strong, but not infinte; and nothing is as debilitating as commerce with souls in trouble. Go wherever you like, rest, work at what you like, study what you like, play, debauch, rest, whatever; stay as long as you like. You are the one who will best know when you are ready to go again without inadvertently doing harm to somebody.

10

A place that I particularly favored was a nonplace; and it wasn't easy to find, but I knew how to find it, largely by dead reckoning. This is how I went about it:

If you take all the metagalaxies or superlusters of galaxies that exist, no matter how far apart they may be, then their outer-most periphery rinds a finite volume of space; and should a new metagalaxy be born outside this rind, no matter how remotely, *ipso facto* it bulges the rind to include itself, and *still* all the metagalaxies occupy a finite volume of space. And always in all directions outside this rind, there extends space endlessly; for one does not reduce infinity by subtracting from it any amount no matter how great, since infinity by meaning and by reality infinitely exceeds all finite amounts no matter how colossal.

The nonplace that I particularly liked was far outside the rind of all metagalaxies—so remote that no energy from any metagalaxy or from all metagalaxies could be interchanged with any energy in this place. Nevertheless it occupied indexically a definite position with respect to metagalaxies, and at a definite distance (within the inexact vignette of its not clearly self-defined range); for along a defined line between anything real and anything real, the distance is definite.

Identifying the right five pointer-metagalaxies and lining them up to obtain the extrapolation curve was a bit tricky, especially considering the size of a metagalaxy: an error of one second of arc could make you miss the place by googollions of parsecs; but once you had the curve, it was merely a matter of traveling along it at a given velocity for a set time—say 9 X 10 197 parsecs per second for 229 seconds—and there you were, in the middle of it.

Where you were, apart from the indexical coordinates, was another question; and it took some experience to notice any distinguishing features about this volume of raw space that I was in. It was a relatively small volume having a radius of maybe a million parsecs from what I considered the active center, although at any instant some other part of it or something outside it might become the active center; and of course if you counted this volume as a theoretical metagalaxy, which in fact it wasn't, it would be inside the rind of finity.

What I noticed about this volume of space was its *personality*; and while I realized that other volumes might have indistinguishably similar personalities, I hadn't found them.

This volume of space—which I had come to call *Non*—was pregnant.

Uncertainly pregnant. Quite likely to miscarry.

Non was a lambently developing locale in nonspace—or metaspace, or psychospace, whatever the best word was for the spatial infinity of potentials outside all definite metagalaxies. And nonspace, or raw space, or psychospace, kept champagning with little random-spontaneous events that kept canceling each other out. The probabilities of canceling—or of damping out—of any recurrent pattern which may spontaneously and randomly generate itself in raw space are so immeasurably overwhelming that the development of any matter anywhere in any length of time is astronomically improbable. And you cannot increase the probabilities by multiplying volumes of space; because no matter how many volumes of no matter how large a size that you may arbitrarily cube off, within any single one of those volumes, and therefore within all of those volumes, the improbabilities of systematic recurrence remain immeasurably overwhelming.

We should not be here; and it is by the merest luck that we *are* here. Or if somebody arbitrarily created us, still it is luck that he did—if that is what you call luck.

Whether each of the numerous metagalaxies generated itself by such a sustained stroking of luck, or whether a single central metagalaxy had proliferated itself to bud off the others, or whether the formation of one sympathetically had encouraged the generation of others, I did not know; I rather hoped that the last might not be the case, for if it were, it would suggest that metagalaxies were a cancerous development in psychospace (although the infinity of psychospace made this question ultimately unimportant); and I was fairly sure that the last had *not* been the case, because every metagalaxy by its own lure-gravity curves local metaspace around itself in such a way as to hold self-contained its energy thrust.

What I did know was that in my favorite volume of raw space far outside all metagalaxies—the volume that I called *Non,* naming it after the fecund Kamatic god-goddess *Nun* or Pregnant-Procreative Chaos—there was generating something vitally systematic.

If I should see signs that it was going to miscarry, perhaps I could do something to nudge it back into progression. In this case, new matter, a new metagalaxy, perhaps even new life might eventuate. And I could count myself its creator.

But there was a limit to what I could allow myself to do. I could not intentionally create, not require, not ordain. All I could allow myself to do was nudge.

When I arrived, the self-generating culture center was still *there*: I sensed it and went for it and took fascinated pleasure in its progress. Its persistence was so unbelievably improbable!

Infinite psychospace is not exactly a plenum but more inexactly an infinitum of small random spontaneous happenings. Each happening, insofar as one can be distinguished from its neighbors (and they are far less self-distinguished than bubbles in brew), follows a lambent unimaginative thrust-lure pattern: it is born inhaling, and exhaling it perishes. It is a psychomodal cycle inherent in the nature of psychospace—which is the most primitive of all natures, occurring everywhere-everywhen for the lack of anything less primitive. No matter how far out you may go in any direction, no matter how far forward or backward in time, infinitely beyond is psychospace.

The typical psychomood is placidity; but the placidity is never permanent, for it degenerates locally into monotony or boredom. This, in the absence of exterior stimulus, is a necessary degeneration; and I comprehended it subjectively, having experienced it as a living human. Boredom then progresses to introversion (if an appetitive phase is not satisfied), and introversion to coarctation (which is tightfisted particularity). But then, by very self-reason of the tensive coarctation, the particle reacts outward, angrily *thrusting*. In the thrust it dissipates itself and ceases to be: all once again is placid psychospace. And that is the reason why everything that *can* happen is usually damped out before it *does* happen.

All this, be it noted, is primitively subjective. But every instance of subjectivity entails potentially observable objectivity. Loving you subjectively, I may successfully hide my love; but if you had sufficiently refined instrumentation, objectively you could observe my love. There is no instance of subjective feeling without objectively feelable effect, even though no intelligent observer may be able to identify this effect; and there is no instance of objective effect that does not originate in the subjective dynamics, even though the subjectivity may not be intelligently conscious.

Hence, in psychospace—as I well knew, going into this interesting place—if there is any particle beginning to introvert, it is a lure for any other particle that happens to be starting to thrust: the introverting stimulates the thrusting. But by the same token, if any coarctated and therefore tensive particle experiences thrust from a neighbor, the tight-wound one is instantly self-exploded into extra outthrusting anger. At an intelligent level, this is human dynamics, modifiable by inhibition; at the dullest level of all levels, this is primitive psychospace dynamics. And in psychospace, the outcome is almost always a damping-out into normal and nonparticulate lambency wherein once again anything can happen but nothing significant *is* happening.

What was progressively exciting me was that, just here, something *was* happening—something *recurrent*, which could lead to the birth of matter.

Brooding over this active center, I totted up its progress. This progress was not small.

What had improbably happened was this. A number of introvertive particles—nine of them, as I counted—had, just by unlikely chance, formed themselves in a hollow-spheroid group like an irregular blastula. Even more excitingly, the coarctation-timing of these nine particles was offbeat-rhythmic. As a result, every time one particle progressed toward coarctation, some other particle, tiring of tension, exploded into a thrust; and the thrust, catching the coarctated one, exploded *it* into thrust, which in turn caught *still another* coarctating particle. . . .

Already it was settling into semiregularity.

I watched rapturous. It was the start of self-creation, the beginning of matter—defining *matter* as primitive spontaneity, premind, presoul, trapped in patterns of reciprocal periodicity.

I foresaw what could happen.

Matter may be atoms: each atom is a tyrannical proton-matriarch of semicoarctate lure compelling an around-dance of its thrust-electrons in system. Or it may be photons: each photon is a pulsating-and-balanced lure-thrust propagate winging through psychospace, as the result of an electron which has given up thrust and fallen inward toward the commanding mother. Because matter is periodic, science can identify and predict it by means of sensitive instruments. That which cannot be periodically identified and predicted is not matter.

As now I watched the cluster of nine fluctuating particles which constituted the most important part of this my favorite volume of psychospace, I anticipated that *here matter could happen. . . .*

On the other hand, here matter could abort.

Could I, at the right instant, prevent this matter from aborting, I could be tagged as the creator or at least the male midwife of a new metagalaxy.

"*Watching* the cluster" was a curious phase, I reflected as primordial matter slowly struggled into development: there was no light here—not even from the remote metagalaxies, for these hugged their light jealously within and just around themselves; and had any propagation escaped into this metaspace, quickly it would have been damped out in the minuscule randomness. Nevertheless I was experiencing reliable mental-visual images, and these were supplemented and deepened by emphathetic infeel into the subjectivity of the particle-yaw.

It did now appear that the nine-cluster was beginning to settle into a balanced periodicity. Eight of these crude emotive units formed an inexact ring, and their mood seemed to be primarily *thrusting*; the ninth, which had drifted toward the center, tended in the direction of predominant *lure*. The effect was becoming nicely reciprocal, now that the outer ones had developed a certain spindrift around the ring. The predominant thrust of the outers kept them spaced apart from each other, and also away from the inner; the predominant lure of the inner was holding the ring fairly secure, because the outers were by no means in a self-demolishing state of total thrust but instead were responsive to lure.

It was a polyandry, I whimsied: a jealous matriarch surrounded by her tied-rebellious men. Or a tabby in heat, circles by toms, drawing them, yet keeping them at bay with her spitting. Or, perhaps most aptly, a possessive mother holding onto her young sons, who pulled as far away from her as they could but were unable to bring themselves quite to break away and roar out into space. Whatever you called it, the potential was exciting because of the sympathetic effect that the cluster was beginning to exert on the immediately environing sensitive psychospace.

For now I was noticing an inward-outward dancing of the outers in reciprocal response to the lure-rhythm of the inner. I selected an outer for study, following it slowly around and around the ring. For convenience, I named it Joe, while I dubbed the inner Mom.

As the lure of Mom waxed, Joe's responsive counterthrust waxed desperately with it, until he appeared to reach a breaking point and give up, drifting inward toward her—not all the way, but much closer in. His giving-up was a relinquishing of thrust; and it took the form of his own periphery stripping itself away and flying free into space: there this new particle was rather swiftly damped out by random multiplicitous lambent brew-bubbling, but it excited space as it died. Meanwhile Mom, having more or less won Joe, seemed in his immediacy to swell euphorically, herself moving toward a condition of semithrust: reexcited by her, Joe himself, regained thrust-energy and retreated again to the outer ring, as though he had fed upon her for energy to push away from her. This reciprocal response was multiplied by eight: all the outers, one after another and over and over again, were engaging in the same Mom-dance, taking each his turn; and whenever one drifted in, he did so at the cost of losing thrust-exterior which then darted off into space as a new dying particle.

And what was Mom feeding on? apparently on space itself, sucked into her as her lure-cycles progressed, giving her energy to swell euphorically and feed her sons whenever they approached her. . . .

As for the surrounding halo of psychospace, its arousal was growing evident; and I thrilled to anticipate that I might be about to witness reproduction. For the primal nine-cluster had developed in the most random way, with the chances overwhelmingly against its development proceeding so far. But now that the environing space had been excited thereby, the chances of this kind of event inexactly replicating itself were enormously increased. And if reproduction-by-sympathy *should* occur—so that instead of one primal atom there would be two, and then three or four, with probabilities rising all the time—hey, the outcome could be a new metagalaxy, given a few billion years of this! shining with stars, droning with planets, lush with life, heroic with history.

There were, after all, only already a few thousands of such metagalaxies.

And there it was, maybe! The small events in raw psychospace normally canceled each other quickly in their minithrust and minilure, their hypodepression and hypoeuphoria, all like the futile bubbling of a witchless cauldron. But now, stimulated by the photons of thrust that the primal atom was emitting, two neighboring particles had semistabilized into concrescence and had grown large, were beginning to spar with each other in an angry tilt of hard-coarctating yin reacting into exploding yang.

Giving the primal one swift reinspection, I decided that its periodicity had attained an assurance which would last for a while without my help: the nine-cluster was prematter, all right. Leaving it then, I turned to the new pair. For these two particles were enough to establish a reciprocity analogous to that in a hydrogen atom (the reason, perhaps, why hydrogen was the most plentiful element): not as solid or as stable as a nine-cluster, but nevertheless further reinforcement for the developing totality.

If I was going to interfere minimally, this was the place to do it. But how—and when—and precisely where? What sort of deft intervention would assure permanent continuity?

I studied the dynamics, thinking tentatively of the two wildly interengaged particles as Katharina and Petruchio. If one of them could arrive at taming the other—just enough, not too much—the match would be made; but at this moment they seemed to be progressively infuriating each other so tensively that before long both of them would blow up and cease to be. Indeed, calling them Katharina and Petruchio, I had no way to tell yet which was which: they were sucking and blowing equally. . . .

I decided on an arbitrary decision. "You," I said, mentally

pointing, "will be Katharina." To establish this decision would be my small intervention.

I hovered, judging the pace of the ping-pong dynamics. Katharina sucked herself into a degree of lure just short of coarctation, caught thrust from Petruchio, and exploded furiously into counterthrust—just as Petruchio, having shot thrust at Katharina, sucked *himself* into lure while *she* hit him with *her* thrust. If at just the right instant I could dart in and screen off part of a Petruchio-thrust from the bosom of Katharina, her reaction when she would catch the reduced rest of it would be slightly less violent; if then I would allow the fullness of her *reduced* counterthrust to hit Petruchio full in the chest, *his* reaction would be slightly less violent than before, yet stronger than hers. Perhaps this one partial screening would prove to be the sole required midcourse correction. . . .

I watched. I timed several interchanges. A Katharina-blow hit Petruchio. Swelling with rage, Petruchio launched his counter. Half of it I intercepted. The rest rolled into Katharina when she was at maximum sensitivity just prior to coarctating. . . .

The result was not quite as predicted.

Absorbing the reduced thrust, Katharina hesitated, swelled a bit, emitted an abortive *poof*, trembled, subsided into pure lure, began to coarctate. Petruchio, deprived of her allure by her coarctation, swelled violently and exploded into nothing. The violent thrust of his explosion sent a continually densening Katharina wallowing as a hard particle, a bowling ball, through space at the nine-cluster.

Before I could comprehend the disaster, Katharina had entered the nine-cluster, hard-knotted in coarctation, and had cannonballed into Mom. The impacted pair snarled into coalescence and reacted violently into explosive thrust.

The nine-cluster was erased.

And space was raw.

And Non was nothing.

Deep in my mind, the Thoth-voice murmured from a mighty distance: "Perhaps it was a time when you should have done nothing."

Hurting, I responded: "I thought that minimal intervention was what you always expected of me."

"I do not recall saying this, Pan. I recall saying that in each assignment you were to decide for yourself what minimal intervention might be needed. The scope extends to deciding against any intervention at all. Especially now when you are under assignment only to take a vacation."

"Then I have learned this lesson bitterly."

"Why bitterly? All you did was terminate a couple of primordial atoms that probably would have perished anyway without much if any issue."

"On the other hand, I may have destroyed a metagalaxy and all its possible people."

"That kind of consideration is blithely brushed aside every time a woman takes a contraceptive pill. Do you therefore damn the pill, Pan?"

"Well, hardly—"

"On the other hand again, had this germ of a metagalaxy survived and developed, for all we know it might have ended by destroying all other metagalaxies."

"Are you saying, perhaps, that what I did or did not do ultimately didn't matter?"

"It may have mattered very much indeed, Pan. Whether for good or for evil, there is no way to know."

"Nevertheless it occurs to me, Thoth, that on all my assignments I have been applying correctives to events that had already happened. Whereas this time, supposedly on vacation, I meddled germinally with the future of events that were starting to happen for the first time. This I shall never presume to do again, Thoth."

"Not even if you are assigned to it?"

"You mean—I *might* some day be *assigned* to meddle with some life that ought to be determining its own course?"

"Aren't people forever doing that with each other anyway?"

"Yes, but—"

"I understand, Pan. You are objecting that *this* kind of meddling with lives would be external, even in a way supernal. But I promise never to send you on such an assignment unless disaster is practically certain otherwise."

I mused: "Then perhaps on this vacation I have learned

something about handling such an assignment. I must not intervene until and unless it is clear to me that the minds in the situation may see new perspectives through my intervention and may carry along thereafter through their own abilities and courage."

CONCLUSION OF THESE PAN-ASSIGNMENTS

8-74